CW00493651

J L ROBINSON lives in a sma
a bearded dragon, and a ca
thinks it does. Their three gi
on adventures of their own.

After teaching in Primary Education for 27 years, she decided to become a supply teacher and is enjoying the variety each day brings. During this change of lifestyle, her love of reading has transformed into a love of writing.

Also by J L Robinson

Stephanie Rhodes Series
Spring Fever

SUMMER MADNESS

A STEPHANIE RHODES NOVEL

J L ROBINSON

ISBN: 978-1-7394040-2-4

For my family.

Contents

1

BACK TO NORMAL

Stephanie sipped her tea thoughtfully while gazing out of her patio doors. It was 8 am, Saturday morning in late June, and the sky was a hazy, summer blue. She watched the white, fluffy clouds glide slowly overhead reminding her of two white piglets Eskimo kissing, so romantic. She continued to watch as the second pig dissolved away, its mouth was the last to disappear leaving the first pig to float away into the blue emptiness, alone.

Stephanie shook herself from her reverie, the weather forecast predicted a glorious, sunny day and Stephanie was looking forward to Hibaldton's Summer Fair. The proceeds would go towards repairs for the village church, and it seemed ages ago that Stephanie had helped to organise it with the Parish Council.

Spring had been an emotional time, so much had happened. Two murders in the village, both discovered by Stephanie, were something you don't recover from quickly. Plus, on top of that, she had made the front page of the local paper and it was a nightmare being careful what to say to reporters.

Stephanie shook her head as she started watering the plants in her garden with her watering can and remembered the awful night when she could have been killed. The police had still not found the killer, which meant that Stephanie had felt safer spending a few weeks living with her boyfriend, Mark, at his house. It had taken weeks for her to stop looking over her shoulder and to stop jumping at shadows. She shivered even though the sun was already beating down. She had insisted that she was ready to move back home, she was determined to get back to normal.

She looked across the crops of wheat to the other side of the field where Mark's house stood peeping through the trees. Stephanie told herself that she should be feeling happy. The weather was warm, it was going to be a fun day, Mark was coming to pick her up soon… so why did she still have dark thoughts?

Stephanie was ready for Mark when he knocked on the door. She unlocked it and walked into Mark's arms. He lifted her to swing her around.

'Morning gorgeous,' he grinned.

'Good morning. Did all the marquees get set up ok last night?'

'Yep. Everything looks great, I hope there will be some interesting beer to try.'

Stephanie locked the front door.

'I'm sure Angela and Ben have it all under control, but we'll be in trouble if we don't hurry to help out before it starts.'

Angela and Ben were on the village committee. They had taken on the responsibility of organising the stalls and planning where everyone should go. To begin with, the Village Council had planned to hold a beer festival, but so many groups of people wanted to be involved, it had turned into a Summer Fair. Stephanie was pleased that the school where she taught, Hibaldton Primary, also had a stall selling the children's artwork and the school choir would be singing.

Mark held out his hand and they walked down Field View Road. It wasn't far to the village hall, only a ten-minute walk. Stephanie looked up at Mark's handsome profile. He was about 6 feet tall, average for a man she supposed, but she was quite tall herself, about 5 feet 7 so he didn't tower over her. His face was very masculine, his chin strong and when he turned to look at her with those chocolate brown eyes, the skip of her heart still surprised her enough to make her face flush. He was wearing a white cotton shirt with short sleeves, hung over dark, blue jeans. Mark grinned as if he knew the effect he had on her.

'You okay?' he asked squeezing her hand.

Stephanie nodded and smiled, there was nothing to worry about she told herself, life was perfect.

They strolled past the empty football field on their left and then turned at the end of the road to walk up Church Street.

It had been a mixture of emotions living together, Stephanie thought, feeling the warmth of his hand around hers. Their teenage attraction had been rekindled when Mark had returned to Hibaldton and for two months Stephanie had felt like she was on cloud nine with him. Extraordinary circumstances had pushed them into living together though, and it had felt too soon. It had been the right decision to move back to her own place, she told herself.

As if echoing her thoughts Mark said, 'I've missed you this week, I was wondering if I could stay over at your house tonight?'

They stopped walking for a minute and Mark bent down to lightly brush his lips against Stephanie's mouth that left a tingling warmth, and a lemon and musk fragrance teased her senses.

Stephanie smiled as they stood, nose to nose, 'I've missed you as well, but I worry that if we spend too much time together, this... excitement we have between us will disappear.'

Mark started walking, pulling her along with him and then slipped his arm around her waist.

'Believe me,' he whispered in her ear, 'I will not let that happen.'

Stephanie believed him and that gave her something else to wonder about.

Stephanie glanced to their left, over the high cracked wall up to the stone church surrounded by weary, grey gravestones leaning at odd angles in the churchyard. Around the bend, they continued, past the village shop where bunting was hanging above the shop window next to a colourful basket full of red and pink geraniums.

'Ben seemed to enjoy himself yesterday, organising where all the marquees should go, he did a good job actually, I'm surprised,' Mark commented.

'You shouldn't be surprised, he is very organised. Did you see his plan? He knew exactly where everything should go, and he researched the costs too. I think he would make a good replacement for Mary, she used to do all that kind of thing.'

Stephanie paused, it still caused a lump in her throat when she thought about poor Mary and how her life had been cut so short.

'She would have been very proud of the way he has stepped up to the job,' Mark said gently.

Mark could tell that the mention of Mary still upset Stephanie and she noticed how quickly he tried to change the conversation.

'Dad's looking forward to his tractor stall. He can't wait to show off his new combine harvester to everyone.'

Stephanie smiled, 'Yeah when I was around at their house the other day, I tried to change the subject.'

'Oh, my dad could talk for hours about farm machinery, it's his favourite subject. Me, I'd rather talk about cars.'

'Have you two been getting along okay lately?' Stephanie asked hopefully. She knew that Mark's dad had been pressuring him to take over the farm, but he had been fighting against it.

Mark sighed, 'We had a row about it the other day. He doesn't understand that I have no desire to run the farm when he's gone, not without…'

Mark suddenly stopped talking and they continued in silence until they crossed the road and walked past the fish and chip shop.

'There must be something that you have in common with your dad,' Stephanie prompted.

'Dad and I used to fish together. We'd all go sit by the river in the evenings, my dad, my brother and me, that was the best time when the ducks had settled for the night, and all was still. We used to fish around the country too,' Mark laughed. 'In fact, Mum would get annoyed at us. Every time we went on holiday, which wasn't often with the farm, but when we did get away, he'd be filling the boot with fishing tackle.'

At the mention of his brother, Stephanie knew that Mark was missing him. She tried to lighten the mood.

'You should take your dad fishing, in fact, didn't you say you would take me? How big was that fish you caught on holiday in Greece?'

'Oh at least this big,' Mark laughed and spread his arms out wide and then caught Stephanie by the waist and tickled her.

2
SUMMER FAIR

When they arrived at the Village Hall, everyone from the Parish Council was looking busy setting up stalls on the field in front of the main doors. Mrs Moore was setting out cakes, Rosie was selling her knitted animals and supporting the local hedgehog rescue. Stephanie pulled Mark over to Rosie's table and they looked down at two cute, spiky balls curled up in a towel.

'Aww they're adorable,' Stephanie gushed.

'I know,' Rosie bent down to pull the towel back further to reveal a pair of tiny eyes and a pink nose.

Lisa, Stephanie's best friend and work colleague, appeared and looked over her shoulder.

'Those two are so cute.'

Rosie pointed at them, 'I'm calling them Terry and June.'

'My daughters will love to see them, and I know they'll want to buy a knitted animal,' Lisa said picking up a pink cat.

'Good, I've been making them all year.'

They all agreed on how amazing they looked.

'Stephanie, we'd best unpack the raffle prizes for our stall,' Lisa reminded her.

'When's your dad turning up with the tractor?' Stephanie asked Mark.

'He's on his way. There'll probably be a stream of kids following him up the road.'

He looked across to the car park.

'They'll love climbing all over it.' Lisa smiled. 'My daughter, Sophia, can't wait, she thinks she's going to be driving it around the field.'

Mark smiled, 'She can come and work for us when we harvest.'

'Haha, I don't think you'd want a five-year-old getting in the way.'

He said goodbye, kissed Stephanie and squeezed her waist.

'See you later, babe.'

He smelled gorgeous and her body cried out to follow him. Lisa pulled Stephanie by her arm and, reluctantly, she dragged her eyes from Mark as he walked across the field, and she followed Lisa to their table which was waiting to their left. Bunting had already been hung along it and their box sat on top.

They started to unpack the prizes from boxes: A bottle of wine, a bottle of whiskey, some toiletries, chocolates, a gift card for the garden centre, sweets and the main prize was a picnic hamper full of food and a tempting bottle of prosecco.

They sat down on a deck chair each and looked around. Most people had already set out their stalls, some were just making the finishing touches. A lady was hanging up necklaces onto her display of branches. Suncatchers twirled in the breeze, every now and again they reflected light, sending out orange, blue and yellow flashes. There were food trucks, a bouncy castle, a beer tent, local craft stalls and games tents each tent was a cream canvas and had red, white and blue bunting flapping and fluttering. All around there was an air of excitement and anticipation as everyone waited for the public to arrive.

A low rumbling noise gradually became louder and then a big yellow tractor appeared and slowly made its way into the field. Sam waved at everyone as he drove past and aimed for where Mark, his son, was waiting.

'Oh, here comes Mrs Moore,' Lisa said, 'You could ask for your mum's casserole dish back.

Stephanie and Lisa had taken a shepherd's pie to comfort the grieving husband of Mary, only to find his body sitting in his chair, eyes glassy and face frozen in horror. Stephanie shuddered at the memory and remembered how while talking to Mabel Moore, she had given the old lady her mum's casserole dish, pie and all.

Mabel marched towards them, her tight grey curls bobbing up and down on her head. Stephanie felt herself lower her body in her chair as if to make herself invisible, she thought about ducking under the table with the pretence of looking for something, but Lisa grabbed her arm as if she could read her mind. The lady halted in front of them and started to scrutinise the prizes with the precision of a judge on Bake Off. Stephanie felt Lisa tense beside her, Mrs Moore always made them feel like they were in trouble and Stephanie found herself staring into a pair of disapproving, blue, piercing eyes. Stephanie noticed her hair had recently been curled and set and saw an opportunity to try to get on her good side.

'You look nice today,' Stephanie complimented her.

Mabel Moore subconsciously put her hand up to her hair and blushed.

'Oh, err thank you, I go to the hairdressers every Friday.'

'I like your brooch,' Lisa joined in.

'This thing? I haven't worn it for ages. My late husband bought it for me at a fair a bit like this, actually.'

Stephanie hadn't heard her mention her husband before, it made her realise that she didn't know much about her. She only saw her at council meetings. Stephanie and Lisa admired her cameo brooch.

'How long were you married for?' Stephanie asked.

Mabel's face looked less wrinkled as her features softened.

'We married when I was only eighteen and he was twenty. He impressed my father by getting a steady job working in the payroll office at the steelworks, he was always good at maths, and he could add up numbers just like that in his head.'

She clicked her fingers and stood gazing into space as if looking at him standing in front of the trees, it sent a shiver down Stephanie's spine. Stephanie wanted to know more about Mabel's life when she was younger, but when Stephanie looked up Mrs Moore was back to normal, her lips pursed in disapproval.

'I don't agree with alcohol for prizes. What if a child wins the prize? Isn't there an alternative?' She sighed as she handed over five pounds. 'Nevertheless, I would like to buy five strips of tickets, please. It is for the church after all.'

Lisa took the money and Stephanie peeled off five strips of tickets and wrote her name on the back of the stubs. They watched Mrs Moore return to her stall across from them.

'You try to get on her good side and still, she bites your head off,' Lisa sighed, 'Like a praying mantis in tweed.'

Stephanie felt sad for Mrs Moore.

'You know Lisa, there's more to that woman than she lets on. I bet there's a good reason why she's so aloof. I think she's lonely.'

'She probably goes to all the church activities,' Lisa replied.

'By activities, do you mean sermons?'

'Yeah, and they have coffee mornings, Knit and Natter and bingo. I know cos my granny goes to them.' Lisa turned to Stephanie suddenly. 'You forgot to ask for your dish back.'

'Damn.'

ADULTS AND CHILDREN started piling in, and soon the field was packed full of excited sunburnt bodies.

Reverend Pierce came wandering over to their table, he wore a black shirt with his usual 'dog collar' but today he wore it with blue jeans. He also sensibly shaded his face from the sun with a cream sun hat, and you could just make out his hearing aid behind his ear.

'Hello ladies, how much is a ticket?' he almost shouted.

Stephanie knew that he often turned off his hearing aid and forgot to turn it on again.

'It's one pound a strip Reverend,' Lisa told him.

'How much?' He adjusted his hearing aid and lent forward.

'One pound,' Lisa said louder and held out a strip of tickets.

Reverend Pierce looked around at the prizes and his face lit up when he saw the bottle of whiskey.

'I'll take two please,' he said cheerfully.

Lisa took the money as Stephanie scrawled his name on the ticket stub.

'You're announcing the winning tickets, aren't you?' Lisa said.

'Yes. Do you think people will think I've cheated if I win something?' he said cheekily.

Lisa and Stephanie chuckled.

'If it's the whiskey… probably,' Stephanie said.

'Drat,' he pretended to be disappointed.

'I do hope that you lovely ladies will be able to get away and enjoy the festival yourselves.'

'Oh no worries, we're going to take it in turns to have a wander,' Stephanie spoke clearly with hand gestures, just so that she didn't have to repeat herself.

Reverend Pierce smiled and nodded, 'That's good, that's good. It certainly looks like it's going to be successful, everyone has worked so hard, haven't they?' He clapped his hands together. 'Our Lord is looking down on us today, we have a great deal to be thankful for.'

'Amen,' chorused Stephanie and Lisa, and then looked at each other wondering why they had said that.

The Reverend laughed and looked around until he spotted Mrs Moore at her cake stall.

'I think I'll go and see Mabel and see how she is getting on with selling her cakes. You know, her fruit cake is very good, but could do with some sherry in it.'

He winked and headed her way slowly.

Stephanie's gaze followed Reverend Pierce and she watched as a woman stopped him for a chat. Stephanie couldn't tell at first who she was as she had a large cream sun hat on and dark glasses. The two of them stood talking and the reverend patted her hand now and then as if he was consoling her. Stephanie thought she looked familiar, then she realised it was Vera Grayling. The memory of her husband made Stephanie stiffen and her first reaction was to be surprised that she had the nerve to show her face at the fair after everything that had happened. Stephanie elbowed Lisa.

'Look, is that Vera?'

Lisa put her hand up to shield her eyes from the sun.

'Oh yeah, I haven't seen her for a while. I'm surprised she came out here today.'

'I know!' Stephanie narrowed her eyes and stared at her, and when Vera looked in her direction she didn't look away.

'I can't believe that she didn't know what her husband was up to.'

Lisa nodded in agreement.

'She must have known something.'

Stephanie watched as the woman got out a tissue and looked like she was dabbing at her eyes under her sunglasses. Stephanie turned away and looked down the field to see two girls running in their direction.

'Oh look who's here, double trouble. It's Phoebe and Sophia,' Stephanie called as they reached the table panting.

'Mum! Can we have our faces painted? Dad said we have to ask you first,' Sophia shouted in excitement.

'Last time you hated it and cried for it to be washed off,' Lisa told her daughter.

'Yes, but that was because I didn't want *all* my face covered,' she pouted.

'She can just have a butterfly on her cheek,' Phoebe suggested putting her arm around her younger sister.

'Ok. Where's your dad?'

The two girls pointed to the tractor in the distance and Lisa could see her husband talking to Mark and Sam. A small crowd of adults and children surrounded the tractor.

'Run straight to your dad and don't go anywhere else.'

'Thanks, Mum,' they both said and hurriedly hugged Lisa before dashing off.

Stephanie watched with Lisa as they raced to their dad, their hair dancing in the wind as they ran. Stephanie remembered Vera and searched the field to find her further away, talking to a couple Stephanie didn't recognise. The woman was wearing a huge hat and long, white gloves. She looked like she had dressed for the races. The man next to her was slightly shorter, wearing a cream suit.

Stephanie's eyes returned to Reverend Pierce who was now chatting to Mabel as she held out a plate of biscuits for him to taste. Stephanie noticed how Mabel's face seemed to light up when they were together.

Stephanie was distracted by Lisa laughing and she looked over to the tractor to see what was happening. She could see Phoebe and Sofia tugging at Martin's arms to stop him from talking to Mark.

'They really want their faces painting,' Stephanie remarked.

Then it was Stephanie's turn to laugh as she watched Mark helping a little boy off the tractor and he had his leg over Mark's head.

'Mark would make a great dad don't you think?' teased Lisa.

Stephanie elbowed her friend.

'I wasn't thinking that.'

'He's great with kids,' Lisa observed. 'Don't you want children?'

Stephanie turned in surprise at the question and didn't know what to say.

'Erm, yes… not yet though, I mean I would if I met the right person… I think. I don't know if I'm ready to give up my life though.'

'What do you mean give up your life?' Lisa sounded appalled.

'Well, you know it's a big life change.'

'It is but it's amazing to have your own family.'

Just then a couple walked past with the woman trying to console a crying little girl. The child had blonde pigtails with red bows that matched her red face as she was screaming for her lost ice cream. She had melted chocolate all over her face and dress and was trying to pick up a cone that had fallen on the floor. Her mum picked her up and grimaced as sticky hands flew into her face and hair. Her husband was pushing a pram and looked like he was going to fall asleep any minute.

Stephanie watched them walk past with her mouth open. She turned questioningly to Lisa.

'It has its ups and downs,' Lisa replied.

'Hi, Miss Rhodes. Hi Mrs Croft.'

Two young boys, William and Noah, arrived at the table with objects in their arms. Teaching at the local school meant that most of the children at the fair would know Stephanie and Lisa.

'Look what we got, I got my mum this lamp,' William said, proud of himself as if he'd just completed a mammoth task.

Stephanie looked for a lamp and then realised a huge, standard lamp had appeared next to her. It was so tall, it towered over the boys and Stephanie wondered how they had managed to carry it. It had an old-fashioned mustard-coloured lampshade with pea-green tassels around the edge.

'Oh,' remarked Stephanie, shocked, 'I…I'm sure your mum will be surprised. I'm amazed you manage to carry this.'

'Noah helped me,' he beamed, 'I got it for my mum's birthday. Can we leave it here while we go look around?'

'Err… ok, I suppose so.'

William lifted the lamp and shuffled behind Stephanie's chair.

'We have these as well,' the boys reached into the pockets to bring out a water gun, four candles, a Chinese cat ornament that waved its paw, a bra wash bag and a bag of sweets.

Trying not to laugh, Stephanie pulled out an empty box from under the table and put the objects inside, they grabbed back the bag of sweets.

'But don't forget to come and get them,' she warned.

'Ok Miss Rhodes, bye.'

'Haha, his mum's going to get a surprise for sure,' Lisa laughed looking at the lamp.

Stephanie looked up and found herself sitting under it.

'Actually, it makes a good sunshade,' she acknowledged with a smile.

A STEADY STREAM of people stopped to buy tickets and then thankfully there was a lull where Stephanie and Lisa could relax.

Ben, Angela and Rosie came wandering over. Angela was licking an ice cream and Ben had a camera around his neck. They must have been at the Village Hall for hours setting everything up Stephanie thought as she gazed at Rosie's shoulder-length, dark hair with a fringe and large, black-framed glasses. She always wore bright 60's style clothes and today she was in an orange flowery sundress. She must have left the hedgehog stall for someone else to look after so she could have a wander around the fair. Angela and Rosie were a similar age to Stephanie and Lisa. Angela was more confident and serious. She had short blond hair and wore a light blue sundress. 'How's it going, have you sold many raffle tickets yet?' Rosie asked.

'A fair few,' Stephanie replied.

Lisa shook the money tub.

'I reckon there about twenty pounds profit in here already.'

'That not bad,' Ben said. 'We've been walking all around the stalls and everyone's doing well.'

Ben was liked by everybody, he was an optimist, always full of energy. He was quite good-looking, his hair was cut very short at the sides and balding at the top. Stephanie thought about advising him to buy a hat to protect it from the sun. Instead, she praised them for their hard work.

'Mark was saying what a great job you two have done to organise the setting up,' Stephanie said.

'Looks like there'll be plenty of money for the church and some for the guides and scouts when it's finished, I bet,' Angela enthused.

The field had filled up with people of all ages. Music had started over by the stage and the sounds of talking and laughter surrounded them.

'The DJ is playing some good music, he's thinking of starting a karaoke at about 11:00.'

'That should be interesting,' Stephanie laughed.

'You know that band that plays in the pub sometimes?' Rosie asked.

'Rocking Robins?' Ben replied, shielding his eyes from the sun.

'Yes, are they going to be playing? I thought I saw the singer talking to the DJ.'

'They will be on stage at 1:00, and the school choir will be singing at 3:00.'

'Oh, I told the children I would be watching that,' Stephanie said.

'Are you buying a raffle ticket?' Lisa asked rattling the tub with a cheeky grin.

'Oh yeah, sure...'

They each got their purses out and handed over the money. Stephanie wrote out their names on the stubs and gave them the tickets.

Ben held up his camera and pointed it at Stephanie and Lisa, so they smiled.

'Thank you. Right, I'm off to take more photos, cheerio,' Ben waved with Angela and Rosie following.

Stephanie smiled as she watched them go. At first, she hadn't been sure about them, they always hung out together and were very possessive over the Village Voice magazine, but since she had worked with them on the Summer Fair, she realised they were fun to be around, they were a bit quirky, but Stephanie liked that about them.

More people came over to their table to buy raffle tickets, and Stephanie recognised three girls and a boy from her previous year's class with his mum Mrs Johnson. Stephanie liked Mrs Johnson as they had often had a chat in the playground at home times.

'Hi,' they all choroused.

'Can we have 5 strips please,' Mrs Johnson asked.

Lisa held out the tub for her to put the money in.

'Are you all having fun?' Lisa asked.

'Yes,' the children all shouted excitedly.

'It's lovely weather for it, isn't it?' Mrs Johnson commented.

'Yes, we're lucky, aren't we?' Stephanie replied.

'You don't mind if we just leave these bottles of pop, do you? Billy bought them over there, but we can't carry them around all day.'

'Yes of course,' Stephanie told her.

'Oh, thank you,' she said relieved, 'they were a bargain, but I didn't think how we'd carry them about.'

Lisa took the bottles from them and put them under the table, out of the sun and they left to wander over to the tractor.

After a while, Stephanie was feeling thirsty.

'I'm going to take a break if that's all right Lisa.'

'Yeah ok. I'll be fine, come back in about half an hour?'

'Ok'

3

HOOK A DUCK

Stephanie stood up and went for a walk to find Mark. She turned to look over towards the stage where a trio of teenage girls were singing and dancing, she couldn't quite make out the song. A small crowd had gathered around the stage, it looked like the karaoke was becoming popular.

Stephanie wandered over to the tractor. Mark's dad, Sam, seemed to be looking after the tractor on his own so Mark wasn't there anymore. She ambled around the field and found him in one of the beer tents talking to Martin, Lisa's husband. The tent was busy, with men and women standing, casually talking and laughing with plastic cups of amber liquid in their hands.

'Thought I'd find you here,' Stephanie teased.

'It's my first moment of peace!' Mark complained with a laugh,

'Those kids are tiring.'

'Yeah, try having 32 of them all day. What are you drinking?' Stephanie asked.

Mark handed her his pint to try and then when she said she liked it, he went to fight his way to the bar to get her one, leaving Stephanie to talk to Martin.

'So, Lisa let you get away,' Martin said sipping his pint. 'I should be a good husband and go take her a drink. How's it going?'

'Great, we've sold loads of tickets. Where are the girls?'

'Oh, they're somewhere...' He looked around vaguely. 'They're fine, I told them not to leave the field.'

'Lisa's gonna kill you.'

'They're running around with their mates from school, I can't keep up with them. They'll come and find me when they've run out of money, I only give them a small amount at a time.'

'Ahh clever.'

Stephanie nodded.

'Lisa sometimes doesn't give them enough freedom. I know you've got to be careful nowadays, but you've got to get the balance right.'

'Yeah,' Stephanie agreed. 'My parents were very protective of me when I was young, and they still are. If I go away anywhere, I still have to let them know I've got there safely.'

'I suppose mothers usually worry more about girls than they do boys. I used to stay out all night sometimes. We used to camp out in the woods sometimes.'

'Which woods?'

'Bluebell Woods. We used to camp next to the lake and go swimming. Those were the days.'

Martin smiled.

'Did you hang around with Mark back then?'

'Not really. He was usually busy on the farm. He used to follow his brother about a lot until he left.'

'I knew he had an older brother, Richard, but he never talks about him. What happened to him?'

Stephanie tried to remember the last time she had seen him. She remembered that he played cricket when she used to hang out at the village hall on match days while her mum made the sandwiches.

'He moved to America somewhere. I remember Mark was upset at the time, he idolised his big brother.'

Stephanie noticed his demeanour change and could sense Mark was returning from the bar.

Martin smiled and laughed, 'Ok, you win, I suppose Lisa probably will kill me if I lose those two monkeys. See you later.'

He nodded to Mark as he stood next to Stephanie.

'Catch you later for another pint?' he said to Mark and walked into the crowded field.

Mark handed Stephanie half a pint. They exited the tent and wandered aimlessly for a while. The sun was warm on their back and there was a soothing, cool breeze. Stephanie was dying to ask Mark about his brother. Why didn't his family ever mention him? Didn't they keep in touch? She looked at Mark as he sauntered next to her sipping on his pint. He looked so relaxed that she decided it wasn't the right time to bring up that conversation.

They walked past an ice cream van and up to a burger truck. The delicious smell of the burgers and the onions was starting to make Stephanie feel hungry, she looked at her watch.

'Do you want something to eat?' Mark asked stopping to look at the menu.

'It's 11:30, I might as well while I'm wandering around.'

Stephanie nodded eagerly as she watched a man expertly stir up the onions and quickly scoop some up neatly onto a burger before popping it on a bun.

'There's not a big queue, it smells delicious.'

Stephanie's mouth watered as they waited.

THEY ATE THEIR burgers while they walked around the edge of the field. A variety of games had been set up at the end of the field. Running races were keeping children entertained with mums and dads cheering them on. A tent with a coconut shy was full of competitive men, throwing balls with such force that they bounced off the back of the canvas.

Stephanie noticed Hook a Duck so she steered Mark eagerly in that direction. It was actually a paddling pool on the grass with some bright, yellow plastic ducks bobbing about in the water. Debbie stood next to a table, she was about eighteen and sometimes worked at the fish and chip shop when she wasn't in college. She had her blond hair in a high ponytail and flushed when she saw Mark walk towards her, never mind that Stephanie was holding his arm. He had that effect on women. She did her best to look happy, but Stephanie could tell she was stressed. She was keeping her eye on a little Jack Russell that kept escaping from its owner because it wanted to get at the ducks.

'When I get hold of that terror…' Debbie wagged her finger at it.

Mark and Stephanie laughed. Under the trees, a group of ladies were sitting on chairs around a picnic blanket. Tied to a chair leg was a Golden Labrador and sitting up on the checked blanket, staring at Debbie, was a cute, brown and white Jack Russell Terrier panting with its tongue hanging out.

'Let's see the fishing skills you've been bragging about,' Stephanie challenged Mark and handed Debbie two one-pound coins.

They put their drinks down on the table and each picked up a rod. Every time Stephanie's hook got near a duck's loop, Mark tickled her.

'Hey stop it,' Stephanie giggled.

Debbie watched them amused and shouted Stephanie encouragement. 'Quick get that one, there.'

Stephanie ran around the paddling pool and tried to hook a duck before he could reach her. On the third go, she caught one and triumphantly held the rod up in the air. Just as she was about to declare herself the winner, a brown and white streak jumped into the pool with a splash, and a hairy, wet body ran through her legs.

'Aargh' Stephanie cried as she fell back into the pool. Her top half landed on the grass, but her bottom fell into the middle sending a wave of ducks onto the grass.

Stephanie sat in the middle of the pool watching as Debbie chased after the dog with a yellow duck peeping out between its teeth. The little scamp ran over to the picnic rug and shook himself, showering the shocked ladies who screamed in dismay. The Labrador jumped up in the commotion and pulled on his chair to chase the Jack Russell.

Mark pulled Stephanie up and they both watched in amusement as the two dogs ran around, the little one hanging on to its prize and the big dog dragging a chair by its lead. At least two of the women were on their backs with their feet in the air with cries of, 'Alfie!' Eventually, the ladies managed to get back control of their pets and Debbie was given her duck back.

'I win…I guess,' Stephanie said standing in front of Mark dripping wet.

Mark's dark eyes slowly looked down Stephanie's body, where the material clung to her hips and dripped down her legs. Stephanie felt his gaze prickle her skin and watched him close the gap between them and he bent down in front of her.

'W…what are you doing?' Stephanie stammered as he knelt in front of her.

Stephanie felt his warm hands on her hips as he smoothed out her skirt and squeezed the water down her thighs. It was too much to take and she had to step back suddenly aware of how it was making her feel in front of all the people around them.

Stephanie continued to squeeze the water out of her dress as Mark handed her back her drink with a smile on his face.

'You look so cute,' he tucked an unruly curl behind Stephanie's ear. 'If it was anybody else, I'd be laughing my ass off. But you look so sexy.'

Stephanie looked at Mark and saw the smoulder in his eyes.

They were interrupted by Debbie emptying the pool and packing everything away.

'Here,' she handed Stephanie a pack of sweets, 'in fact, take the box, I've had enough. That devil of a dog will just come back to steal the ducks.'

'Has he been doing it for long?' Mark asked looking towards the dog that had taken up its position on the rug once more. It did look like a coiled spring ready to pounce, its eyes were focused on the poor ducks that now lay in a sad, yellow pile on the grass.

'It's been stealing my ducks all morning. Look…' She bent down to pick up a couple of the ducks. 'You can see the holes where its teeth have been, so they keep sinking.'

'That's a shame, at least you had a happy customer.'

Debbie sighed and laughed, 'I might as well throw him these two to play with and here are the sweets. At least I can go and watch the band now.'

She gave the bags to Stephanie and started to pack away.

'Thanks for the sweets, I'll use them for prizes.'

Stephanie and Mark walked about in the hot sun so Stephanie could dry off until she noticed the time and said she ought to return to Lisa.

WHEN SHE GOT back, it was after 1 o'clock, the Rocking Robins had started playing and people had started to dance in front of the stage. At the table, Lisa was sitting and talking to Serina, another teacher from school. Stephanie noticed that as well as a standard lamp and bottles of pop, there was now a toddler's red and yellow car and a tricycle.

'We seem to be getting more junk,' Stephanie remarked placing the box of sweets on the table.

'I know, all the kids keep leaving their stuff here,' Lisa moaned.

Serina smiled at Stephanie and Mark as he had his hand on her shoulder and was playing with Stephanie's hair.

'You make a cute couple,' Serina said.

Stephanie looked up at Mark and he grinned.

'That's cos we are a cute couple,' he said. 'Now then, I'd better go see how Dad is doing. See you later.'

He quickly kissed Stephanie and left. Stephanie walked around the table, and Lisa got up for her to sit down. Stephanie could still feel the tingle on her neck where Mark's hand had been. Lisa waved goodbye and strolled off to find Martin and her girls.

'Oh, you've got it bad, girl,' said Serina, laughing, 'and I don't blame you, he *is* gorgeous.'

Stephanie watched Mark walk back over to the tractor wondering what it would be like to be married to Mark. It was something she could get used to, but it was a scary thought. Stephanie frowned, she had to stop thinking thoughts like that, she still didn't know how long he was staying in Hibaldton for, he was only supposed to be there to help his father with the farm.

'So, are you here with anyone?' Stephanie asked, changing the subject.

'My sister and my cute nephews.'

She pointed to a young woman with long, black hair down to her waist, standing with two boys.

'They're over there with the parrot man,' she said, pointing to their left.

'He lives in the village, doesn't he? Oh, hasn't he been into some of the school assemblies?' Stephanie asked.

'Yes, his name is Ron, his parrots are amazing, he keeps them in his garden. The blue parrot can talk and the red one walks along the perch, and when Ron's back is turned, it reaches its beak into his pocket and takes out a cashew nut. They're very clever.'

'The parrots are beautiful aren't they.'

Stephanie watched Ron for a while. He was in his sixties, with grey hair and black glasses. She smiled at his white, jungle print jacket with a yellow shirt and pale blue trousers.

Serina pointed to the birds walking up and down a wooden railing.

'My grandmother, in India, has them in her garden. She thinks they're a pest because they steal her fruit, she grows grapes and mangoes, and she says they are called Ringneck parrots.'

'Wow, her garden sounds amazing,' Stephanie sighed.

They sat chatting and listening to the band. The rush for raffle tickets had died down, most people had sat down to listen to the music or were in the tents having a drink. The band eventually finished, and the DJ resumed his playlist.

A group of children came running over to the table.

'Miss, can we leave our bags here?'

'Oh no, you'll have to carry them about with you,' Stephanie ordered.

'But Betsy said she left her car here.'

Stephanie looked at all the bags they had in their hands. It was getting hotter, and they looked tired.

'Ok then, but make sure you come back for them.'

'We will. Are you coming to hear us sing? We'll be on in half an hour, Mr Bradshaw has asked us to round everyone up.'

'Don't worry, we'll be able to hear you from here,' Serina promised.

The children ran off to find their friends and Stephanie looked towards the stage that had been set up near the Village Hall. The local DJ had set up some speakers and a microphone, and a few people had been taking it in turns singing in between his playlists. Now she could see the school choir gathering at the side with Mr Bradshaw the music teacher, ready for their performance. They were putting on their blue school hoodies for the performance and Stephanie wondered if he needed any help.

'I did say that I'd go to watch,' Stephanie told Serina, 'but I don't know where Lisa is.'

'You go…*go*, I'll stay here for you,' Serina urged Stephanie to leave.

She walked towards the choir and Mark caught her up.

'Hi, where are you going?' Mark asked.

'Over to the choir, they're singing songs from Grease.'

'Are they learning about Greece for geography or history?' Stephanie looked at Mark.

' Grease -the musical,' she laughed.

As they approached, she could see the children had started to line up on the stage, one of the children had noticed them and was giggling. Just as the DJ turned on the music, a girl next to one of the microphones waved at Stephanie and said quite clearly, 'Hi Miss Rhodes. Look it's Miss Rhodes and her boyfriend.'

Her voice came out of the speakers loudly and everyone looked round and laughed. All Mark and Stephanie could do was look embarrassed and wave back. They stood waiting with other parents and families who had by now gathered around.

After the songs had finished, Stephanie and Mark clapped and cheered with the crowd. Stephanie felt so proud of the children for singing so confidently, they had obviously enjoyed every minute up on the stage.

ON RETURNING TO the stall, Stephanie could hardly see Serina for all the things around her. It seemed that half the village had left their items with them. Mark thought it was hilarious and so did Martin and Lisa when they got there.

'I'm sure everyone will come and take their things away,' Stephanie said, partly attempting to reassure herself.

Serina was sitting under the lampshade, its tassels swaying in the breeze.

'I'll go and get the microphone to tell everyone to claim their stuff, and call Reverend Pierce over for the announcement,' she shouted over her shoulder as she ran back to the stage.

When she got there, she grabbed a mic off its stand. Then she decided it would be better to stand on the stage, that way she would get more notice.

She climbed up the steps to stand in the middle. People were still hovering about after the choir's performance and when they saw Stephanie, they turned to look at her.

'Great,' thought Stephanie, 'a captive audience.'

She coughed and tapped the microphone.

'Can I have your attention everyone?' she began confidently.

'It's not on!' shouted a man from the crowd.

Everyone laughed. Stephanie frowned and looked for a switch on the side. She couldn't see one, so she waved at the DJ to turn it on.

'Hello everyone, thanks for coming today.'

There was a horrible whistling noise from the speakers, and everyone put their hands to their ears. A little girl, who was standing next to one of the speakers, started to cry so her mum moved her quickly and hugged her.

'Oh sorry,' Stephanie put out her hands to gesture an apology.

'As I was saying…' she continued carefully.

'What are you going to sing?' A teenage boy with short blond hair, shaved at the sides shouted out.

'What? Oh, I'm not...'

'Sing that devoted to you song,' shouted out a woman who was near the stage, 'I was waiting for that one, it's my favourite.'

Just as Stephanie was trying to say that she was not going to sing anything, music started playing.

Stephanie started to panic. She glared at the DJ, who just thought it was a last-minute decision, he was keen to show his skills at playing requests quickly. The crowd started to sway, and when Stephanie didn't start singing, they thought she must be shy so were encouraging her by joining in.

Stephanie didn't know what to do, everyone was waving for her to start and so she eventually found herself singing, quietly, at first into the microphone, looking around for support from anyone she knew in the crowd.

As the song progressed, Stephanie felt herself relax, especially when a couple of women got onto the stage next to her. And as the song came close to the end, she found that she had absolutely got into the swing of things.

'*But now,*' the song gathered in momentum and Stephanie, by this time, had totally gotten carried away. She happened to look up to see Mark, Lisa and Martin standing gobsmacked at the back of the crowd, but she couldn't stop now. She finished off with what she thought was a soulful and emotional end... '*to yooooo oooo*.'

She pointed with dramatic effect towards Mark, who was grinning from ear to ear, the two women on either side of Stephanie were pointing at each other and then impulsively knelt, so Stephanie put her arms up for a dramatic finish.

Everyone went wild, clapping, cheering and laughing.

When it had all died down, Stephanie shouted into the microphone as quickly as she could, 'If you left your belongings by the raffle table, could you move them, please? The raffle will be announced soon by Reverend Pierce. Thank you.'

She climbed down the steps and hurried with her head down back to the table. She didn't even stop when people tried to talk to her, even when she passed Mark.

Panting, she reached the table.

'Was that you singing on the stage?' Serina asked wide-eyed.

'Who, me?'

A group of children from the school came racing over.

'That was amazing Miss!'

They all were chatting, thrilled that their teacher had put on such an entertaining performance. Stephanie started to relax and soon everyone had come over to move their things.

About an hour later, Reverend Pierce and Mrs Moore appeared at the table after announcing the raffle, and all the prizes had gone.

'Well done, Stephanie,' said the reverend.

'I love that song, Stephanie, you were a bit squeaky in places… but well done.' Mrs Moore said enthusiastically.

Stephanie forced a tight smile and wished the ground would open up and swallow her.

4

SUMMER NIGHTS

It hadn't taken as long as Stephanie thought to clear up the field at the end of the day. Everyone pitched in, including members of the public who helped to pick up litter on their way out.

Ben and Angela were the last to sit down at the round table in the corner of the pub. Ben sank in his seat and looked exhausted.

'I'll get you a drink,' Martin said getting up. 'What would you like Ben?'

'Oh, I don't care, as long as it's cold and got alcohol.'

Martin disappeared towards the bar while they discussed the fair.

'Do you have any idea yet how much we've made?' Lisa asked Ben.

'No, not yet. We decided to count it all tomorrow.'

'We're all too hot and bothered to count properly anyway,' Rosie agreed.

'The stage was a great idea, it was good that your school could lend us the stage blocks,' Angela added.

'Yes, we can do that again as long as we're not using them,' Stephanie told her.

Mark put his arm around Stephanie and said, 'As long as we can have a repeat performance from you Steph.'

Stephanie went bright red and laughed pushing him away.

'Don't mention that again. It wasn't my idea to sing, the crowd just expected it and… I don't know how it happened really.'

Everyone started laughing and couldn't help teasing Stephanie for a bit longer.

Lisa added, 'The finale with you and those two girls was fab. It looked like you'd rehearsed it.'

Stephanie had to think for a moment to remember.

'It's all a blur,' she laughed, 'but no it was just instinctive talent.'

Martin came over with a drink for Ben and a couple of plates of chips. Stephanie reached for a few and sat back to take it all in. Martin stood behind Lisa who was busy chatting to Angela. Rosie was telling Ben about the hedgehog rescue and how much money she had made on her stall. Mark sipped his pint smiling lazily with his arm resting on her leg. It had been a fun day and Stephanie hoped that they all could get together more often.

IT WAS ABOUT 7 o'clock when Stephanie and Mark were back at Stephanie's house. Mark was still humming 'Hopelessly Devoted to You' now and again, so Stephanie threw a cushion at him.

'Oh, why does this kind of thing always happen to me?' Stephanie moaned.

Mark pulled her hands away, 'Haha, I don't know but it's one of the things I love about you.'

34

They both froze for a second when they realised what he'd said.

'I'll go make us a drink,' Mark walked into the kitchen and Stephanie plonked herself down on the settee. Damn, was that an 'I love you' statement or was it just a casual 'I love that about you' thing? What did he actually say? 'That's one of the things I love about you.' He didn't actually say he loved her… but should she have said she loved him? Did she love him? Was he expecting her to say that? She twiddled with the belt on her skirt as she listened to him opening a bottle and the glugging sound of wine as it was poured into the glasses.

She watched him for some clue as he sat down next to her with a glass of wine in one hand and another for her in the other. She accepted it and they both took a sip, and then he stood up again. He seemed nervous about something. Oh my God he was going to say he loved her, and she did love him, she knew it with all her heart. She had come to realise, that a 'first love' holds a piece of your heart forever and the moment Mark stepped back into her life, that piece had slotted back like completing a jigsaw puzzle. Her heart started thumping in her chest.

'Is there something you want to say?' Stephanie eventually said as the suspense was killing her.

Mark stood up and nervously looked down at his feet, then he looked up and swallowed.

'I… have to go back to London… tomorrow,' he said.

5

SUMMER LOVIN'

ow long are you going for?' Stephanie eventually said after a long pause.

She was taken by surprise and couldn't hide it. Mark sat down next to her and turned to look at her.

'My boss has been annoyed that I haven't been into the office in months. I've been putting them off but now they want me in.'

'How long will that take?' Stephanie asked again slowly.

'A few months.'

'Months?'

'The rest of the summer. I was thinking that I can still come up to visit on weekends, and you can come and stay in the summer holidays. We'd been planning on going to London anyway.'

Stephanie thought about it and tried not to seem disappointed.

'Of course, you need to go, it is your job after all. I will miss you.'

'You're not mad at me?'

'No of course not.'

She tried to sound like she wasn't disappointed, but inside she felt like her heart had just stopped.

'Oh good.'

He sounded relieved.

'I thought you'd get upset or something.'

'We'll have to have a good night then,' she said forcing a smile.

'Today has been just the thing I needed. I'll have some great memories to take with me… Sandy'.

Some memories to take with him? What a jerk! Stephanie put her glass on the floor, not caring that it spilt, and sprang to her feet. Was that all she meant to him? Someone to stop him from feeling bored while he was away from the big city. Mark stood up and spun her around to face him, without thinking she punched him on the arm.

'Do you feel better now?' he asked. 'I only found out a couple of days ago, and I've been trying to find the right time to tell you. I don't want to go, so I put it off. Honestly, I will miss you *so* much.'

Mark slowly cupped her face with his hands and looked into her eyes.

'I'm sorry Steph, I love being with you.'

Looking into his brown eyes, was like melting in a pool of seductive, silky, chocolate, it wasn't long before she regretted spoiling the mood.

'I'm sorry too, it won't be the same without you.' Stephanie whispered.

Her lips reached up to his, and each kiss was tender. He kissed her on the mouth, her nose, her eyelids and then back to her lips.

His slow, gentle kiss became more demanding, and Stephanie reacted. He walked her backwards until her legs were against the settee, causing her to fall back onto the soft cushions. She lay back to allow him to unbutton her dress. The buttons only went to her waist. He stroked her arm lightly as he moved the thin strap over her shoulder and started to leave a tingling trail of kisses down her neck.

'Oh Steph,' he murmured into her ear which sent shivers down her spine. 'I need you.'

'Yes,' Stephanie answered.

His hands stroked up her legs and found the hem of her dress and pushed it higher exposing her thighs. His tongue traced the contours of her neck and across her collar bone, he smiled, and his eyes grew dark with lust as Stephanie purred with pleasure at his touch.

'Your skin is so soft,' he whispered in her ear. His deep chuckle made Stephanie melt even further against his warm body.

Mark had this effect on her that no other man had before. Her body shivered as he kissed inside her thigh which made her cry out. Her hands moved up to the cushion and she grasped it tightly, her annoyance with him was forgotten. Things hadn't changed, they would still see each other often.

Mark couldn't take his eyes off her.

'You're so beautiful,' he groaned, 'I can't believe you're mine.'

Wrapping his arm around Stephanie's back and the other underneath her knees, he lifted her off the settee and carried her up the stairs.

REALITY ARRIVED WITH the morning coffee. They sat on opposite sides of the table drinking and eating their toast in silence. On waking up, Stephanie couldn't help but feel upset again that he was going back to London. Doubts that he would be returning kept coming into her mind. She tried to not be in a bad mood but when Mark woke up as if nothing had happened, she had snapped at him.

'I should go back to my house after this so I can pack.'

Mark looked down at his coffee and seemed to be avoiding Stephanie's gaze.

'You might as well set off early to avoid the traffic.'

Stephanie tried to keep the emotion out of her voice, but instead, it made her sound like she didn't care. Mark looked up and reached out for Stephanie's hand, but she pulled it away and stood up to take the empty plates to the sink. She needed to be busy, or she knew that she would cry. Stephanie was annoyed at herself for feeling this way. She didn't want Mark to think she was pathetic and couldn't live without him.

'Pathetic,' Stephanie spoke to herself but said it out loud.

'Why am I pathetic?' Mark asked standing behind her.

Stephanie turned to face him.

'No…I'm being…'

Stephanie sighed and forced herself to smile.

'Go and get your things together. I'm going to be busy at work. The Summer is always the most hectic with report writing and exams, so we wouldn't see much of each other anyway,' she spoke quickly.

'I'll ring you when I get there… I'm sorry.'

'You have nothing to apologise for.'

'It will only be a few weeks before we'll see each other again. London's only a short train ride away and you'll come and stay in the holiday?'

Mark looked concerned, his eyes looked deep into Stephanie's until she could see that he meant what he said.

'I won't go now if you don't want me to.'

'No, you should go. I'm fine honestly.'

'Are you sure?'

'Yes, now go.'

Stephanie kissed his stubbled face and warm lips.

Mark picked up his car keys from the table, smiled at her and then walked to the door. Stephanie watched him bend down to pick up something from the doormat.

'You've got mail,' he said handing it to her.

Stephanie looked at the postcard in her hand. On the front it showed a picture of a river with the moonlight reflected in the dark water. There were narrow houses on the side of the river and a bridge with bikes leaning on the side. Amsterdam?

'I didn't know anyone was on holiday,' Stephanie said as she turned the card over to look at the back.

On the right side was Stephanie's name and address. On the left was just one phrase:

'You are always on my mind.'

'Who do you think it's from?' Mark asked puzzled.

Stephanie shrugged, 'I don't have a clue.'

'Strange that it's not signed, where's the postmark from?'

They both looked, but there wasn't one.

'That's funny, it means it's been hand-delivered. Have you got a secret admirer you're not telling me about?' Mark asked teasingly.

'Don't be silly.'

'Anyway, I'll go now. Take care of yourself and I'll see you soon.'

He opened the front door and Stephanie closed it behind him, first looking up and down the road in case she saw a clue of who might have put it through her door.

Stephanie walked back into the kitchen and sat at the table. She breathed in deeply and knew she would see him soon. She couldn't believe how her body was reacting to him returning to London. She felt panicked that she wouldn't see him again, was that it?

'Get a grip girl!' she told herself. 'What is wrong with you?'

She shook her head and wondered why she didn't trust him with her heart. This man had risked his life for her a few months ago, protected her, made her laugh when she needed cheering up... but there was something she couldn't figure out.

Was it maybe her?

Was Stephanie scared of change? Did she worry that he might want her to move to London? She had broken up with her ex when he wanted to move to Wales.

Stephanie realised she had been turning the postcard around in her hands. She looked at it for any clues, then stood it up against a vase.

Suddenly she felt so exhausted from psychoanalysing everything. The night before, she and Mark had stayed up late watching movies and, well, there had been plenty of sex. Now with the tension of the morning, Stephanie had a throbbing headache, she needed to go back to bed and get some more sleep.

6

BARBARA, MALCOLM AND GRANDMA BETTIE

The bed was buzzing. Bzzz bzz…what was that? Stephanie pulled herself out of her slumber… her parents' number lit up her phone.

'Stephanie, is that you? It's your mother.'

A shrill voice screamed in Stephanie's ear. She scrunched up her eyes and wished she could do the same to her ears.

'Yes, it's me, what's going on? What time is it?'

'Oh, thank God. Malcom, It's Stephanie, she's ok,' Barbara announced.

'We thought you'd had an accident.'

Stephanie sat up, bleary-eyed, and looked at her phone. It was 1 pm.

'I fell asleep again, I'm sorry. Why do you always have to fear the worst?'

'It's because we love you, you'll understand when you have children.'

Stephanie had heard this a million times before.

'I'll get dressed and be over as soon as I can.'

'Don't rush, I don't want you to drive fast and have an accident.'

'Mum, there's hardly any traffic on the road between here and Rigby, there's not much chance of that.'

'Remember, my friend Rita's son's girlfriend's neighbour's cousin had an accident on that road.'

Stephanie rolled her eyes and slowly got off the bed.

'Yes, but she was trying to overtake two tractors, and she didn't have an accident, she just got flashed at. And before you say anything, I won't overtake anybody. Now I'm going to take a shower and I'll drive carefully and see you soon. Save some food for me and don't let grandma eat all the Yorkshire puddings. Byeee.'

Stephanie sighed and tossed her phone onto the bed.

Every Sunday, just about, Stephanie had her lunch at her mum and dad's house. Her Grandma Bettie lived with her parents, and Stephanie had bought her grandma's old house. Ever since the terrible events in the Spring, her family had been overly concerned about her. Stephanie hadn't told them the whole story, but they had heard rumours, which possibly might have been ten times worse.

Stephanie walked towards the bathroom, and she realised that her headache had nearly gone, and it was now her stomach that was complaining and needed food. A memory of the morning with Mark flashed into her mind as she stepped into the shower. She hoped that standing under the powerful flow of water would wash it all away.

AN HOUR LATER, Stephanie was in her parents' kitchen sitting down for lunch.

Stephanie remarked, 'You didn't have to wait for me, I could have had leftovers.'

'You see, I told you we didn't have to wait,' Grandma Betty piped up.

Barbara gave her mum a hard stare.

'I'm not giving leftovers to my daughter when she can have the real thing. It was ok, I hadn't made the veggies anyway.'

Barbara and Malcolm finished putting dishes of food onto the table and then they all started to help themselves. It wasn't long before they were tucking in.

'Are you all right?' Barbara was staring at her daughter as she ate her lunch.

'I'm fine,' Stephanie reassured her mum as she popped a roast potato into her mouth.

'Where's Mark, is he not joining us today? I made extra.' Barbara asked.

'No, not today, he's had to go back to London.'

'Oh, he won't be gone for long,' Barbara said soothingly.

'I used to love being in London,' Grandma Bettie started to reminisce.

'All those exciting dance halls to go to… I remember we used to stay out all night dancing to rock and roll, the boys used to throw us around, my legs used to get up this high…'

Grandma Bettie threw her arm up in the air enthusiastically and a lump of beef flew off her fork. They all watched it soar through the air and land in the sink.

'No wonder you walk with a limp,' Stephanie's dad chimed.

'Malcolm!' Barbara warned him.

'Those were the days. We knew how to have a good time then,' Grandma Bettie finished grumpily.

'I always love listening to your stories Grandma, but Mark's gone to work. I also have a lot of work to do as well so I would have been too busy to go with him anyway.'

Stephanie used her fork to make a little mountain out of her mashed potato and then let the prongs slide down the sides.

'Don't play with your food dear,' Barbara said disapprovingly.

'Here's some ketchup. You could make it look like a volcano,' Grandma Bettie winked.

'It's not Close Encounters, good film though,' Stephanie's dad said as he finished off his food.

'You work so hard, every time I see you, you're busy.'

Stephanie ate a bit more meat and then realised she had lost her appetite.

'It's always busy in the Summer Term, lots to finish off before the holiday and reports to write.'

Bettie patted her arm in sympathy. 'It will be the holiday soon, won't it?'

Malcom grunted, 'Another holiday, you teachers get more holidays than I have hot dinners.'

'Dad, I'm not getting into this conversation with you right now and I'm not in the mood.'

'Would you like me to put the rest of your dinner in a box?' Barbara asked, concerned.

'Yes, please mum. Do you mind if I don't stay long? I have a pile of tests to mark.'

'Of course, I'll do it now.'

As Stephanie watched her mum put the leftovers in a plastic box, she remembered the postcard.

'Do any of you know anyone who's gone on holiday to Amsterdam?'

'No.' They all shook their heads.

'Why?' Barbara asked.

'I got a postcard from what looks like Amsterdam, but it was hand posted.'

'Doesn't it say who it's from?' Malcom asked.

'No, it just said, 'You are on my mind.'

'Maybe, it's from a secret admirer,' Grandma Bettie suggested.

'A secret admirer sends a Valentine's card, not a holiday card,' Stephanie pointed out, 'and why does everyone ask that?'

'Maybe he only started admiring you recently,' Barbara said.

'It might not be from a man, it could be from a lesbian,' Grandma Bettie announced.

'Oh, for heaven's sake,' Malcom groaned and stood up to leave. 'I'm going to go and finish my crossword. Take care of yourself Munchkin.'

He stopped to kiss Stephanie on the top of her head, walked out of the kitchen and headed for the living room.

'I don't understand where your mind wanders, I really don't mum,' said Barbara shaking her head.

'I don't know it just goes there.'

'Thanks, you've been a great help.'

Stephanie rolled her eyes and stood up to go.

'Thanks for the delicious lunch.'

She kissed them on the cheek, picked up her food box, shouted bye to her dad and set off for home.

7
STAFFROOM CONFESSIONS

Monday, at school, Stephanie found herself discussing Mark in the staffroom at lunchtime.

'It's a shame he's had to go back to London,' Lisa said unwrapping her sandwiches.

The five friends sat in a circle with sandwich boxes on their knees. Lisa was sitting on Stephanie's left, Tracy and Serina opposite, and Rita, a teaching assistant who worked with Tracy, was sitting on a chair to Stephanie's right.

'You two didn't say anything about it on Saturday.'

'No, I didn't know then.'

The others looked surprised and shook their heads.

'Why didn't he tell you?' Serina asked.

'He said he didn't want to spoil my day,' Stephanie replied.

'Men.' Tracy sat back in her chair. 'They can't decide what they want.'

'He has to go back to London sometimes, he can't work from here all the time.'

To her surprise, Stephanie found herself defending him.

'But he was out of line not keeping you in the loop,' Tracy replied biting down on her sandwich with vigour. If Mark had been there, he would have been crossing his legs.

'He wasn't given much time to tell me,' Stephanie continued, 'I acted like an idiot as well, I was so upset when he told me.'

'I'm not surprised you were upset. I'd be upset if Martin told me he was going away the next day.' Lisa comforted her best friend.

'Yeah, but I made a fool of myself and hardly spoke to him in the morning.'

'The bastard got what he deserved.'

Tracy shook her half-eaten sandwich at Stephanie and Serina nodded in agreement.

'You shouldn't feel like you did anything wrong, you should be able to show your feelings.'

'He said he was sorry and that he wanted me to visit in the Summer holidays,' Stephanie said.

'Well, that's big of him. So, you can visit, what for a few days?' Tracy asked.

'No, he wanted me to stay with him for the holidays.'

'He's going for a long time then,' Lisa said surprised.

'He's not helping with the harvest?' Rita asked.

She knew quite a lot about farming as her husband worked on a farm nearby.

'No, he doesn't help his dad with the farming side of it. He helps with the technical side of things.'

They sat in silence while they ate.

'I don't know how I'm feeling, it might be that I'm worried that he won't want to come back. I'm also worried that he will ask me to move there.'

Stephanie felt better for saying it out loud and wondered what her friends thought.

'It would be exciting moving to London,' Tracy said. 'There's nothing to do around here and the men are drips…'

Tracy paused and looked around the group who stared back at her, sandwiches paused in front of their mouths.

'Apart from your partners of course -- I need a strong man to whisk me away.'

'I'll whisk you away Tracy love,' came a voice from the back of the staffroom.

They all looked round to see Dave, the caretaker, washing up his mug. He gave them a cheeky wink.

'You keep promising but you don't deliver,' Tracy shot back. Dave chuckled and left the room.

They were used to Dave. He liked to listen in to female conversations in case there was a chance for a flirtatious joke, but he was harmless -- unless he had a screwdriver in his hand. Ironically, DIY wasn't his strong suit. They turned back to their conversation but talked more quietly, now more aware of the rest of the staff in the room.

'The two of you, on Saturday, looked very much in love. I am sure he will be missing you just as much as you are missing him,' Serina smiled.

'We haven't mentioned the word 'love' yet though.'

'You've only been going out for a few months,' Lisa said.

'Lust comes before love,' Tracy nodded knowingly.

'Loves grows in time,' Serina said.

'Do you guys believe in love at first sight?' Stephanie asked.

'I believe it could happen…but it didn't happen to me. Martin annoyed the hell out of me when I first knew him.'

Serina said, 'I had a kind of arranged marriage. He was a friend of the family and we dated because it was expected, but he is the love of my life now, and I am his.'

'That's romantic,' Stephanie sighed.

'Was it love at first sight for you and Mark?' Tracy asked.

'If seeing him makes you feel like your heart is going to explode and you feel faint and all you want to do is look into his eyes for eternity.'

Tracy blew a long, whistle. 'Is that what you felt like when you first saw Mark?'

Stephanie nodded, 'But that was when I was sixteen, does that count?'

They were about to continue that debate when the bell rang for the end of lunchtime.

8
ANOTHER POSTCARD

When Stephanie got home, she was closing the door when she saw another postcard waiting for her on the mat. She quickly looked up the road but there was no one except for a man standing next to a blue car. He was a few doors away on the other side of the road, but he seemed to be watching her. A chill ran through Stephanie at the thought of Sergei but as she stared at him, she realised that he was much slimmer and couldn't be him. He leaned against his car and there was a cloud of vapour wafting above his head. Stephanie shook her head and turned away telling herself to not be paranoid, he was probably just waiting for someone.

Stephanie picked up the postcard from the mat and tentatively turned it over. She didn't really think she had a secret admirer, then she wondered if maybe Mark was leaving her clues about a holiday. She looked at the back first and the same handwriting was there, this time it said,

'I will never forget you.'

She turned it round to look at the picture. It was a speedboat on a river with a man fishing in the reeds. It was a peaceful image, nevertheless, it sent a shiver down her spine as the last time she saw a boat on a river, she had been forced onto it. It was a memory she'd rather forget. Stephanie stood puzzled. She enjoyed working out crosswords with her dad, but this was tricky. Surely Mark wouldn't send her a card with a boat on, he had bad memories of that night too.

'I will never forget.' Stephanie read it out loud.

She closed the door and walked into the front room to put the postcard with the first one. 'Your brain is on your mind, where your memories are… an elephant never forgets… is it an anagram? I'm stumped.'

STEPHANIE WAS SITTING at home in front of the TV when her phone rang. She looked at the screen and her pulse quickened at Mark's name. She took a deep breath before she answered it.

It was their first phone call since he returned to London and she wasn't sure how it would go.

'Hi.'

'Hi, how are you?' Mark sounded as worried as Stephanie did.

'I'm fine, I'm just watching TV and marking some test papers.'

She looked around at the piles of papers all around her feet.

Mark laughed, 'I bet your room's a mess right now.'

'You know me too well,' Stephanie laughed, feeling more at ease. 'What are you doing?'

'I've just ordered a takeout and I'm sitting on the settee in front of the TV. I've just closed my laptop for the night. I'm sorry I didn't ring when I got here.'

'You texted. I'm not your mother you know.'

'I know. I wanted to talk to you, but I felt grumpy by the time I got in, I wouldn't have been good company.'

'Sounds like that's the time when you should talk, it might have helped.'

Stephanie paused the TV and put her pen down.

Mark sighed. 'When I left you, I popped in to see my parents.'

'Ah, that explains it.'

'Dad wanted me to explain how the new software works again. He makes out that he doesn't understand but he doesn't try. I told him that I can help him over the phone when he needs it.'

'Does your mum use a computer?'

'No not really. I told them they should hire an assistant to help with the admin and that didn't go down well.'

'Why doesn't he hire someone to help?'

'Oh, he's stubborn… and I suppose he's been down this road before.'

'With your brother, Richard?'

There was a pause and Stephanie was worried she shouldn't have mentioned him.

'You remember him? Yeah, I guess you would, it was about 10 years ago when he left, and he was about my age.'

'Maybe your dad's worried that *you* might emigrate,' Stephanie said softly, she could hear the emotion in his voice. When he didn't reply she continued. 'It sounds like you and your dad should talk about what happened.'

'It was my dad's fault that he left. Richard wouldn't have moved to America if Dad hadn't been so bloody single-minded.

They used to argue all the time, and when I finished Uni, I made up my mind that I wasn't going to go through all that with him.'

'So that's why you haven't worked with him until now,' Stephanie realised.

She was beginning to understand the tension she had noticed at times between Mark and his dad.

'Is that why you've gone back to London?'

'No, I really had to show my face for a while. To be honest, me and Dad… it was nearly working, but I'm just not ready to commit yet.'

His voice trailed off as if he was deep in thought.

Stephanie wondered if he felt like that about their relationship too. 'Are you coming up this weekend?' Stephanie asked.

'I might be able to next week. Hopefully, I can finish early on Friday after a morning meeting. Would you like to get a takeaway at my house? Then on Saturday, we could go over to see if Dad has thrown the computer in the lake.'

Stephanie laughed and then remembered the postcards.

'Are you thinking of us going on holiday?' she asked feeling excited.

'Where are you thinking of going?' he asked.

'Maybe somewhere where there are elephants? Maybe India?'

'India?' Mark sounded surprised, 'Maybe… if you want.'

'Oh, I don't know, I've been puzzling about it all night.'

'I have ten days of leave, we can go anywhere you like.'

'How about America to see your brother?' Stephanie suggested.

'I don't know Steph, we haven't talked in a long time. He might not want to see me.'

'I bet he would. Think about it. You are on my mind too you know.'

'I'm always thinking of you Steph. I can't wait to see you.'

'Ok, I have to ask you Mark, who are you getting to send me these postcards?'

'What?' Mark asked.

'No really, stop teasing me.'

'Did you get another postcard?'

He hung up the phone and then rang again on a video call.

'Hi,' Stephanie answered.

'Show me the card,' Mark said.

Stephanie took the phone over to the dining table and put the cards out for him to see.

'Turn them over,' Mark ordered.

Stephanie turned them over.

'Didn't you send them?'

'No, I didn't.'

'What's it all about?'

The way Mark was acting, was starting to make Stephanie feel worried.

'I don't know, don't worry, it's probably nothing but keep them and let me know if you get another,' Mark sounded calm, but Stephanie could tell that he looked worried.

'Someone's probably got the wrong address, maybe it's meant for one of the neighbours,' Stephanie suggested.

'Has anyone been, you know, hanging about your house?'

'No, not like Sergei if that's what you mean. Don't worry Mark, I'll be fine.'

Mark looked annoyed.

'It's typical that this has happened when I go away.'

'Look, I shouldn't have mentioned it. It's nothing really.'

Stephanie sighed and felt awkward, she hadn't meant to make him feel guilty, she was feeling fine about him being back in London. She made an effort to make him see that she was fine.

'How is work in London? I'm looking forward to staying there with you.'

'I can't wait to show you around, I'll show you my office and we can see the sights if you like.'

'Is it close to the centre?'

'Not far, but everywhere is close by when you can get the tube.'

'A bit different to Hibaldton. I suppose it's nice for you to get the best of both worlds.'

'Yes, I suppose so, but I'm here for work remember so I'll save the sight-seeing for when you get here.'

9
THERE WAS NO BREAK IN

The next day, Stephanie was feeling much happier. The weather was hot and sunny, perfect for working outside with the children. In the morning, the class had spent the maths lesson measuring the playground with rulers and measuring tape. The children sat huddled in small groups, busily recording the data in their books. After that lesson, a rugby coach came to teach the children out on the field, it gave Stephanie some time to reflect on the night before.

They had talked for hours later that night, the conversation continued when she got into bed, and they watched the same TV programme until Stephanie had fallen asleep. She remembered listening to his deep voice, promising things he would do to her when they saw each other again. Stephanie suddenly realised where her mind had wandered, it made her look around guiltily as if someone might have read her thoughts and guessed what she was daydreaming. She stood up to take some photos of the rugby game for the school website.

After school, Stephanie and Lisa walked to the shop on their way home.

'You've seemed a lot happier today,' Lisa observed.

'Yep, it's been a good day today,' Stephanie smiled and stopped walking to turn to her friend.

'Plus, Mark rang last night.'

'I thought he might have,' Lisa grinned. 'What did he say?'

'We had a good talk actually about his relationship with his dad and he told me that he's coming home soon.'

They continued to walk past the church. The sun was hot on their faces as they rounded the corner, and a group of children came out of the shop tearing the wrappers off ice lollies.

'Ooh, I so need an ice lolly, I think I'll get an orange one. It's so hot,' exclaimed Lisa fanning her face with her hand.

'I know, why does it get so hot in Summer around 4 o'clock? I think I'll get a Cornetto.'

The door to the shop was open and inside stood Mrs Cook behind the counter talking to two ladies. Stephanie recognised them but didn't know who they were. One of the ladies was older, in her seventies, and was looking quite upset, the other was younger and was soothing her with a hand on her shoulder.

'Are you sure you didn't lose your earrings down the back of the drawers?' Mrs Cook asked her.

'I am certain. I put my earrings and a bracelet in a little bowl by the mirror, like I do every night, and when I went to put them on this morning… only the bracelet was there. I looked everywhere,' the lady said, waving her arms to impress how hard she had searched.

She turned her head and noticed Stephanie and Lisa.

'Oh well, I'll have to keep looking I suppose. Maybe you are right.'

She shrugged and the two ladies walked out of the shop.

Stephanie and Lisa looked at Mrs Cook with puzzled expressions.

'She's so upset because those earrings cost a lot of money-diamonds apparently,' Mrs Cook shrugged. 'Now then, what can I get for you today?'

Stephanie and Lisa pointed over to the freezer and they all walked over to choose their iced treats. Stephanie also reached for a bottle of milk from the fridge.

'It's funny,' Mrs Cook mentioned as they handed over their money, 'Margaret is the second person to lose her jewellery today. It must be the heat.'

'Oh?' Stephanie asked, 'Who else lost something?'

'Mabel Moor. She believes that she was burgled.'

'She would,' Lisa noted.

'It can't have been a robbery though,' Mrs Cook explained, 'because there was no break-in.'

'That's odd,' Stephanie agreed. A man then entered the shop, so Stephanie and Lisa turned to leave.

Outside, they put their wrappers in the bin and started to walk back towards the church. When they stopped at the junction, Stephanie looked up the road that went behind the church to where Mabel Moore lived.

'I probably should go visit Mrs Moore, she still has my casserole dish.'

' Let her keep it, it's not worth it,' Lisa said, mouth full of lolly.

'It is my mum's dish!' Stephanie said.

'You'll probably see her at the next Parish Council meeting, I think there's one next week.'

Stephanie didn't take much persuading, she hadn't been up that road since Mary and Gordon's death and as Mrs Moore lived opposite Mary's cottage, Stephanie had no desire to venture that way any time soon, although she had been wondering if Mary's relatives had started to empty her house yet.

'Yeah, you're right I suppose...' Stephanie decided not to reveal her thoughts to Lisa, her friend would only tell her off for living in the past.

The two young ladies carried on walking together until it was time for Lisa to branch off towards her house. They stood on the corner for a final chat.

'I've been getting some strange postcards by the way,' Stephanie said.

'What kind of postcards?'

Stephanie told her about them and how she thought Mark had sent them at first.

'Maybe he's just not letting on.'

'No, he didn't seem to know anything about the second one. So, you haven't heard of anyone else receiving mysterious postcards then.'

Lisa shook her head. 'Not me. I'll see you tomorrow then.'

'Bye.'

Stephanie continued to walk down the road thinking about the postcards. A niggling thought kept telling her that it wasn't a coincidence that they were both pictures of rivers and boats and she wondered if the puzzle might become clearer if there was another one waiting for her when she got home.

As she walked up her road, she noticed the blue car again and looked over the road to see if anyone was inside. The driver's window was partly down, and a cloud of smoke or vapour was drifting out. It was difficult to see who was sitting in the car, but it looked like the same man as before. He had dark hair, a slim build but that was all she could tell. Stephanie walked quickly into her drive feeling for the door key in her bag, she wondered why he was sitting in his car like that. Maybe his wife didn't like him smoking.

As she opened her door, she looked down expecting there to be a postcard waiting for her, but there was nothing.

10

AN EXCITING INVITATION

All week, Stephanie worked hard after school to finish marking her class's tests. It was Thursday and she needed to enter the results by Friday and her reports also were due soon.

She was sitting at the dining table, thinking how much she had to get done when her phone rang. It was a video call from Mark again and Stephanie hated those. When talking, her eyes would always flit to the camera where she would see herself from an awful angle and then she would spend the rest of the call fiddling with her hair or changing position. Maybe she would not answer it and check herself out in the mirror first. Her desire to see Mark made up her mind for her, and she managed to answer it before he hung up.

'Hi, had a good day?' Mark asked.

He looked like he was at his desk in his flat. Suddenly Stephanie was curious to see what it looked like.

'Busy,' she answered, 'but I'm glad you called. I've got this last paper to mark and then I can input the data before you come back.'

'That's good,' Mark replied.

'Hey, give me a tour,' Stephanie pleaded.

Mark looked around then slowly stood up with his laptop in his hands.

'Ok, but it's kind of a mess... So, this is the lounge.'

Stephanie stared transfixed at the screen as he showed her around his place. It was a lot bigger than she thought. The kitchen was a wall of white, glossy cupboards above a black work surface that opened out to the lounge. She couldn't see any mess either, Mark was tidier than she was, only the small, round table had some clutter of a beer bottle and a dirty plate left over from dinner. There was a black, leather sofa which faced a wide-screen TV and a black and white rug covered the wooden floor in between.

'It's amazing,' Stephanie said excited at the prospect of staying in the holidays. 'Show me the view from the window.'

Mark laughed at Stephanie's enthusiasm as he pushed back the blinds for her to see the view of the street.

'I bet you can't wait to come to stay in London,' Mark said and then seemed to have an idea. 'Why don't you come over this weekend instead of me going there?'

'What, I go to you, in London?' Stephanie felt excited but unsure.

'I've got a lot of work to do though, I've got reports and planning for next week.'

'You could work here, and then we could go out at night.'

There was a pause while Stephanie thought about it.

Mark continued, 'Actually, there's a gathering I've been invited to. It's a work's do at a wine bar. Come with me, it'll be fun.'

'This weekend?'

'Tomorrow night.'

'I don't know, I won't know anyone and it's short notice.'

Mark frowned, 'I would like you to come with me. I've told my friends about you, and they'd love to meet you.'

'I don't know, I suppose I could work on the train down,' Stephanie could feel herself getting excited again, she realised that she'd be silly to say no. Besides, she looked into Mark's brown eyes, and she couldn't wait to be in his arms again.

"I know someone who'd love to see you again…'

'Who?' Stephanie asked.

'Kate. Every time I hear from her, she keeps moaning that we need to meet up and I've been instructed to bring you.'

Stephanie laughed at the memory of Kate gate-crashing Hibaldton in the spring.

'It would be fun to meet up with her again, and if I don't go down to London, she's likely to come and tell me off!'

Stephanie thought back to when she first experienced the whirlwind called Kate. With her long, dark hair, model-like body and tasteful clothes, Stephanie had to admit that she had felt intimidated. But Kate grew on her, and it turned out that she and Mark were good friends from Uni, she was just very demanding that's all.

'Ok, I'll come down,' she beamed.

'Great.'

Mark looked slightly surprised that she'd agreed to it, but he also looked excited too.

'Do you want to book the ticket? I'll send you the money if you want as it's my fault you're having to go.'

'No, I'm ok thanks. You can pay for food and drinks though when I get there.'

'It's a deal. I'm sorry to spring it on you, I'm glad that you're coming. It's fun to do things on the spur of the moment.'

'I suppose so. It is exciting, but sometimes girls need a bit of notice to buy clothes or get their hair done, that kind of thing.'

'Don't go to any trouble, it's not a party, just a few friends meeting up, plus, you look gorgeous whatever you wear. I'll ring Kate and see if she can meet up. I'm only going to say that we're available Saturday evening, otherwise, she'll have the whole weekend planned.'

After booking the train, they said goodbye so that Stephanie could finish the paper she was marking. It was hard to concentrate and she couldn't wait to tell her friends at work.

11

TRAINS, BRAS, AND PROSTITUTES

It had been a hot night, even with both bedroom windows open, Stephanie had had little sleep. In the morning, she was annoyed that she was so tired as she knew it was going to be a hectic weekend in London.

In the staffroom, everyone was talking about the weather and had kept their bedroom windows open. The caretaker came round delivering an electric fan to each classroom and the children took it in turns to say how poorly they felt so they could sit next to it. In the afternoon, Stephanie took the art lesson outside to draw under the shade of some trees and then she allowed the children to make paper fans while they listened to the class story.

At the end of the day, after the children had gone, Stephanie discussed her trip to London with Lisa and Tracy in the classroom.

'I'm so jealous Stephanie,' Tracy moaned. 'Make sure you take lots of photos.

'Yes, and you're not allowed to work when you get there, have fun,' Lisa ordered.

'If you insist,' Stephanie laughed. 'I need to hurry, the train leaves at 10 past 5. I've already packed, I just need to grab my things.'

They laughed as Stephanie quickly picked up her bag and gave them an excited hug goodbye before rushing to her car to drive home.

As she was checking she had everything, she suddenly realised she hadn't told her mum where she was going. Damn, she didn't want to be late for the train, but then again, her dad could drive her to the station and then she wouldn't have to pay for parking.

Stephanie rang her parents, they still had a landline and her mum answered.

'Hello?' Barbara answered, louder than necessary.

'It's Steph, can I speak to Dad?'

'Why?'

'I just want to ask him for a favour?'

'What favour?'

'God mum, I'm in a rush.'

Stephanie took a deep breath, she hadn't meant to sound so impatient.

'I'm going down to London to see Mark and I was wondering if Dad could take me to the station. The train leaves at 10 past 5.'

'Why isn't Mark coming to see you? Why is he expecting you to go there?'

Stephanie closed her eyes and tried not to sound annoyed.

'I want to go, it'll be exciting. He's meeting me off the train, now can you ask Dad? Please?'

FINALLY, STEPHANIE COULD relax. She leaned back against the seat of the train with her bags on the seat next to her. It had been a while since she had travelled to London on the train, she remembered there was a hectic train change, then after that she could get some work done. She had booked a seat with a table and if she worked solidly, she might finish her reports, then she only had to read them through.

The changeover went smoothly, despite the platforms being busy. So many people going about their lives. Stephanie wondered where they were all going, and why? She walked along the platform, carrying her bags, searching for her carriage, and then climbed on board picking up her small suitcase and putting her laptop bag on her shoulder. Once inside the compartment, she moved along with difficulty until she found her seat. She felt relieved when she saw it was empty, and before long, she had opened her laptop and got to work. The carriage was about half full as the train pulled out of the station.

The first thing she did was to text Mark.

'On the train. Got a table!'

'Great, can't wait to see you.'

'Me too! Where are you taking me first?'

'The bedroom of course.'

'Hey!'

'Babe, I miss you so much, we might only get as far as the hallway.'

Stephanie blushed, put her phone upside down on the table with a smile and decided to focus on her work.

Every now and then, she paused to look out the window at the fields whizzing by. The constant vibration and gentle hum of the train felt soothing as people read and quietly chatted with their companions. Stephanie felt like she was going on an adventure, and she smiled at the thought of Mark waiting for her when she arrived.

Shortly after a stop at a station, Stephanie glanced up from her laptop to see a man sitting at the opposite side of the table. It surprised her as she was so engrossed with her work that she hadn't noticed him arrive. He wasn't paying attention to her, just looking at his phone and drinking from a train station plastic cup. She continued writing her reports and then looked up again to see chocolate and white foam under his nose. Stephanie wondered whether she should tell him or not. She continued with her work, telling herself to mind her own business but when she looked up it was still there. Stephanie coughed to get his attention, he looked up briefly and then continued with his phone.

'Excuse me,' Stephanie ventured.

He looked up again with raised eyebrows. He wasn't very communicative she thought.

'Erm,' Stephanie pointed to her top lip with her finger.

He continued to stare at her.

'Wow he was slow,' she thought.

'You have something on your lip,' Stephanie eventually said.

He moved his hand to his lip and brushed it. He looked so annoyed.

'It's called a moustache.'

With horror, Stephanie realised it was his moustache, not cappuccino foam. How was she to know moustaches could be a different colour to your head hair? Before she could say anything, he got up and moved.

She bent her head behind her laptop and pretended to be busy, not daring to look up. After a few minutes, she started to giggle at the mistake, putting her hand on her red face. She decided to text Mark.

'Just tried to let a man know that he had foam on his lip- turned out it was his moustache!'

'Ha ha. Trust you LOL. Meeting up with Kate Saturday night for a meal.'

'Cool.'

'I meant it about the hallway…'

After a while, the train started to slow down for the next station. The low rumbling noise became a distinctive 'clickety clack', 'clickety clack' over the tracks. A row of houses slid past revealing neat gardens in full bloom, some with children's climbing frames and a paddling pool. The houses turned into allotments where Stephanie could make out tall plants of beans climbing up sunflowers, a couple sitting next to their work shed and men busy pushing mowers. Next, the allotment became garages and workshops, an industrial estate which then turned into rubble and abandoned train carriages. 'Click-e-ty-clack' was followed by a 'shhhhh' as the train came to a stop at a busy platform. Stephanie turned back to her laptop, not bothering to see the name of the station.

A few more people boarded. A little hand grabbed the laptop and Stephanie had to reach for it to stop it sliding off the table.

'Stop it! Oh sorry,' an alarmed voice cried.

Stephanie looked up as a woman carrying a toddler squeezed past with a young boy behind her.

Next, a young couple approached and then stopped at her table. Stephanie smiled at them as they checked the number of the seat and sat down. Stephanie returned to her work and when she finished the paragraph, she looked up to stretch. The guy opposite was stroking the girl's arm and they were holding hands, they looked so in love Stephanie thought. The girl reached up to touch his cheek and Stephanie thought about how much she missed Mark. She'd be seeing him soon, she looked at her watch and realised she'd be in London in half an hour. As she looked up again, she realised they were kissing. Stephanie thought they looked cute. They were so oblivious to anything around them; so romantic. Stephanie returned to her laptop and counted how many reports she had left to do- ten more.

As she was writing, the table started rocking so she looked up to see that the couple had moved on considerably from romantic kissing to full-blown tongue-down-throat, eat-each-other-up kissing. Jeez, get a room!

Stephanie lowered herself in her seat behind her laptop, she could hear people around her turning around and muttering. She was just wondering whether to move seats when the train started to slow down and thankfully the couple stood up and left.

Stephanie closed her laptop to talk to a couple of women in the seat across from her.

'I didn't know where to look,' said one of the women laughing.

There were older than Stephanie, probably in their late thirties.

Stephanie joined in, 'It was when the table started rocking that I looked up.'

The other woman said, 'It doesn't bother me if people want to kiss in public but that was a bit much. You couldn't ignore them.'

A new lady arrived and sat down in the kissing couple's place.

'We were just talking about the couple who were sitting where you are now.'

'You are now in the 'love seat'.' The two women laughed and the lady opposite Stephanie looked uncomfortable. She checked her seat as if it were dirty.

'What were they doing? Or shouldn't I ask?'

The lady looked about sixty, with pearls around her neck and a matching cream twin-set cardigan and top. Her silver hair was short at the back and sides with a wave on top.

'Oh, nothing major, they were just getting a bit too carried away.'

Stephanie smiled at the newcomer as she opened up her laptop once more.

'Are you having a good journey?' the lady enquired as she looked across at Stephanie with interest.

'Yes, I thought I'd take the opportunity to do some work while on the train,' Stephanie replied.

'It must be difficult working on the train.'

'No, I'm a pro.'

'Will you be working in London?' the lady asked.

'Probably,' Stephanie nodded. 'I'm going to fit it in when I can.'

'Well, I hope your weekend is not going to be too tiring,' she smiled.

'Oh no, I'm also going to be with my boyfriend, he understands how busy I get but we'll have time to have fun too.'

'That's nice.'

The two women leant towards them.

'We're going to London to see 'The Lion King', it's her birthday.'

'Happy birthday,' Stephanie and the lady said together.

'Thanks. We thought we'd go down tonight and see the show and then tomorrow do some shopping before going back home. We're just staying one night.'

The silver-haired lady smiled. 'That show is fantastic, it is worth seeing just for the costumes and of course, the music is wonderful. Have you seen it?' She looked across at Stephanie.

'No, but I'd love to. I'll be coming back to London in the summer, so I'll add that to my 'to-do' list. I will be staying for a few weeks so there'll be plenty of time.'

'That sounds fun, where will you be staying?'

'My boyfriend has a flat. He works in London, so we see each other at weekends but I'll spend the summer holiday with him. I'd better get ready, we'll be arriving soon, and I still have work to do.' Stephanie noticed as the build-up of buildings caught her eye through the window.

Stephanie picked up her handbag and in one movement she stood and stepped into the aisle. The train was moving quickly, and she was startled when it lurched sideways throwing Stephanie into a man's lap.

'Oops,' she giggled, and her embarrassment was made worse by the fact that she found it difficult to stand up with the carriage's swaying motion. The man helped her up and then followed her down the aisle. Stephanie staggered towards the toilet as if drunk, and nearly fell on two more people.

'Oh, I'm so sorry,' Stephanie apologised and stood up only to knock into a guy carrying a cup of coffee. It spilt all down the front of Stephanie's white top.

After more apologising, Stephanie locked herself in the toilet and stared at herself in the mirror.

'Oh no!' she gasped as she dabbed at the coffee stain.

She looked around and decided to try to wash it off the best she could. Pulling the top over her head, she held it under the soap dispenser and dribbled on a bit of soap then started to rub the material together.

'This is going to work,' Stephanie said out loud.

To her relief, the stain was getting fainter. Ok, so now all she had to do was dry it. She spread her legs to try not to fall as she was jostled from side to side in the rickety cubicle.

'You are kidding me,' Stephanie shouted when she realised there were paper towels instead of a blow drier.

What should she do? First, she pulled out some paper towels and dabbed at the damp material. Next, she tried to shake her top but that just sent water spraying all over her. She looked around again for inspiration and saw the window. What if she opened the window and hung it out to dry? Genius.

Stephanie put her damp top in the sink while she pulled at the window. She successfully managed to open it halfway, the sound from the railway roared in her ears along with the wind as the train rocketed down the tracks. She pushed the window up a bit more until the air was calmer, then hung her top over the window. That was when she realised that she needed to pee.

She sat down on the toilet when she heard a knock on the door.

'It's busy!' Stephanie shouted.

Stephanie stood up and reached to see if the top had dried in the wind. It wasn't there. Frantically she searched the cubicle, she looked out of the window, but nothing.

'Oh, my God!' Stephanie screamed.

The knocking on the door grew louder. Stephanie saw her reflection in the mirror and nearly died. She was wet through and was only wearing a lacy bra on the top half. Why did she have to wear a sexy bra instead of a T-shirt bra? Because she was meeting Mark that's why, and she'd be arriving any minute.

'Why do these things always happen to me?' Stephanie cried at her reflection. 'What am I going to do? I can't go out in my bra!' she whispered in horror.

The knocking continued so Stephanie slowly unlocked the door and opened it slightly. She peeped out to face an annoyed and intrigued line of people. She gulped.

'I don't suppose someone could get me my jacket, could they?'

The man in the front looked confused. He was about Stephanie's age and just stared at her, wondering why this girl was refusing to come out and didn't seem to be wearing much. He tried to see around the door.

'Have you finished?' he asked.

'I've had an accident and I need my jacket.'

A teenage girl, standing behind him, showed more concern. 'I'll get it for you, where is it?'

'Oh, thank you,' said Stephanie relieved. She pointed down the carriage. 'it's the table with the laptop, on the right.'

Stephanie waited with her face showing in the crack of the door for the woman to return. There was an awkward silence as they waited. A little boy was wiggling about, holding his mum's hand.

'Why is that lady stuck in the toilet?' he asked pointing at Stephanie.

'I don't know,' the woman replied with an annoyed look.

Stephanie winced and willed the girl to return quickly with her jacket. Head sticking out of the door, Stephanie could see that the girl had stopped and was talking to the silver-haired lady who didn't seem keen on letting her take the jacket. They both held a sleeve each, the young girl pointed in desperation towards Stephanie and the lady looked up the carriage. Eventually, the lady gave in, and Stephanie watched with relief as it was carried up the aisle.

'Does she need help to wipe her bottom?' the little boy said too loudly to his mum.

His mum looked embarrassed and the guy standing in front of Stephanie sniggered.

By now a few passengers had begun to notice something odd was happening so when the girl arrived at the door, Stephanie grabbed her jacket.

'Thanks, I'll be right out,' she added to the waiting people.

Stephanie closed the door and quickly put on her jacket with the carriage still jostling her from side to side.

Stephanie appeared, flustered, back in her seat and saw that they were pulling into the station.

'That was close,' Stephanie said smiling across the table.

She rushed to put her laptop into her bag and turned to the lady to say goodbye. Stephanie could see her staring and remembered that she was only wearing a lacy bra under her jacket which was gaping open.

The train came to a standstill, and the lady stood up, eyes round with her mouth open.

'I see what you mean when you said you fit your work in when you can. It doesn't take long does it!'

'Sorry?' Stephanie was puzzled.

'How do you arrange to meet your clients on the train?'

Stephanie didn't have a clue what the woman was saying.

'Do they contact you on your laptop? I suppose prostitution has to move with the times like everything else.'

Stephanie paused as the words sunk in and she replied in shock,

'I'm not a prostitute!'

The lady was taken aback by Stephanie's alarmed voice that she quickly turned and shuffled away down the carriage.

The two women she'd been talking to turned to stare as Stephanie tried to explain, 'I spilt coffee,' she told them as they stood up to leave. 'On my top…I wasn't with that couple.'

At last, Stephanie stepped off the train and walked down the platform as quickly as she could. Mark was standing against a wall with a big grin on his face watching Stephanie's approach. His eyes looked her up and down, mainly down her jacket as he gave her a welcoming kiss.

'Hello,' he said, 'nice jacket.'

'I was wearing a top,' Stephanie began.

'I like what you're wearing, or not wearing,' he said as they started to walk through the train station.

'Have you come in the car?'

'No, we're taking the tube.'

'I need to change then. I'm not going on the underground in just a bra and this jacket is really hot.'

'You can say that again! Why are you not wearing a top?'

Stephanie saw the toilet sign and reached for her case from Mark's grasp.

'I'll explain later,' she said.

12

THE EXCITEMENT OF LONDON

Stephanie felt relieved entering the cool, calmness of Mark's apartment. She dropped her bags, took her shoes off and turned to face Mark. He pulled her towards him.

'I just want you to know how it was torture standing so close to you on the Tube and not be able to do anything.'

Mark's voice was low and sexy. He pressed her up against the wall and started to kiss her neck.

After a few moments, Stephanie managed to ask, 'What time are we meeting your friends?'

Mark spoke in between kisses. '8 o'clock.'

'In that case, I need to have a shower before I get ready.'

Mark's eyes lit up. 'I'm right behind you,' he grinned.

THE EVENING WAS warm, the air heavy as Stephanie and Mark strolled hand in hand through the streets of Soho. All of Stephanie's senses were buzzing as she took in the sights and sounds around her. Young people laughing and talking, standing outside bars, sitting at tables, music wafting from open doorways and windows.

'Is it always this busy?' Stephanie asked.

'Just about every night,' Mark laughed, 'It feels a million miles away from Hibaldton, doesn't it?'

'I bet it feels like being on a constant holiday, living here.'

'It soon gets tiring though, I'm enjoying it much more being here with you.'

'What are the plans for tomorrow?' Stephanie asked excitedly, giving a little skip.

Mark laughed at her reaction and squeezed her hand.

'I thought we'd have a lie in…'

Stephanie rolled her eyes at him, but before she could complain he added, 'Then I thought we could wander around Covent Garden and have lunch there.'

'Oh, I'd love that! Can we go round all the little shops?'

'We can do anything you want.'

'What about Saturday?'

It was time for Mark to roll his eyes this time.

'You're as bad as Kate is with needing an itinerary."

'I just want to know what to look forward to…'

STEPHANIE WANTED TO carry on walking about, but soon they stopped in front of a bar with doormen standing outside.

'This is it,' Mark said showing the way.

'You go first,' Stephanie suddenly felt nervous.

Mark led her into the bar, and they weaved through the noisy crowd until he spotted his group sitting in the corner. Faces looked up as they approached, some smiling, some staring with interest at Stephanie.

'Hi.' A tall thin man stood up and smiled at Stephanie.

'This is John, he works at the desk next to mine,' Mark introduced him. 'John's my lunch buddy.' Mark almost had to shout to be heard.

When Stephanie looked confused, he continued, 'We go out at lunchtime for a wander and grab something to eat.'

John nodded, 'Do you want a beer? What can I get you to drink Stephanie?'

'Err, a gin and tonic please.'

Mark took Stephanie's hand and walked towards the table. Stephanie sat next to two women about Stephanie's age and Mark sat opposite her. Stephanie regretted wearing her summer dress as they were wearing tight-fitting, black outfits more suited for evening wear.

'Hi, I'm Laura,' said the woman next to her with a smile, 'and this is Tammy.'

Stephanie said hello back and smiled nervously.

Laura had a friendly round face with long wavy blonde hair. She had large, silver hooped earrings and a feather tattoo on the outside of her lower arm. Tammy's look was more scrutinising. She smiled with her mouth, but it didn't seem to reach her eyes. She was tall and thin, like a model Stephanie thought. Her fair hair was tied up in a high ponytail, her eyelashes were thick and long and her lips bright red.

She leaned forward across the table to talk to Mark, her mouth so close to Mark that her lips were almost brushing his ear. Laura leaned forwards causing Stephanie to look at her.

'How long are you in London for?' Laura asked Stephanie.

'Just the weekend. I have to go back to work on Monday.'

'You're a teacher aren't you, what do you teach?'

'I teach Primary, so every subject really.'

Stephanie smiled and felt pleased that Mark had talked to his friends about her.

'Do you work in the same office as Mark?'

'Yes, but I don't do the same job. I'm a personal assistant, so I organise meetings and make sure my boss knows where he needs to be, that kind of thing.'

'So, you keep things running smoothly then?'

Laura seemed to like the compliment.

'Yes, absolutely,' she smiled. 'Now what I need is for you to come to work with me on Monday to tell my boss that!'

Tammy leaned back and reached for her drink, so Stephanie took the opportunity to find out more about her. She could tell that Tammy was someone she should be wary of.

'So, Tammy, how do you know Mark?'

Tammy's smile reminded Stephanie of a lazy cat that had just licked some cream.

'Mark and I work closely together,' she purred.

Stephanie raised her eyebrows and looked towards Mark, he was quick to add, 'Her desk is next to mine.'

'Tammy used to work next to me,' a voice spoke, and Stephanie looked up to see a man standing next to her. 'I'm Pete,' he said holding out his hand.

Stephanie reached forward for a handshake but was surprised when he held on for longer than necessary. He stood slightly bent towards her and held her gaze. 'Pleased to meet you.'

Stephanie felt uncomfortable and for a minute was worried that he was going to kiss her hand. She didn't want to appear rude, but the guy was a bit creepy, her mind raced to think of how to escape from the awkward situation. She decided to laugh it off and stretched her hand out to be clear she'd had enough, luckily, he immediately let go.

'It's so nice to finally meet Mark's friends,' Stephanie said and looked towards Mark.

'I've told them all about you Steph,' Mark said reaching his hands out across the table, so Stephanie did the same and held his hands.

'We've all worked together for about 3 years now.'

'Apart from John, he joined last year,' Laura added, 'and Mark is always talking about you, Stephanie.'

Tammy glared at Stephanie and Pete walked off towards the bar just in time for John to replace him.

He had returned with drinks for everyone on a tray and sat next to Mark.

'Cheers,' he said lifting his pint glass.

'Cheers,' Stephanie, Mark and Laura clinked glasses with him, 'Thanks,' Stephanie said.

Stephanie chatted with John for a while, who asked her questions about what she did for a living and told her how patient she must be teaching children. Stephanie asked him about his work and discovered he was married, had no children yet and lived just outside London.

The crowd in the bar thinned out a little, making it a bit easier to talk without shouting.

Stephanie was worried that she would have nothing in common with Mark's friends, but she found herself having fun. She told the embarrassing story of how she lost her top on the train, it was the first time she'd told Mark as well.

They all laughed, and Mark shook his head and chuckled, 'This girl never fails to surprise me, she is the most impulsive person I know.'

'I'm not that impulsive, I just make the wrong decisions sometimes,' Stephanie shrugged laughing.

'She is always trying to help people too,' Mark continued.

'Don't attempt to help people in London,' John warned.

'Everybody just minds their own business here,' Tammy agreed.

'In my village, everyone knows everyone's business, but at least we look out for each other.'

'That sounds nice,' Laura said.

'It would drive me crazy,' Tammy said shaking her head.

'It can be funny reading the village Facebook comments,' Stephanie continued. 'People are always complaining about new houses being built, or kids wearing hoodies riding bikes with no lights on.'

'That sounds like where I come from. Adults are always blaming kids, but there's nothing to do but ride bikes up and down the streets.' John said.

'Are you in a neighbourhood watch group or something?' Laura asked.

'No, but I am on the Parish Council, so we meet up to discuss things like that and what we can do to help.'

Pete, who was now sitting on the other side of Mark, leant over the table. He seemed like he'd had a bit too much to drink, Stephanie noticed he was drinking whisky.

'Parents need a good talking to by the sounds of it,' Pete said.

'You'd fit right into our village,' Stephanie replied sarcastically.

'You know Mark, I wondered what the countryside had to offer, and now I can see why you didn't want to come back,' Pete said.

'It's one of the reasons,' Mark looked at Stephanie and smiled.

There was something about Pete that Stephanie didn't like. Maybe it was because he was tipsy but she didn't like the way he looked at her. It reminded her of the way a cat looks at a mouse who's trapped under its paw. After what felt like a long stare, he looked away.

'You always can pick 'em, I'll give you that.' Pete lifted his glass in the air before downing the rest of the drink.

When Mark didn't respond he continued,

'There'll be girls all around in tears when they see Mark has finally settled down.'

'Give it a rest,' John warned Pete.

Laura touched Stephanie's arm, 'Don't take any notice of him, he's had too much to drink.'

Tammy looked at Stephanie and leaned over to say, 'He's jealous because Mark's so popular with the ladies, if you know what I mean.'

Stephanie looked at Tammy, not sure exactly how to react.

Mark looked uncomfortable and turned to Stephanie, 'Are you hungry? Shall we go find something to eat?'

Stephanie nodded, 'I'd like to have a walk about, I haven't been to London for ages.'

'You should definitely go for a look around then,' Laura said to Stephanie.

She leaned in closer and put her hand on her arm.

'Mark is smitten with you Stephanie, I can tell.'

'Really?' Stephanie asked.

'Yeah. Since he's come back, he's much happier, don't you think Tammy?'

Tammy stared at Stephanie.

'When did you two meet up?'

'We were at school together,' Stephanie replied.

'Oh, that's so romantic,' said Laura.

'Well, we weren't dating, but we liked each other. Then Mark came to London, and I went into teacher training.'

'So, you've not been going out for long then?' Tammy asked.

Mark stood up and was saying goodbye to everyone.

'Make sure you come out with us again,' Laura said hugging her.

BACK IN THE streets, it felt cooler, and Stephanie realised how hot and stuffy it had been inside.

'So, apart from Pete, how do you like my colleagues?' Mark asked.

'They were nice, very welcoming, I had fun,' Stephanie nodded.

They stopped for a slice of pizza and walked towards Mark's flat, with the intention of stopping at some bars on the way.

'What was wrong with Pete?' Stephanie asked.

'He doesn't like me,' Mark shrugged. 'He's always been weird with me, I just stay out of his way.'

'He acted jealous of you,'

'It was the drink talking, but he probably does have a reason to not like me.'

'Really?'

'I sort of… erm… he was going out with someone and…'

'She fancied you?' Stephanie interrupted.

'We went out for a while.'

'Did you know they were dating?'

Mark looked sheepish.

'It was a couple of years ago. I don't deny it was a shitty thing to do…but yeah, I knew.'

He shrugged and sighed looking guilty.

'It was her decision too. You didn't deliberately steal her from him, did you?'

'It's difficult to turn off my charm,' he grinned, and Stephanie hit him on the shoulder.

Stephanie wondered again how much she could trust him. Women flirted with him all the time, even when they bought pizza or got a drink.

As if he could read her thoughts, Mark stopped walking and tilted her face up to his.

'I only have eyes for you, you know?'

He looked worried and bent to kiss her on the lips, softly.

'Let's pop in here for a drink next, we come here sometimes to unwind, it's got a relaxing atmosphere.'

THE NEXT MORNING, Stephanie turned over sleepily and felt a familiar hand gently stroke her shoulder. She opened her eyes and smiled at Mark as he lay facing her. Sunlight streamed through a gap in the curtains and Stephanie wondered the time.

'What time is it?' she asked lazily.

Mark moved his hand from her arm to her waist under the covers and he pulled her towards him. He nuzzled his face into her neck, she complained as his stubble rubbed her throat, so he started to kiss it better with slow, light kisses and blew a titillating pathway down her body which made her shiver. They made love as if time ceased to exist, nothing else mattered in the world. Stephanie sensed every goosebump that came alive on her skin, under her fingers she felt Mark's body react in the same way.

Hunger finally coaxed the two lovers outside into the London streets. Mark led the way and it wasn't long before Stephanie realised they were in Covent Garden. They followed the crowd of shoppers into a courtyard, where classical violin music wafted from below. They wandered, hand in hand, past rows of shop windows which looked so inviting. After pausing at nearly every shop, they eventually headed downstairs to see where the magical music was coming from.

A young lady stood in a corner playing the violin. Stephanie was in awe at how the music seemed to flow through her, her long blonde hair swayed as her arms danced with her bow across the strings. They walked over to small glass tables and sat down to watch along with other couples in front of a restaurant. Stephanie leaned her head on his shoulder, and they sat like that until the music stopped.

A crowd had gathered around on the balcony above, and everyone clapped. Mark got up to put some money in a box and returned with a rose. He sat down and gave the rose to Stephanie with a grin.

'Why do you only have eyes for me? Stephanie asked Mark taking the rose and smelling it.

Mark was silent for just a minute before he spoke.

'I have never met anyone like you before Steph. You are sensitive, caring, daring, feisty, sweet and interesting. I… haven't felt this way about anyone before.'

He held her hands in his and kissed her fingertips.

A waitress in a crisp white blouse and a black apron appeared to ask what they would like to eat. They chose a bottle of wine from the menu and then, as the waitress walked away to get the drinks, they sat close together to decide what to eat.

After their wine was poured Mark held up his glass and looked into Stephanie's eyes.

'Let's drink to our future together,' Mark grinned holding out his wine glass.

Stephanie clinked her glass against his.

'Our future, together…'

AFTER RETURNING TO Mark's flat, Stephanie finished her reports and they got changed to go out again. This time, Mark booked a taxi to take them to a hotel to meet up with Kate.

When they entered the foyer Stephanie couldn't stop looking around, it was so grand. The ceiling was high with sparkly chandeliers, and a marbled black and white floor twinkled as if it were encrusted with diamonds. Mark and Stephanie walked towards the restaurant and saw Kate immediately, sitting at a table, one long slender leg crossed over the other in black high heel shoes.

When she looked up, everyone in the restaurant knew about their arrival.

'Mark and Steph darling!' she squealed, standing up with arms outstretched.

She kissed Mark dramatically on both cheeks and to Stephanie's surprise, embraced her in a giant bear hug that nearly squeezed the air out of her lungs. After a great deal of Kate complaining that it had been far too long, and there wasn't going to be time to catch up with all the news, they eventually settled down to order their meal.

'I would insist on waving you goodbye tomorrow Steph but I will be at the airport. I can't believe I will have to get up so early, I am not an early bird.'

'That sounds very exciting," Stephanie said, taking in Kate's amazing figure-hugging dress which was silver with a low neckline.

Kate sighed, 'It sounds exciting, however, it will no doubt be extremely tedious. Most of the day will be spent sitting around a table pretending to be interested in a bunch of misogynistic middle-aged men who won't be responsible for making any decisions. I might as well be in London.'

Mark laughed, 'I am sure you will be a breath of fresh air, or maybe a hurricane would be more accurate- you'll blow their boring grey socks right off.'

Kate pursed her lips and replied, 'You are right of course darling.'

After ordering, they sipped wine as Kate demanded to know how Stephanie was. She leant forward in concern when she discovered about the postcards and her large, hooped earrings jangled as she looked from her to Mark.

'What are you doing back in London Mark? Stephanie can't stay on her own with a maniac on the loose!'

Stephanie spoke firmly, she was just getting her confidence back, and this was the last thing she needed.

'There is no reason to blow it all out of proportion Kate, I am perfectly fine, I wish we hadn't mentioned it now.'

'If you hadn't told me, I would be very upset. You are very special to me and that's what friends do, they look after each other. If I weren't travelling to New York, I would come up and stay with you for a while…'

Stephanie's mouth fell open at the thought of having to entertain Kate once again, and it wasn't until the food arrived, that the discussion of Stephanie's safety was put to one side.

Every item of food tasted like heaven and a new bottle of wine was brought to the table to complement each course. They were all fairly tipsy by the time a taxi was called to take them out clubbing. It was a very happy, exhausted Stephanie who fell asleep as soon as her head hit the pillows in bed that night.

13

BACK TO HIBALDTON, BACK TO REALITY

Stephanie lay in bed not wanting to get up. The alarm had gone off, but she wished that she could wake up with Mark beside her. The weekend had flashed by, if it hadn't been for the rose on her bedside table, she would have believed it to be a dream.

Stephanie got ready for school, thinking about Monday's lessons and if there was anything she would need. The weekend had been so action-packed that she felt like she'd been away for a week! It was going to be difficult to get back into work mode.

Lisa was already in the classroom when Stephanie arrived.

'Hi, how did the weekend go?' Lisa asked as she sat trimming some worksheets.

Stephanie sat down opposite Lisa with a huge grin on her face.

'That good, eh?' Lisa laughed.

'It was amazing, his apartment is amazing, the night out was romantic… and amazing,' Stephanie laughed reliving the moment in her head.

'And how was the sex?' Lisa joked.

'Amazing,' Stephanie nodded.

They both laughed.

'Did I hear the word sex?' Tracy popped her head around the door.

'Trust you to come past at *that* moment,' Lisa teased.

'Oh, and we had dinner with Kate.'

'How is she? I bet you ate at a classy restaurant.'

'You know Kate. We had the most amazing meal in a fancy hotel. She's in New York now for a few weeks, but yes it was fun to see her again.'

'Glad you had a good time in London,' Tracy interrupted, 'but you did miss a good night out in Rigby.'

'Oh yeah? Anything to share?' Stephanie asked.

Tracy walked further into the room.

'I ended up going out with Rita and we just had a good laugh, met up with some lads in the Black Bull.'

'Did you meet anyone in particular?' Lisa inquired.

'Maybe…we're meeting them at the airfield in a couple of weeks, there's a band on. D'ya fancy coming?'

Stephanie looked at Lisa and they both agreed they would think about it.

'Ooh, best get a move on,' said Stephanie noticing the time.

AT LUNCHTIME, STEPHANIE told her friends in the staffroom about her disastrous train journey, which they all found hilarious.

After hoots of laughter, Lisa said, 'That could only happen to you Steph.'

'I can't believe you hung it out of the window!'

'I closed the window on it,' Stephanie defended herself. 'Mark's friends thought it was funny too. I think they were expecting me to be more sensible.'

'Why? Because you're a primary teacher?' Tracy scoffed. 'Some people expect primary teachers to be Miss Goodie-Two-Shoes as if we're not human.'

'Sounds like Mark has been telling his colleagues about you,' Lisa said.

'He's a right charmer, I remember him from school.'

Tracy had also been brought up in the area, she lived in a small village near Rigby.

'Afterwards, we went to Covent Garden, it was very romantic,' Stephanie sighed.

'A shame you had to come back to reality then.'

Rita looked sympathetic.

'To change the subject slightly,' Tracy said getting out her phone. 'Have you seen the competition that Hibaldton parachute club is running?'

The others said they hadn't. Tracy showed them the post on her phone and explained…

'You just have to 'like 'the post and share it, and then you get entered into the competition. The winner gets a free parachute jump.'

'Count me out,' Stephanie shook her head.

'Oh, come on, it'll be fun,' Tracy said.

'You are never getting me up there, not in a hundred years.'

Stephanie pointed up at the sky.

'It's a tandem jump so you're not on your own. Anyway, Craig said that they just need the publicity.'

'Who's Craig?' Lisa asked.

'He was one of the lads I was telling you about from the Black Bull, they parachute jump regularly. We were sitting on the pub right, and there was a group of guys standing nearby. Craig kept looking at me, so I went up to them.'

'You didn't!' Lisa gasped.

'I did. We got chatting and there was this other bloke who said he'd started a competition and asked if I knew anyone in Hibaldton who'd be up for it.'

'Did they persuade you to have a go?' Lisa asked.

'Craig asked me and I said I'd be well up for it. Anyway, we were talking, and I said I'd try to get my friends at school to share the post on social media.'

'Why Hibaldton?' Stephanie asked.

Tracy shrugged, 'Craig's friend said it would be good if the locals were part of it. He was a bit slimy actually, I don't like men with moustaches, they remind me of a seventy's porn star. Come on then you two, get your phones out.'

Stephanie and Lisa reluctantly got out their phones and looked at the post briefly, clicked on the blue thumbs-up, and then shared it.

'There's going to be a band at The Skydive Bar a week on Saturday, and the winner will be announced. Do you all fancy going?' Tracy asked.

'So will *Craig* be there on Saturday?' Stephanie asked.

'Yeah, and so will the others.'

Tracy looked a bit flushed so, of course, they all teased her about it.

Lisa turned to Stephanie, 'I've just remembered, are you going to the Parish Council meeting on Wednesday?'

'Yes, I'll be there. Did you see the email about John Barry stepping in as Chairman?'

'Yeah. I wonder who the clerk will be to take over from Mary?' Lisa asked.

'I don't know, guess we'll have to wait and see what tomorrow brings. One thing's for sure… our meetings always bring a surprise,' Lisa predicted ominously.

14

THE DITCH OF DOOM

After school, Stephanie was walking home and the sun was so relaxing after being in a sweaty classroom all day, that she decided to go for a walk.

Instead of turning right along Field View, she continued straight on down the lane that ran past John Barry's farm. John Barry's farm and Sam Proctor's farm worked closely together even though the two men hadn't always seen eye to eye.

The crops in the fields were still green but they were growing tall, and Stephanie could hear the breeze whispering through the ears of corn. Birds were quiet in the hazy sun, only the rooks squawked and screeched in the branches ahead. Looking up into the trees, Stephanie could see why those birds were thought to bring bad luck. Their black wings beat a foreboding warning overhead.

As Stephanie reached the crossroads, she paused to look over the fields that stretched towards the river. Those fields were a brilliant yellow of rape seed which Stephanie loved to see each year.

She thought about popping in to see Mark's mum when an engine noise came up behind her and a car pulled up next to where she was standing. Stephanie turned to look at the blue car and noticed someone sticking a camera out of the window and taking photos of the view.

Stephanie glanced at her watch and decided to head home instead.

She lazily wandered back the way she came, thinking about what she should make for tea when she heard a car behind her. She turned to look and saw the blue car was heading towards her slowly.

It annoyed her that cars drove up and down the lane as it was such a lovely place for people to walk, take dogs or ride bikes.

She quickened her pace a little and looked over her shoulder to decide whether to stand on the grass to let it pass. Weirdly it was crawling along, and it looked like the driver was still taking photographs through the windscreen. He shouldn't be taking photos while driving she thought and she didn't like the fact she was in his view, so she stepped on the grass to wait for him to pass. He stopped, and just sat there staring at her.

Stephanie stared back and wondered now if he was the man she had been seeing on her road. She took her phone out of her pocket and decided to take a photo of his car registration, but as she did so suddenly his engine revved and without warning he sped up towards her.

Instinctively, she turned and ran and a clamour of rooks all took to the sky with a frenzied KAAH! There were trees to her left and a ditch which she didn't want to dive into, she knew there was an opening to a field somewhere close. Her feet stumbled on the uneven ground as the sound of the car got closer but, just before she could reach the opening, the car sped past leaving a dust cloud behind it.

Stephanie leapt sideways and fell into the ditch of doom. Her hands grabbed tree roots to steady her fall. Leaning over, hands on knees to catch her breath, she looked up, but the car was gone.

'Idiot!' she screamed.

She knew he couldn't hear but it made her feel better. She rubbed her hands together and dusted herself down. Luckily there was no water in the ditch, she decided to sit on the bank until her legs had stopped trembling. She looked at her phone to see if she'd got a clear photo of the car, but she'd moved when he sped up so only part of the car could be seen. From the photo she could see the windscreen wiper looked worn, that was all she could tell.

She set off walking again as the birds settled back in their nests. When she got to her road, she scanned the street for the blue car, but it wasn't there. She wasn't even sure if it were the same car. It could have been anyone, there were often maniacs who drove recklessly down that lane.

15

NEW FACES

Wednesday soon arrived and Stephanie sat in the Village Hall waiting for the Parish Council meeting to begin. There was a low buzz around her as people chatted. For Stephanie, it had been difficult returning to the meeting room as it held awful memories: the tragic loss of a kind friend, and the betrayal and greed of a village council member. Deception and sorrow lingered in the air, a ghost from a recent past that would never be forgotten.

Stephanie looked with fondness at the group as they sat around the wide wooden table. On her left were sitting Angela, Rosie and Ben. Ben was still buzzing about the Summer Fair the week before.

'You did a fantastic job, Ben, it was a great success,' Rosie congratulated him.

'Oh, I can't take all the credit guys,' Ben gushed fanning his face in mock embarrassment.

'You did most of the organising,' said Angela.

'I was so worried no one was going to turn up. It was all down to your publicity Angela and Rosie,' Ben complimented them.

'Don't forget all of us,' Mabel Moore huffed from across the table.

'Oh of course Mrs Moore, and when it comes up on the agenda, I will thank everyone properly,' Ben flushed.

Mrs Moore was sitting across the table next to Reverend Pierce. He was busy talking to Mr and Mrs Cook, who ran the village shop.

Sitting opposite Stephanie was Sam Proctor, Mark's dad. Stephanie was pleased to see him again, but she wished that Mark were sitting in his dad's chair.

Sam smiled at Stephanie and leaned forward, 'We've missed seeing you Steph, you should come and visit.'

She nodded, 'Yes, I will.'

Just then, a few people were led into the room by Sam's business partner Farmer John Barry. They sat down on a row of chairs reserved for members of the public. It had been a while since anyone had attended a council meeting who wasn't a member. Everyone turned to watch with interest.

Stephanie recognised the lady who had lost her earrings and her friend, she also knew Mrs Johnson, a mum of a child from school.

Next to her, the local community police officer, PCSO Manning sat down. Stephanie often saw her walking around the village, and she recalled how friendly she had been to Stephanie when she found Mary that awful morning. Stephanie noticed from the agenda, that she was there to discuss recent thefts in the neighbourhood.

Next to him, was a man and woman whom Stephanie didn't recognise.

Stephanie whispered to Lisa, 'Do you know them?'

'I think they live in the new large house that's just been built,' Lisa whispered back.

Stephanie was keen to find out more about them as their house had been the talk of the village while it was being built. It was easily the largest house in the neighbourhood, it looked like something out of a Jane Austin novel.

She remembered when they had gone for a walk a few weeks ago, they had stopped to admire the house.

'Who lives in a house like this?' Stephanie had pretended to be Lloyd Grossman in the old version of the TV show 'Through the Keyhole.'

'You need to talk more down your nose,' Lisa laughed.

Stephanie had tried again in a deeper, more nasally way and the two of them had creased up in stitches.

Back in the meeting room, Lisa whispered in Stephanie's ear, 'You're staring.'

'Who lives in a house like this?' whispered Stephanie to her friend.

Lisa giggled, 'Now you sound more like David Attenborough.'

Stephanie continued, 'Through the trees, you can just make out the dwelling of the new Hibaldton species.'

'They both look very smart, don't they?' Lisa whispered noting the soft, elegant material of the lady's dress and the style of the man's jacket. He was quite short but slim, in his 50s, and his wife was a bit taller than him and looked a bit younger. She was wearing a pearl necklace and a brooch that also had pearls nestled in curls of gold.

'Hey and who's that just sitting down? OMG.' Lisa's eyes grew wide.

Stephanie looked from Lisa's shocked face into the eyes of a god. 'Henry Cavill move aside there's a new Superman in town,' Stephanie whispered under her breath.

Time seemed to be in slow motion as he sat down with a shy look on his rugged face. A lock of black hair fell over his forehead as he looked up, his sharp blue eyes scanned the room and locked on to Stephanie's. His dazzling smile nearly blew Stephanie's socks right off and it wasn't until John Barry started the meeting that Stephanie realised that she had been staring at the gorgeous hunk with her mouth open.

'Hello everyone,' John Barry said from the head of the table. 'I must admit it feels strange to be sitting here in this chair.' He laughed nervously but was encouraged by everyone in the room.

'I will be Chairing our meetings for a while until a permanent chairperson is voted in. Before we start the meeting, I would like to welcome members of the public at the back. There are some new faces in the village if you'd like to introduce yourselves, please feel free.'

The elegant lady spoke first, 'Hello everyone and thank you for the lovely welcome. I am Sylvia Smith, and this is my husband, Gavin. We only arrived in Hibaldton two weeks ago, and we are bowled over with the friendliness of everybody we have met so far, haven't we Gavin?'

'Yes, absolutely.'

A positive murmur circulated the room.

Sylvia continued, 'We came along because we wanted to meet people from the village and find out more about it.'

Everyone round the table said hello and Mrs Moore promised to talk with them after the meeting about some village clubs they could join.

Next, everyone's eyes settled on the well-built man sitting looking slightly uncomfortable. Stephanie noticed how his jeans were tight on his thighs, showing pure muscle under the fabric, and how his T-shirt fitted closely over his shoulders and chest.

He smiled and lifted his hand to give a brief wave.

'Hi, my name is Lucas. I've also just moved into the village and wanted to introduce myself.'

His voice had a southern, possibly London accent, Stephanie thought. He looked around the room and his blue eyes stopped at Stephanie. She felt a prickle of attraction as she returned his gaze and was surprised that she found it difficult to look away.

John Barry continued, 'We all are very pleased to see you at our meeting. If there are any issues you'd like to bring up, then please let us know now, otherwise you can bring it up at the end. By the way, you are welcome to leave anytime you wish, these meetings can go on a bit.'

There was a pause, but no one said anything so John Barry continued, 'To start the meeting, I would like you to meet Jane Farrow who will be our new Clerk until someone else is voted in.

It was then Jane's turn to speak, her voice was quiet and high which seemed to match her small size.

'Hello everyone, it is my honour to cover for Mary as your Clerk, and I am deeply sad for your loss. I work, as Mary did, at Rigby Council, although I didn't work with her, I was a friend… I am here to advise you and make sure your meetings run smoothly until two more council members can be found to replace those you have lost. Thank you.'

Then she sat down and opened her laptop looking emotional.

Everyone fell silent for a moment until Reverend Pierce spoke.

'I know that I speak for all when I say that we are grateful to you both for stepping in. Furthermore, for it to be another friend of Mary's, is comforting. Thank you.'

John continued, 'First of all, I assume you have all read the minutes of last month's meeting, do we all agree with them?'

Everyone around the table nodded.

'Second, on the agenda is appointing a new chairman.'

John looked towards Jane for support.

Jane began, 'John Barry is offering to be the Chairperson full time, and this would be a good time to ask if there is anyone else who would consider this post.'

'I'd be happy for John to take over,' Mr Cook spoke up.

'I second that,' Sam Proctor said.

Everyone nodded in agreement, while John Barry looked around the table.

'Well then,' John swallowed and took a deep breath, 'shall we vote on it?'

Jane nodded, 'Show of hands for John Barry to be the new Hibaldton's Chairman.'

Everyone around the table raised their hand.

'Congratulations Mr Barry, Chairman.'

Everyone clapped and John's face went flushed for a second.

He coughed to clear his throat and then moved on to the next thing on the agenda…

The meeting continued, mainly discussing the spending costs of the village upkeep and the proposal of building more houses and extensions of properties in Hibaldton.

Ben was fidgeting in his seat Stephanie noticed as the report on the Summer Fair came closer for discussion.

'Number twelve, The Summer Fair, it was a great success, wasn't it Ben?' John looked up for Ben to take over.

Ben almost exploded with enthusiasm, 'I have been dying to tell you that we have made enough profit to pay for the church and some extra.

He looked down at his notes.

Everyone clapped and there was a buzz of conversation around the table.

'I would like to say a great big thank you to everyone for putting up with me the last few months, and all the hard work you have put in to make it happen.'

It reminded Stephanie of a thank-you speech at the Oscars. She nearly said something but liked Ben too much to steal his thunder.

'I have a cheque for you Reverend Pierce for the church repairs.'

Ben stood up and quickly walked around the room to give the reverend his cheque.

'Oh my! Well done everyone. That means we can go ahead with the repairs, wonderful.'

Ben walked quickly back to his place.

Jane spoke up, 'If you look at the next page, we can see the quotes for the repairs and how much money the Parish has set aside for this matter. With the money from the festival and the council's addition to that, we can begin getting the contractor in. Do we agree on the first quote?'

Stephanie's mind started to wander at this point, as it usually did when money matters were involved. Instead, she watched

Lucas as John Barry spoke. He was wearing a gold signet ring on his right hand, his hands looked strong and were at that moment clasped together casually on his lap.

Ben's voice pulled Stephanie from her daydreaming.

'The rest of the profit will be split between the scout's group and the primary school.'

'Thank you, Ben. Next item - children riding bikes without lights.' John continued.

Mrs Moore's voice pierced the air like an arrow.

'I understand that young people do not have much to do in the evening, however, I don't like the way they hang about on the streets.

'Mabel, this is about bikes,' John said gently.

Mrs Moore continued, 'Like the boys in the black hoodies who gather outside the fish and chip shop on their bikes.'

Rosie agreed, 'I was driving down Church Street the other night, and I nearly ran a boy over. I was only going slowly, but one of them dashed in front of my car before I could see him- no lights of course.'

Mr Cook added, 'We are forever putting out messages to parents about that, but they still ride without lights.'

'Young anti-social behaviour is a plague these days,' Mrs Moore complained.

'Could we have some reflectors or cheap lights that we could buy and give out at school maybe?' Mrs Cook suggested.

There was a murmur of approval at the idea. Stephanie looked over to the community officer who was keeping her face devoid of emotion.

Stephanie's mind flashed back to when she nearly got run over by the blue car. She decided to say something about that.

'Adults are sometimes driving recklessly in the village. I was walking down the lane the other day when I was nearly run over by an idiot driving far too fast.'

All eyes looked at her in concern and Mrs Cook was the first to respond.

'Stephanie my love, that's terrible, are you ok?'

'Yes, I'm fine. I was shaken a little bit but it's not the first time that cars have driven fast down there.'

'That is true.' John Barry agreed, 'I can hear cars speed down there when I'm in my office, what can we do about it?'

Stephanie suggested, 'What about if the children at school designed some road signs to tell people to slow down?'

There was a murmur of agreement around the table.

'That's a good idea,' Ben said.

'You didn't say you were nearly run over!' Lisa said.

'If you could see to that please Stephanie and we shall discuss it again at the next meeting.'

John Barry smiled and then continued, 'The last thing on the agenda is a worrying spate of robberies in the village I see. Has anyone got anything to say about that?' John asked looking around.

'My brooch was stolen,' Mrs Moore said.

'Have you spoken to the police about it?' John asked.

'Well, our local officer here but not officially… There was no sign of a break-in you see, so I wasn't sure at first, but I have looked everywhere, and I know it's not in my house anymore.'

'Could you have dropped it outside?' Sam Proctor asked.

'Was it the same brooch you wore at the fair?' Stephanie asked.

'Yes, it was but I didn't lose it, I know that I put it on my dressing table upstairs.'

'That's just what Margaret said,' said Mrs Cook pointing to the lady who was sitting at the back of the room. 'She swears she put her earrings in a bowl and the next day, they were gone but no sign of a break-in.'

'On social media, people are suspecting the black-hoodie gang,' Mrs Moore said pursing her lips.

'It sounds to me to be more of a cat burglar than a kid. Did you lock all your doors that night Mabel?' Rosie asked Mrs Moore pushing up her glasses as she leaned forward.

'I certainly did, I never forget.'

Stephanie's brain started to engage. This meeting started to become fascinating.

'Does anyone know if there have been any other thefts?' Stephanie asked.

'Reverend Pierce looked up, 'Yes, let me think… the lovely young couple who live across the road from here, Sandra and Mike Davies, they were at the service on Sunday. They told me that Mike's watch has gone missing, but they thought their little boy had put it somewhere.'

'It sounds like there could be something to this… a thief who is only stealing one item, so the owner isn't quite sure if it is a burglary or not,' Stephanie thought aloud.

'A clever idea, if it's true,' Rosie agreed.

'Oh dear,' gasped Mrs Moore, 'so my brooch was stolen, and someone was in my bedroom while I was asleep!'

'Don't get upset Mabel,' Sam tried to calm her down.

Mrs Moore continued to get upset, and Sam and Reverend Pierce did their best to soothe her. Ben poured out a glass of water and walked around to give it to her. Stephanie looked at Lisa, she felt guilty for upsetting the old lady.

'Now then Mabel,' John finally said when things had returned to normal. 'let's not be hasty, we don't know for sure if that's what happened. Maybe you should contact the police and see what they say.'

'Huh,' scoffed Mr Cook, 'a lot of good that will do.'

Mrs Cook agreed. When we had a break-in at the shop, they wouldn't even dust for fingerprints. I had to do it myself with icing sugar and they wouldn't come back to look.'

Stephanie noticed throughout the whole thing that Lucas was listening intently. He seemed quite impressed at Mrs Cook's ingenuity with the icing sugar, however, the police officer at the back had grimaced at the comments but managed to keep quiet.

'What we need to do is gather evidence together. We need to find out how many people have had things go missing recently,' Ben suggested.

'That could be everyone in the village,' Rosie said.

'Not if we narrow it down to a value of… how much would you say your brooch was worth?' Stephanie asked Mrs Moore.

Mrs Moore shrugged and shook her head.

'Oh, I don't think it was worth anything. My husband bought it for only a few shillings.'

'Margaret's earrings were diamonds though so they must have been worth at least a thousand pounds,' Mrs Cook pointed out.

'How do you propose we gather the evidence?' John asked.

'We could put it in the Village Voice and on social media. We have a Hibaldton group,' Ben said.

'Can you arrange that then Ben? We shall see what happens. You all have my number and email in case you need to contact me.'

Ben looked pleased that he had been given a job.

'That was the last point on the agenda, so now for any other business. Is there anything that anyone at the back would like to add?'

The community officer cleared her voice and stood up.

'I would like to say that I agree that there's not a lot the police can do about the robberies if people don't officially tell them. If you are putting a message up on the village group chat, then put on my number to contact for advice. I'll give it to you at the end.'

'Thank you, PCSO Manning.'

The officer sat down and there was a movement from Gavin Smith a few chairs along.

'I just think I should add, in case you don't know, we live in the newly built house in the village…'

'Oh, it's a lovely house,' Rosie piped up and then looked embarrassed that she'd interrupted.

Gavin continued, 'We also had something go missing, didn't we sweetheart?'

He turned to his wife who looked surprised at his outburst.

'It was her favourite bracelet. It is the same story as before, she put it on her dressing table and the next morning it was gone.'

'Seems like there is a pattern,' Lisa said to Stephanie.

'I wonder if the thief is targeting expensive properties,' Ben said.

'But Mrs Moore's house isn't big, and her brooch isn't worth much…no offence,' Angela commented.

Mrs Moore was taken aback and was thinking of something to say.

'Mabel, if it weren't for you, this whole mystery wouldn't have come to light,' Mrs Cook said.

'Yes, we have you to thank Mabel,' Sylvia said firmly, 'Don't we Gavin?'

After the meeting, a few people gathered to talk before going home.

Rosie, Angela, Ben and Lisa stood with Stephanie to talk about the possible burglaries.

'Stephanie, this is just up your street, you should investigate,' Ben said.

'Why me?' Stephanie looked surprised.

'Who discovered the criminal gang on our very doorstep? Who discovered the murderer?' he pointed at Stephanie.

'More like I was kidnapped by the murderer,' Stephanie pointed out.

'You could talk to the victims and see if you find out anything new,' Rosie suggested.

'Don't bring me into it,' Lisa said.

Stephanie started to feel excited about trying to solve the mystery.

'Oh, come on Lisa it will be fun to investigate it together.'

Lisa rolled her eyes at her friend.

'I must admit, we do make a good team.'

'So, are you an amateur detective, Stephanie, isn't it?'

Stephanie turned to see Lucas standing there. They all moved to let him into their circle.

'No not really,' Stephanie laughed, 'but I must admit it is intriguing.'

'I agree with you, it sounds like a mystery that's begging to be solved. Thank you, everyone, for such an interesting meeting, I admit, I thought it was going to be boring.'

'Our meetings are far from boring,' Lisa said looking up at him. Lisa was quite short, so she was almost tipping backwards to look up into his eyes.

'Yep, this is a typical meeting to be fair,' Ben agreed smiling up at him.

'I look forward to the next one then,' Lucas laughed.

Stephanie's heart jumped into her throat at his laugh, it was so deep, carefree and sexy.

'Why don't we carry this conversation on at the pub?' Ben suggested, 'Lucas, you have to come along too, we need all the support we can get.'

Everyone in the group agreed and Lucas was soon persuaded to join them.

16

WHO IS LUCAS?

Standing in front of the bar, the group decided what they wanted.

Stephanie and Lisa were the first to get their drinks and then headed over to the large table in the corner where they could all fit around.

'So, what do you think of Lucas?' Stephanie asked Lisa.

They watched Ben chatting to him as Angela and Rosie stood at the bar.

'Do you think he's gay?'

Stephanie practically spat out her drink across the table.

'What makes you say that?' Stephanie almost shouted.

'Shhh!' Lisa pulled Stephanie to sit back, 'He's just so bloody perfect, he's like a Greek god.'

Stephanie's eyes went wide as she looked at her best friend.

'That's what I thought. Well, the god part not the gay part, not that he has a gay part, what am I saying? Ben likes him but he has a partner anyway.'

'So does someone else I know,' Lisa raised her eyebrows at Stephanie.

'I know, to be honest, I bet even Mark would fancy him. Look at him.'

'Fair,' Lisa agreed.

'Wow, Lucas must work out twice a day, have you seen his muscles?' Angela said breathlessly as she sat down next to Lisa.

Rosie sat next to Angela and said excitedly, 'He's renting a house in the village, and he has a German Shepherd called Bruce.'

They fell silent as Ben and Lucas approached. Lucas slipped onto the corner seat next to Stephanie and she immediately felt the warmth of his body which made her tense, she sat up straighter and inched closer to Lisa. As if he sensed Stephanie was feeling uncomfortable Lucas moved slightly further away. Ben sat opposite Stephanie and raised his glass to everyone.

'Here's to the start of the next Hibaldton mystery- the case of the missing jewels,' Ben declared dramatically.

'Are you planning on writing a book?' laughed Lisa.

'That isn't a bad idea Lisa,' Ben pretended to take it seriously.

Stephanie took off her jacket, pulled her phone out of her pocket and placed it on the table.

'We should make a list of the people who have had things go missing. I know where everyone lives apart from Margaret, but we need addresses,' Stephanie said.

'I can get that,' Rosie said, 'I'll be the clerk if you like, I'll set up a chat and email group.'

'When we find out the items that are missing, I can do some research into their potential value,' Angela suggested enthusiastically.

'So that leaves a job for me, Lisa and Lucas,' Ben looked at Stephanie expectantly.

'You could take photos.'

'I do have a great camera,' Ben agreed.

'When are you going to show us the photos from the Summer Fair?' Lisa asked.

'I've just finished editing them actually, they are fab-u-lous.' Ben gushed.

Stephanie thought about something.

'Hey, have you got a picture of Mrs Moore?'

'Yeah, I'm sure I do.'

'Have a look at that because she was wearing her brooch that day,' Stephanie said.

'That's a good place to start. Mabel said she hadn't paid much for it.'

'She told us that her husband bought it at a fair for a few shillings, but that doesn't mean it's not worth a lot now.'

Angela agreed, 'That's right. I watch a lot of antique programmes and go to places like that all the time. Most objects are passed down generations or get bought for a few pence and, well look at Antiques Road Show, nearly every show a person finds out that their object is worth a lot more than they thought.'

'It sounds like we have a great team,' said Stephanie looking around the group. 'Angela knows her antiques, Rosie's good at getting information, and Ben's the photo expert.'

'You're good at finding clues,' Ben said.

Stephanie looked at Lisa, 'Will you come with me to interview people?'

Lisa looked unsure. 'I'm not keen on finding dead people,' she said shaking her head. 'Remember last time?'

'Who said anything about finding dead people?' Stephanie raised her eyebrows.

'You didn't think you were going to find any last time either.'

'Lisa, I promise there won't be any dead people…I am almost sure there won't be any dead people.'

'Do you usually find dead people?' Lucas asked with surprise.

'Look, will everyone stop saying…' She whispered the next words, ' *dead people*… and I only found two.'

Lucas chuckled, he sat back and shook his head in disbelief.

Stephanie wasn't sure whether he was laughing at them or with them so she faced him and asked, 'So, Lucas, what can you bring to the table?'

Everyone stared at him and suddenly Lucas seemed not so confident.

He thought for a few seconds, 'I suppose I'm your muscle.'

He flexed his biceps and Stephanie ogled at how his arm filled his shirt sleeve, her face flushed.

'Touché,' Lisa quipped.

'I'll drink to *that*.' Ben nodded in Lucas's direction and downed his glass of lager.

'So?' Stephanie asked Lisa, 'Do you feel safer now muscle man is with us?'

Lisa thought about it for a minute, 'It could work. But I might not be able to come every time.'

Lucas coughed and Lisa realised what she'd said and went crimson.

'That's not a problem for me,' Ben sniggered.

Lisa tried to kick him under the table, and then they all burst out laughing.

Stephanie tried to bring things back to some kind of order.

'I'm free tomorrow after school if that suits everyone. We should go see Mabel first.'

'I can meet you at her house about half five,' Ben said.

'Yes, I can ask my mum to look after the girls,' Lisa added.

Stephanie looked over at Lucas and hoped he'd say he was busy.

'Yep, count me in. Pass me your phone please Stephanie.'

'Why?'

'I thought I'd give you, my number.'

'Why?'

'I thought you could share it with the group.'

He led out his hand and Stephanie reluctantly passed him her phone.

'Can I have your face?'

Stephanie looked blank for a moment then realised he wanted to unlock her phone.

'Oh yes.'

Stephanie leaned across as Lucas pointed the phone towards her face. Her eyes strayed towards his chest, it was huge and pulled his shirt tightly in all the right places. Briefly, she wondered what he looked like without his shirt. She looked down at his arm resting on the table, she felt an urge to stroke the dark hairs, to feel how soft they were and run her fingers up to his biceps.

Stephanie bolted back to Lisa, almost knocking into her. Stephanie finished her cider while she waited for her phone to be returned. She had to control the images she was imagining, she felt so guilty thinking these thoughts about someone else than Mark.

She looked at Lisa and said, 'We should be going now, don't you think?'

Stephanie was restless to be away from this man sitting far too near for comfort. Her body was confusing the hell out of her right now, she needed to get away. She was obviously missing Mark, that was it.

'Yes, yes Martin will be wondering where I am,' Lisa agreed and looked surprised when Stephanie encouraged her to shuffle faster along the seat until they were standing.

'Right, well, I'll see you at Mrs Moore's and now I have your number, I'll text you, Lucas. Bye team, great meeting, good work,' Stephanie called as she walked backwards, knocking into a table on her way out.

'WHAT IS WRONG with you?' Lisa asked when they got outside.

'Nothing why?'

'Cos you're acting weird that's why.'

'I was just feeling too hot all of a sudden and needed fresh air,' Stephanie put her hand to her cheek, which felt flushed.

The two women walked past the church, the air was warm, and the moon was bright in the night sky.

'Wow…so Lucas he's going to be with us when we go to visit Mrs Moore…' Lisa sounded like she could hardly believe it was happening.

'Hmm hmmm,' Stephanie replied, trying to not give her emotions away.

'Just checking I wasn't dreaming this whole thing.'

Stephanie pinched her on the arm.

'Ouch!' Lisa screamed and they both laughed. 'Gee, thanks.'

'Who *is* he?' Stephanie said when they'd stopped giggling.

'I don't know. We just need to ask him I suppose,' Lisa said.

'I guess we'll find out tomorrow. It's not a mystery that he's moved into the village as such, but who moves in and joins a council meeting?'

'Maybe he thought it was a good way to meet people.'

'Looking at him though, you'd think he'd meet people at the gym or martial arts or something like that, you know?'

'Hmmm. I wonder what he does for a job.'

By this time, they'd reached the road where Lisa lived, and Stephanie realised that they'd spent all the time talking about Lucas.

'See you tomorrow at school, we can have fun making up possible jobs for him then,' laughed Stephanie who always enjoyed imagining what people did, unfortunately, reality was often more boring.

'Bye then,' Lisa called.

Stephanie continued down the road, glancing at a person leaning against a fence on the street corner. It was dark so difficult to tell for sure, but it looked like a man with his hood up, and as Stephanie passed by, she felt uneasy. He was standing in the empty street, and a slight sickly smell of a vape wafted in Stephanie's direction.

Stephanie couldn't help looking over her shoulder and realised the figure had turned and seemed to be watching her. Stephanie quickened her step and didn't slow down until she was home.

17

MRS MOORE'S HOUSE

Thursday evening came quickly. As it happened, work had been so busy that Stephanie and Lisa had not really had time to discuss Lucas and it was now that Stephanie found herself thinking of him again as she walked to Mrs Moore's house.

Getting out her phone, she looked at her emails and saw that Rosie had sent everyone Mabel's address. Good, that meant that she didn't need to text Lucas. She noticed that his email was lucasl007@gmail. That didn't give his surname away. 007 though, very James Bond, she thought rolling her eyes.

Stephanie walked along Field View, her road meandered past a small football field on her left then Stephanie walked around the corner onto Church Street. She looked at her watch and realised she had five minutes to get to Mabel's house as they had agreed.

The previous evening had given her a lot to think about. She had talked to Mark on the phone and told him about the Parish Council and how a group of them had got together to look into the burglaries. He found it amusing and said he was glad she was keeping occupied, but he did have a good idea that they could call themselves the 'Mystery Club'. Two things annoyed her though: one was that he wasn't taking the burglaries seriously, and two he didn't seem bothered about Lucas appearing on the scene. Of course, Stephanie didn't tell him how Lucas was Thor's body double, or how he was making her turn to jelly. Still, she thought as she turned into East Street where Mabel lived, it would have been nice to think Mark would be a little jealous. She had thought about telling Mark about the car which nearly ran her over, and the vaping man who she'd seen the other night, but she still wasn't certain that it meant anything.

Stephanie stopped at Mabel's gate and breathed a sigh of relief to see only Lisa standing there. Why was she nervous about seeing Lucas again?

'No Ben or Lucas?'

'They're already inside chatting to Mabel.'

Stephanie was surprised that the two men were so keen. Ben opened the door, and they walked straight into the hallway. Stephanie heard the deep voice she knew was Lucas by the way the hair on her arms stood on end. Then she heard Mabel Moore actually giggling.

'Oh, you are a charmer, Lucas. Yes, I was not bad looking in my younger days, and my husband was so handsome.'

Mabel was standing in the middle of the room holding a framed photograph.

'Oh, hello everyone, do come on in and take a seat. I'll just go get the teapot.'

She put the frame on the fireplace and disappeared through a door which led to the kitchen.

Stephanie looked at Lucas who was leaning against the fireplace and he nodded hello. As his eyes met Stephanie's he grinned, and she noticed how his lips looked soft and how he had a cute dimple in his cheek when he smiled. Stephanie pulled her gaze away from his to look around the room, anything to take her mind off Lucas.

Ben was sitting in the chair by the window where Mabel usually sat to watch people pass by. Stephanie noticed the two-seater settee where Lisa was moving to, so she did the same.

'Mabel's in a good mood,' Lisa whispered in Stephanie's ear.

Mabel brought out the drinks of tea and a plate of biscuits. She was wearing an apron decorated with white ducks and daisies over a brown blouse and tweed skirt, she walked over to Lucas first who stood up straight and reached out for a biscuit.

'Mmm, these biscuits are delicious Mabel,' Lucas said taking a bite. 'Did you make them yourself?'

Mabel flushed with the praise, 'Yes I did, would you like another?'

Lucas nodded and took another before she moved on to offer the plate to Ben.

'It is very good of you to not mind us popping around like this,' Ben added.

'I don't get many visitors so it's a pleasure.'

Mabel offered a biscuit to Stephanie and Lisa, then there was silence while they ate and watched her pour out the tea. The biscuits were quite good Stephanie thought, oaty and not too crumbly.

'Did you bring the photograph?' Stephanie asked Ben while they drank their tea.

He smiled and brought out a brown envelope from his bag. Slipping the photographs out slowly, he carried them as if they were precious and everyone gathered round to look at the image of the brooch.

'Yes, that's mine,' Mabel acknowledged.

'And this photograph is a close-up of the brooch.'

'That's some great photography work Ben,' Lucas nodded.

'Yeah, well done,' Lisa and Stephanie agreed excitedly.

The photograph showed an oval cameo brooch, gold round the edge with four tiny pearls spaced out on the sides. The centre contained the profile of a beautiful lady wearing a pearl necklace. The face was cream on a blushed-pink background.

'It is beautiful,' Stephanie sighed. 'We need to get it back for you.'

'I've already emailed the photo to Angela and she's on the task of finding out if your brooch is worth anything Mabel,' Ben announced.

'I don't care about that. It was more for sentimental reasons I want it back.'

'We understand, and that's why we are here,' Stephanie looked up and smiled. Shall we take a look at where you think you left it?'

Mabel led the group up the stairs to her bedroom. It was a tidy house with decorating tastes that reminded Stephanie of her Grandma Bettie. Lucas and Ben carefully moved the drawer unit, in case it had fallen behind it, while Stephanie and Lisa walked over to the window and looked down.

'Did you say the window was open?' Stephanie asked.

'Yes, it was the left one,' Mabel pointed.

Lisa opened the window, and they leaned out to peer down to a flat roof below.

'It could be possible to reach this window from the kitchen roof, don't you think?' Stephanie asked Lisa.

'It looks like it, and someone could have used the bin to climb on.'

'We'll go down and check it out from there, come on big boy,' Ben called, and the two men disappeared.

Stephanie and Lisa exchanged amused looks.

'Big boy?' Lisa mouthed.

'So, is there anything you'd like to know?' Mabel asked.

Stephanie looked at Mabel and asked, 'Another idea could be if the person used a ladder. Do you have a ladder that would reach up here?'

'No,' Mabel shook her head. 'My husband, God bless him, wasn't very good at DIY. We have a step ladder but that's it.'

Lisa's eyes grew wide, 'What if something flew in the window.'

'Like a bird?' Mabel said.

'I'm thinking, what about a trained parrot?' Lisa was remembering the parrots from the fair. 'Is it possible to train a parrot to fly into bedrooms and steal jewellery?'

'That might explain the odd items going missing,' Stephanie said not convinced, 'but is it possible to train a parrot to do that?'

'I saw a film once where a man trained a monkey to climb in through windows and then went to open the front door to let him in.'

Stephanie pulled a face imagining it.

'I don't think anyone owns a monkey in Hibaldton. Would a parrot be able to open a door?'

The voice of Ben carried from outside.

'Yoohoo, we are in position.'

Stephanie and Lisa looked down to see Ben looking very professional, taking photos and Lucas standing looking amused by it all.

'Do you think it's possible to climb onto the roof?' Stephanie called down.

She could see Ben and Lucas talking, Lucas was shaking his head and then pointed to Ben. Ben was then shaking his head.

'What's going on down there?' Lisa asked.

The next moment, Lucas had his hands out and Ben was lifting his foot onto Lucas's hands.

'I don't think I can do this,' Ben's voice could be heard down below, put your hand lower.'

'That's it,' Lucas encouraged him, 'put it there and push up.'

'Not so fast!' shouted Ben loudly.

Lisa and Stephanie looked at each other.

'I hate to think what the neighbours are thinking right now,' Stephanie laughed.

'What on earth are you two doing down there?' Lisa called when suddenly Ben appeared, standing waist-high to the kitchen roof, looking rather dizzy.

'Oh, bloody hell,' he called, in a wobbly voice, his face was white, 'don't let go of me.'

Next, he was getting higher and then somehow, he managed to pull himself up.

Stephanie and Lisa realised they had been holding their breath and Lisa reached out her arms as Ben walked gingerly towards them. He now stood below the window but could only reach with his hands.

'Can you pull me up?' he asked.

'I doubt it, how much do you weigh?' Lisa inquired.

'Does that even matter?' Stephanie said. 'We'd never be able to pull him up through the window. Can't you pull yourself up?'

'I'm not strong enough, have you not seen my puny arms?'

'Lucas would be able to do it,' Lisa said. 'He did say his muscles would come in handy.'

Stephanie said quietly, 'And boy, I'll never get tired of watching him prove it.'

'Excuse me, ladies, Muscle Man to the rescue,' chuckled Lucas from inside the room.

Stephanie and Lisa jumped when they realised that he was right behind them. Stephanie avoided looking at him as she moved aside and wondered in horror if he'd heard her practically admit that she had been ogling him, again. Still, she watched in awe as Lucas leaned through the window frame and seemed to pull Ben up with little effort. Ben slipped through the window frame rather ungracefully hands first on the carpeted floor, and then fell with a heavy thump onto a heap.

He stood up on wobbly legs with everyone standing around him.

He asked in a shaky voice, 'So Mabel, do you think that would have woken you up?'

'I most definitely think it would have, I'm not deaf.'

Mabel looked unimpressed so far, so they all decided to go downstairs and reconvene in the front room.

'It would have been possible though if you were strong enough to pull yourself up,' Stephanie said as they walked down the stairs.

'A cat burglar could have done that much more quietly,' Lisa supposed. 'Not to scare you, Mabel.'

'I am never going to open my window again at night. Oh, the thought of someone slipping in at night sends shivers all over my body.'

'Me too, me too,' Ben shook his head looking down.

There was a pause while the others held their breath to stop laughing and no one dared look at each other until they arrived back in the front room.

Stephanie saw how Mabel looked upset, so she walked over and put her hand on Mabel's shoulder.

Lucas said, 'Mabel, I work in security, and I promise that I will go round your house to make sure you are safe. I have some sensors I can install to make sure no one will be able to even walk up your drive without setting them off.'

Mabel smiled and seemed much happier.

Stephanie thought about who else might have access.

'Do you have a window cleaner?' Stephanie asked.

'Yes, I do, I'll show you I can never remember his name.'

Mabel soon returned with the Village Voice and opened it to the advertisement.

'Dan, Dan the window man.

We wipe, you see,

How clean your windows can be.'

Stephanie read out the cheesy poem.

She passed the leaflet to Ben who had his hand out.

'We swipe, your jew-ell-ry,

And we get away scot-free,' Ben joked.

They all laughed apart from Mabel.

'You don't think it's Dan the window man, do you?' Mabel asked eyes wide.

'Oh no, we don't but it's worth looking into. Don't share anything we've spoken about, will you?'

'Oh of course not. I understand that at this moment *everyone* is a suspect.'

Mabel tapped her finger to the side of her nose as if it were a secret code.

Stephanie smiled. She was warming to this old lady who seemed to be thoroughly enjoying herself. 'I'll just pop outside to look in the garden for myself if you don't mind?'

'No help yourself, go through the kitchen dear.'

Stephanie looked at Lisa, 'Do you want to come?'

Lisa nodded and they walked to the kitchen and up to the door.

'Stephanie first of all noticed her mum's casserole dish on the oven. It was a heavy pot with a lid and was a distinctive deep blue.

'Look,' Stephanie whispered, 'that's my dish.'

'You can ask for it later,' Lisa replied, hand on the door handle.

'Wait a minute,' Stephanie put her hand on Lisa's arm to stop her.

This door doesn't have a very secure lock, not like the front door. Someone might have picked the lock.'

'I suppose so, but look, she keeps the key in the door,' Lisa noticed.

Lisa tried the handle, but the door was locked so she turned the key. It easily turned and the door opened.

Outside, the evening was still light. They had a quick look around. There was a small garden at the rear enclosed by well-established trees and bushes. Next door's fence was too high to climb over so no one could have gotten through that way. Stephanie could hear the clucking of hens coming from over the fence, and she remembered when she had been attacked by one of the chickens a few months before. She recalled its sharp scratchy feet and the feathers in her hair, she shivered.

'Are you cold?' Lucas was behind them, and it made the girls jump.

'You gave us a fright!' Lisa exclaimed.

'Again.' Stephanie added.

'Sorry, I'm good at sneaking about quietly,' Lucas admitted.

'Stephanie's scared of chickens,' Lisa told him.

He raised his eyebrows in amusement.

'It's just that…' Stephanie tried to explain, 'I was just remembering the time when we were questioning next door about Gordon's murder, and she put a chicken in my arms… it was a surprise that's all.'

'Was he killed by a chicken?' Lucas asked.

'No! Could a chicken kill someone?' Stephanie asked appalled at the idea.

Lisa continued, 'We never found out for sure, but we saw pills under his chair and a bottle of whiskey.'

'Why did you think it was murder?' Lucas asked, intrigued.

'It happened shortly after his wife's death,' Lisa began.

'She was attacked at the Village Hall,' Stephanie added.

'I'm sorry, it must have been awful. I'd like to hear that story sometime,' he said seriously.

'It's a long story,' Stephanie said grimly. She didn't feel like discussing it in Mabel's back garden.

Lucas seemed to read Stephanie's body language and changed the subject.

'So, any thoughts?' he asked looking round the garden with his hands in his pockets.

'My thoughts are concentrating on the back door.'

They walked back to the door and Stephanie looked through the keyhole at the key inside.

'Is it possible to pick a lock with the key in?' 'It's possible if you have a tool to push the key out. Any decent burglar would have a range of tools on him,' Lucas pointed out.

'That's true.' Lisa said.

The door opened from the inside to reveal Ben and Mabel in the kitchen.

Lucas stood in the doorway and pointed at the key.

'Mabel, do you remember if the key was in the lock that night?'

'I always leave it in the lock.'

Stephanie sighed with disappointment.

'But now you mention it,' Mabel continued, 'I do remember that in the morning, the key was on the floor. I thought it was strange at the time, so I just picked it up and put it back in the lock.'

'Can you lock a door from the outside, without a key?' Stephanie asked Lucas, who seemed to know what he was talking about.

'Yes, you can, it's just a case of reversing the operation… if you have the right tools. Or someone might have locked the door after leaving… then posted the key through the letter box.'

18

LUCAS'S HOUSE

Back in the street, the group huddled to discuss their next move.

'Are you ruling out Dan, Dan the window man?' Lucas asked with a grin.

'It's too early in the investigation to rule out suspects Lucas,' Stephanie laughed.

'Spoken like a true detective,' Lucas grinned.

'I really should be getting home now,' Lisa said looking at her watch.

'Shall we get something to eat?' Lucas asked. 'Anyone for fish and chips?'

Everyone nodded apart from Lisa.

'Martin will have made tea, but you guys go ahead,' she encouraged them to go on without her.

As Lisa walked down the road, the remaining threesome walked up to the chip shop on the corner.

'We swipe your jewellery…' Stephanie tried to remember Ben's clever rhyme.

'And we get away Scot-free,' Ben finished. They all laughed louder this time.

'Very clever,' Stephanie admitted.

AFTER PICKING UP their fish and chips, in open trays, they ate as they walked down Church Street.

'What we need is an HQ,' Ben said with his mouth full of chips.

'We can meet at my house if you like,' Lucas said.

Stephanie looked up at him, she was so curious to see where he lived, she admitted to herself.

'I live in this direction anyway,' he said.

They agreed and continued to walk to the end of the road and then they turned right. On their way, they passed a small number of people wandering about and some walking their dogs. Stephanie smelt the sickly vape aroma again and couldn't help but look up to see where it came from. Was it the women who had just passed by or the man across the road? Did that parked car have someone sitting in the driver's seat?

'Everything ok?' Lucas asked.

'Yes, why?' Stephanie replied casually.

'It's just that you've been looking around for the past five minutes as if you think we're being followed.'

'Why would anyone follow us?'

Ben wafted a chip in the air nervously as he spoke, 'Do you think the thief knows we're investigating the break-ins?'

'If there were any break-ins,' Stephanie corrected him, breaking off a piece of fish.

'You should trust your intuition,' Lucas said so gravely that Stephanie looked at him.

'I just smelt the vape cloud that drifted over in the breeze and it reminded me of something.'

'Something good, or something bad?'

Stephanie paused, not sure how much to say. 'This sounds crazy, but there has been someone hanging about the area. When I see him, he's just standing, staring in my direction.'

'Go on,' Lucas prompted.

'Sometimes he's in a blue car and once he was on the street corner… there actually.' She pointed. ' I was walking down the lane when I think he tried to run me over.'

'What?' Ben gasped in horror. 'The idiot driver you talked about in the meeting?'

'Well, it wasn't until just now that I realise it could be the same person.'

The trio turned right onto Field View and carried on walking. Ben was the one now looking over his shoulder.

'Maybe you should take the car and stop walking on your own for a while,' Lucas suggested. 'You have my number if you're worried.'

'Gosh Steph, do you think it's anything to do with Mabel's murder?' Ben asked.

Stephanie saw how worried he was and started to feel like she was being silly.

'I don't think so… that's all over now.'

'Isn't this near where you live Stephanie?' Ben piped up.

'Yeah,' Stephanie said, 'I was just wondering the same thing.'

They both looked up at Lucas.

'I'm renting a house at the end of here.'

He walked a bit faster and the other two were struggling to keep up with his long legs.

He looked behind him, 'Sorry am I going too fast?'

'Just a bit,' Ben was a bit out of breath, 'It's hard to eat and walk at the same time.'

Stephanie noticed that Lucas had already finished his food.

'So, Lucas, what do you do for a living?' Stephanie asked.

'I'm in security.'

'No wonder you know about picking locks,' Ben exclaimed.

'How come you didn't say that when we were in the pub?' Stephanie's eyes narrowed.

Lucas turned to look at her.

'Sorry, I guess I went with the comedy answer.'

They continued to walk, getting closer to Stephanie's house. She stopped, looking extremely confused.

'Where do you live?' she asked.

'I live over there,' Lucas pointed to the road that led off Field View and was in direct line to Stephanie's house. Stephanie froze with her mouth open. She was surprised that she hadn't seen Lucas when he moved in.

'Are you coming?' he asked and walked on.

As soon as they entered, they were greeted by a large German Shepherd with huge, adorable brown eyes and pricked-up ears that twitched as he listened to everyone.

'Sit,' Lucas commanded in a firm voice, and the dog sat down immediately. 'This is Bruce, he's well trained, don't worry.'

Stephanie could tell that he was dying to meet everyone, his tongue hung out as he panted excitedly.

Stephanie walked over with the last piece of fish in her hand, and she held it out for Bruce. He gave it a suspicious sniff before delicately taking it from her hand. She knelt next to him to scratch behind his ears.

Lucas stared in surprise. 'He doesn't usually take to strangers so quickly.'

'Well, we're not strangers anymore, are we boy?' Bruce nuzzled and licked at her hands as she smiled down at him.

Ben excused himself to find the bathroom, while Lucas threw their rubbish in the bin. Stephanie stood up and decided to have a look around.

Inside his front room, Stephanie stared out of his window across to her house.

'Is everything all right?' Lucas stood next to Stephanie.

'It's just funny because… I live in that house over there.'

She pointed across the road and watched his face closely to gauge his reaction. His eyebrows moved up in surprise.

'Really? Wow, that's a coincidence.'

'Yeah. I didn't see you move in.'

'I've been here a few days now, err I didn't see you either.'

Stephanie was thinking that she didn't believe in coincidences when Ben came in and then paused wondering what he had interrupted. 'Are we sitting in here? I was thinking we should sit at the dining table.'

Lucas looked like he was going to say something, and then he turned to follow Ben into the kitchen.

'I'll make a drink. Tea? Coffee? Something stronger?'

Stephanie could hear him asking while they were in the kitchen.

Stephanie quickly glanced around the front room, to try to get some clues about this man of mystery. There wasn't much to go on, no personal items around. Bruce trotted towards her, sniffed her hand and when he saw there was no more fish, he walked back into the kitchen, looking over his shoulder for her to follow. She shrugged and decided to join the others. Ben was sitting at the table, bending over Bruce, stroking his head.

'Drink?' Lucas asked.

'Oh, tea please,' Stephanie replied. 'This place seems a bit empty Lucas.'

'Yeah, I haven't had a chance to move much stuff in yet. A lot of my things are in storage.'

He spoke as he moved about the kitchen, opening cupboards which looked quite full of food, and brought out a tea caddy.

'Where have you come from?' Stephanie asked, intrigued.

'Scotland, I was living in Glasgow for a few months, I tend to move about a lot with my job.'

'That's where you're originally from?'

'No, but I lived there for a while.'

'Your accent sounds southern, London?'

Lucas laughed, 'Yes, spot on.'

'You work in security?'

'Yes.'

The kettle had boiled, and Lucas poured the water into three cups calmly.

'What does that involve exactly?'

'Mostly guarding things. You know buildings, property, people.'

He handed out the cups and Stephanie took a sip when Ben's voice broke into her thoughts, 'What we could do with…' he looked around the kitchen diner, 'is a big wall to pin up suspects and join them up with string, you know like in detective films.'

'It's a good job you're not in my house,' Stephanie had to laugh.

'My partner, Simon, is a neat freak so he probably wouldn't be happy either.'

'I've got just the thing,' Lucas said.

He walked out and they could hear him running upstairs. He was very agile for such a large-set man. Bruce stood up to follow him and waited at the bottom of the stairs. Lucas was soon back carrying a large whiteboard with Bruce following like his shadow.

'Oh, that's perfect,' Ben clapped his hands together excitedly. 'We can write on it, is it magnetic too?'

Lucas looked around and picked up a magnet from the fridge- it stuck.

'Is it ok if the group meet here?' Ben asked.

'Yes, fine with me. Do you agree Stephanie?' Lucas glanced at Stephanie as he sat down, he looked concerned that she wouldn't say yes.

'Yes, why not.' Stephanie shrugged and laughed at the two men who seemed so eager.

'You know Mark, my boyfriend,' Stephanie quickly looked at Lucas then back at Ben, 'suggested that we should call ourselves 'The Mystery Club'.'

'Oh perfect,' Ben laughed, 'tell him we'll have to get some badges printed. How is he enjoying London?'

'Fine, he enjoys the big city. I suppose he thinks we have to occupy ourselves with solving mysteries to make our lives less boring, as we live out in the sticks.'

'Maybe we do, and I don't care do you Brucie boy?' Ben was leant over fussing over Bruce again who seemed to enjoy the attention. They watched Bruce as he walked over to Stephanie and lay down on the floor at her feet, tail thudding on the floor. Eventually Ben said with a thought,

´Simon, works late on Wednesdays, is that evening okay for us to meet up?'

Stephanie and Lucas agreed, and Ben got his phone out to ring Simon up for a lift home.

Stephanie turned to Lucas and said quietly, 'I'll email the group and see if Wednesdays are ok with everyone. I hope that we can solve this mystery.'

'Are you going to tell me about the other mysteries you've solved?' he asked.

'There was only one, a few months ago, it's a long story,' Stephanie said quietly looking down at the table.

'Did you say there was a murder, here in Hibaldton?'

Stephanie still found it difficult to recount all that happened, her face must have shown it because Lucas added, 'You don't have to tell me the details, it must have been upsetting.'

She looked up at Lucas and noticed the concern in his eyes and also that he looked interested.

'To cut a long story short, I spied on some criminals in the woods by the river, who were smuggling drugs it turned out. Some people think I was stupid, some think I was crazy…'

'And some think you were brave,' Ben interrupted as he got off the phone, 'you got the evidence to catch the drug runners and found they were part of the Russian mafia.'

'We don't know if it was the mafia,' Stephanie laughed.

'You're telling me that you hid out in the woods, on your own, to get the evidence?' Lucas asked in surprise.

Stephanie nodded and added, 'But not everyone was caught…'

As if sensing Stephanie's mood, Bruce stood up to put his head on her lap. She looked down and stroked the top of his head with a smile.

'It wasn't your fault, you can forget about it now,' Ben tried to cheer her up.

'Bruce is such a sweet dog,' Stephanie said.

'He is, he was also trained in the military.'

'Really? Were you in the military?' Ben asked.

'Yes, we have been a team for five years.'

Bruce sat up and gave a small bark as if agreeing with him and they all laughed.

There was a beep from outside and Ben looked up.

'That's Simon, I'll be off. Thanks for tonight and can't wait to meet up again.'

They went outside and stood in the driveway to wave Ben and Simon goodbye. As they stood outside, Stephanie felt Bruce's wet nose push against her hand.

'He seems to like you,' Lucas said softly.

Bruce whimpered and pushed himself against her hand so that she couldn't help but kneel to hug him.

'Dogs are very intuitive you know,' Lucas continued.

'What do you mean?' Stephanie asked, stroking Bruce's back.

'They can smell our emotions. They know who to trust and who needs comforting.'

Stephanie slowly stood up and stepped away.

'I'll be off then,' Stephanie pointed to her house awkwardly. She suddenly felt like she was going to cry.

'Before you go,' Lucas said quietly, 'I can tell you were surprised about me living so close to you, I hope it's not made you uncomfortable.'

He looked so concerned that Stephanie felt she owed him some sort of an explanation.

She took a deep breath. 'When the criminals were caught, there was one man, the leader I think, who got away. He…he sort of stalked me and, well he stood there actually.'

Stephanie walked across the road and stared at the fence where Sergei used to stand. A shiver went down her spine that she hugged herself.

She looked up at Lucas and saw his jaw had set in a firm line, his eyebrows were drawn together in a deep frown.

'And tonight, you were watching everyone we walked past. Then that man you've been seeing…'

'He's not Sergei. I'd know his figure anywhere,' she shivered.

I promise you, Stephanie, that you have nothing to fear from me. If you ever need anything, anything, you can call me, text, hell even shout and 'I'll come running. Ok?'

Stephanie was taken aback by how strongly he declared this promise.

'Goodnight Stephanie, and remember I mean it. It's what I do and I'm good at it.'

'Thank you, I appreciate that.'

Stephanie entered her house and closed the door, locking it behind her. She stood in the darkness thinking about what Lucas had said. Could she trust him? She didn't know why, but her gut told her that he was telling her the truth… maybe not the whole truth but she felt safe with him and Bruce living close by.

19

GARDEN SECRETS

Saturday soon came around. Stephanie was making breakfast in her pyjama shorts and T-shirt, the sun shone in through the patio doors enticing her to step into the garden.

The familiar whir of the aeroplane overhead made her look up, her eyes searched for the Skydive plane, watching it ascend into the cloudless, blue sky. She waited with anticipation for the engine to cut, and then squinted against the sun, hoping to catch a glimpse of the skydivers. Tiny dots plummeted downwards, then a sudden flapping noise reached Stephanie's ears like panicked wings and the dots turned into a spiral of fluttering sails, and then silence. The sails became silent pterodactyls soaring on invisible air currents. Time seemed to stand still as they floated past. Serenity was rudely interrupted by the refined roar of an approaching vehicle at the front of the house, her heart raced as she recognised that sound as being Mark's car.

Bolting into the front room, through the window, she watched Mark ease himself out of his red Ferrari. She opened the door to welcome her boyfriend as he walked up her driveway.

He jumped in and lifted Stephanie by her waist in his arms. His mouth found hers as he slowly let her slide down his chest until she stood shakily back on the floor.

She pulled herself away and he closed the door behind him.

'I wasn't expecting you this early!'

'I know, I thought I'd surprise you. I set off early to beat the traffic. Ooh, do I smell toast?'

Mark ran into the kitchen to grab Stephanie's toast from her plate.

She chased him but was too late.

'Toast thief,' she laughed.

'Aww, mmm this is good,' he mumbled with his mouth full. His eyes roamed down Stephanie's bare legs to her pink-painted toenails.

'You have it, I'll make some more,' Stephanie laughed and popped two more slices into the toaster.

'So, what's new?' Mark sat next to Stephanie outside at the patio table while they ate their breakfast in the sun.

'Since I last spoke to you… not much. You know about us going to Mabel's house and that's it.'

'It's Mabel now is it?'

'Yeah.' Stephanie sipped her cup of tea. 'She's not that grumpy when you get to know her, I feel like we're friends now.'

Mark raised his eyebrows. 'She didn't argue with you about everything you decided to do?'

'No, she seemed pleased to have company to be honest. Plus, that new guy I told you about…'

'Luke?'

'Lucas. He was like some old grumpy lady whisperer or something. When I got there, she was eating out of the palm of his hand.'

'I hope not literally,' he laughed.

'Err, what a thought,' she laughed, 'no, actually Mabel is all right when you get to know her.'

There was a pause while they finished their toast.

'So… you like this guy then?' Mark asked.

Stephanie kept a straight face and swallowed.

'He's all right. Although I was a bit freaked out when I found out where he lives.'

'Oh?'

'Across the road.' She pointed through the patio doors into the front room.

'Oh yeah, the house over there was up for rent I remember.'

'We're going to be using his house as a base for the Mystery Club.'

Stephanie looked at Mark who was now looking at his phone, typical. Well, if he wasn't bothered about it then… Stephanie huffed.

Mark looked up. 'What's wrong?'

'Nothing,' She stood up and gazed across the field where the wheat had now grown quite high and was glistening in the sunshine.

Stephanie felt confused that Mark didn't seem to be jealous that a new man had entered her life when Mark wasn't around. Then again, why should he? He obviously trusted her. Stephanie frowned, and of course, nothing had happened between her and Lucas. She sighed deep in thought.

Mark got up and stood behind Stephanie, he wrapped his arms around her waist and kissed her left ear.

'What's wrong?' he whispered.

Stephanie closed her eyes and leaned into his body.

'I just thought you might be a little jealous.'

'Should I be jealous?' He leaned her back in his arms so he could see her face.

'Of course not,' Stephanie cried as she was tipped back then he stood her up again.

'Good. Maybe I should remind you what I've got to offer.'

Stephanie stood with Mark's strong body behind her. She closed her eyes and could feel his arms relax letting his hands slowly move across her stomach. His right hand moved under her T-shirt and up to her breast, just cupping her soft curves, his thumb stroking up the side gently. His left hand moved lower to just inside her shorts.

Stephanie's breathing became heavier, and she arched her back in anticipation.

With one swift movement, Mark lifted her top off over her head so that she stood, topless. He left light kisses on her shoulders and his hand moved back to her breasts causing goosebumps.

'It's a good job the patio can't be seen by the neighbours,' Stephanie breathed.

She turned her body to face him, his eyes were heavy and his smile wicked.

'Maybe we should continue this further down the garden then.'

He put his hands on the waistband of her shorts and slowly pulled them down. Mark closed his eyes and bent his mouth towards Stephanie's, his mouth tasted of sweet strawberry jam. His hands stroked down her back to her bottom and then he held her cheeks in his hot palms.

'I think we should take this inside,' Stephanie said as she pushed him back into the kitchen.

'You read my mind,' Mark grinned.

As Stephanie stood inside the patio doors behind Mark, she could see the road as the curtains were open in the front room. She saw a man in jogging shorts looking at his phone. He looked like he had been running fast and was bent over slightly as if to get back his breath. Stephanie's heart stopped as she realised it was Lucas, and she had no clothes on.

'Stop,' she ordered Mark and froze to the spot with him shielding her.

As she spoke Lucas stood up and looked straight into her front room window. She couldn't tell if he could see her or not, then in a flash, he turned to call Bruce and he sprinted to his house.

Mark turned round to face the window.

'Don't worry, no one can see you if we run fast,' he laughed and pulled naked Stephanie quickly through the front room and upstairs.

20

STEPHANIE'S PARENTS

Lazy Sunday mornings were heaven. Stephanie loved waking up with Mark and this particular morning they talked about what to do after they had lunch with her parents. Mark was busy looking up the weather, it seemed a perfect day for the beach when his phone rang.

'Don't bother getting anything together,' Mark sighed after a brief conversation.

'What's the matter?' Stephanie pulled back the duvet to sit on the edge of the bed.

'That was my mum on the phone, she wants me to go over and talk to Dad about some problems he's having. I'm sorry Steph.'

'That's ok, does it have to be straight away, or can it be this afternoon?'

'I told her we were going to your mum's so it can be later. You don't have to come.'

'No, I'd like to come, I haven't seen them for a while. We can go for a walk down to the river after.'

'Come on then, let's visit our families this week and do something more fun next weekend.'

As soon as Stephanie and Mark entered the Rhodes household, it was all hands on deck. Mark got busy setting the table, Barbara started to fill the serving dishes with potatoes and vegetables and Stephanie moved them to the table.

Grandma Bettie wandered in and sat down to motivate everyone into working quicker. 'I'm so starving hungry, I could eat a whole cow,' she said to anyone who was listening, 'I hope you remembered to make extra Yorkshire Puddings as Mark's here.'

'I did mum, don't worry.'

Malcolm entered the kitchen and stood in the doorway to watch everyone almost collide with each other as they bustled about.

'It's like Paddington Station in here, what's the rush?' he asked.

'Grandma's hungry,' Stephanie said as she sat down.

Malcolm walked over to a cupboard and started to rummage about.

'Where's that bottle of wine we got? I fancy a glass of red wine today.'

'I don't know dear, which wine do you mean?' Barbara called over her shoulder as she finished stirring the gravy on the stove.

'You know, the one Dave and Ruth got us.'

'I don't remember, we probably drank it,' Barbara answered and turned off the gas.

Mark went over to help him look, lifting out a bottle at a time for Malcolm to scrutinise the label.

'No. that has to be drunk with fish,' Malcolm shook his head, 'and that one we got for Christmas, and I don't like it, it's too sweet.'

'Bring it over here, I like a sweet wine,' Grandma Bettie said eagerly.

'You're not having any wine mum, you know it messes with your medications,' Barbara warned her. 'Come on dinner's ready.'

'There, that one, I knew we had it. 1993, I remembered Dave telling me that was a good year.' Malcolm started to hunt around in the drawer.

'Honestly Malcolm, dinner's getting cold,' Barbara moaned. 'Everyone help yourselves.'

'You don't have to ask me twice,' Bettie said as she popped three Yorkshire puddings onto her plate.

'Mark lad, will you get the cork out for me while I carve the beef?'

Mark stood up and walked over to take the corkscrew from Stephanie's dad.

'So, what's so special about this wine?' Stephanie asked, intrigued.

'My friend, Dave, knows a lot about wine and keeps a few bottles to mature, he gave it to us and said it would be worth keeping.'

'Not for twenty-odd years!' Barbara declared shaking her head.

'Well, you hid it right at the back, I'd forgotten all about it.'

'She probably hides the wine from you because you get drunk so easily,' Grandma Bettie said in between chewing.

Malcolm ignored her and started to carve the beef. 'You know he stores it in a proper wine rack, at an angle, in his cool cellar.'

'And for nearly thirty years, you've kept it upright, with the vinegar, in a hot kitchen, it'll be disgusting,' Barbara tutted.

'We'll see.'

Malcolm carried the plate of beef and set it on the table as if it were a masterpiece to behold.

'About bloody time,' Bettie grumbled and picked up a piece to plop it onto her plate.

Malcolm continued to pretend she wasn't there and looked around for the wine glasses. Stephanie rolled her eyes and got up to get them, they were kept in the cabinet in the front room for some unknown reason. She couldn't believe that her dad was causing such a fuss.

Finally, they all filled their plates with food and watched while Malcolm excitedly poured out the wine, even Grandma got a little bit.

Malcolm licked his lips in anticipation.

'Right, everyone, cheers and down the hatch.' He held his glass high and slowly brought it to his lips. Everyone else cautiously copied him, yet stopped to wait to see what his reaction would be as if it might be poisonous. Malcolm took a big gulp, swallowed, paused, and everyone held their breath it seemed, frozen in time with glasses to their mouths.

Sure enough, the spell was broken with Malcolm gagging, gasping and reaching for a large glass of water. In unison, the others put their wine glass back down without touching a drop, not at all surprised.

'Wine connoisseur of the month award goes to…' Bettie cackled with laughter.

'Mother!' Barbara glared at her across the table.

Stephanie sighed and rolled her eyes while Mark tried his best not to laugh.

21

MARK'S PARENTS

On the way to Mark's parents' house, Stephanie let out her frustration in the car.

'So, Dad does nothing to help with dinner, waltzes in just as it's nearly ready and then has to create havoc, making out that he has something important to do. Of course, everyone else has to pay him attention because he can't do it on his own. And to make matters worse, we never *have* wine! When was the last time we drank wine with our Sunday dinner?'

Mark started to laugh and soon Stephanie was joining him.

Mark nearly had to stop driving he was laughing so much, he eventually spluttered, 'Nearly thirty years, your dad has had that wine!'

'I know, and then blames my mum for hiding it.'

'You know that men expect something to be where they last saw it.'

'Not you, you're tidier than I am.'

'That's because I'm still at the impressing you stage. Wait until we're married, then I'll turn into a slob.'

There was a pause when they both realised what he'd said.

Stephanie laughed nervously, 'Right, next it's your parents' turn. Let's see how much better that will be.'

'Believe me, probably more depressing and tense. At least your family gives us a good laugh.'

Mark pulled into the driveway, his expression more serious.

'HELLO BEV, HOW are you?' Stephanie smiled at Mark's mum as they entered the kitchen.

Beverley was finishing tidying away the dishes, she looked up with a smile and walked across to hug Stephanie.

'All the better for seeing you two. Thanks for coming, I hope we're not stopping you from doing anything fun.'

'Not at all, we were just going to go for a walk, and we can do that here.'

'Is Dad in the office?' Mark asked and when his mum nodded, he squeezed Stephanie's arm and wandered out to find him.

'Cup of tea?' Beverley asked Stephanie.

Stephanie sat on a chair at the large rustic table while the tea was being made. She gave a recount of the dinner at her family's house and her dad's disastrous wine tasting.

'Oh dear,' Beverley chuckled, 'I remember when we used to make our own wine, most of that ended up in the bin. We don't usually drink it now, Sam's more of a lager drinker.'

'I don't mind American lagers,' Stephanie said and as soon as she had mentioned America, she decided to bring up Mark's brother. 'Richard moved to America, didn't he? Whereabouts does he live now?'

Beverley sat down at the table opposite Stephanie and took a sip of tea from her mug slowly.

'He's been there for, let's think, oh over 10 years, he lives in South Carolina with his girlfriend. He met her over there while he was working as a chef.'

'I didn't know he was a chef.'

'Yes, he always liked to cook. He used to fish a lot with his dad, and they would bring fish home for tea. Sam used to show the boys how to gut the fish and clean them, I think that's how he started with cooking. He's got his own little restaurant now.'

'Do you speak to Richard often?'

'I ring him sometimes and we did a video call at Christmas. Though he didn't stay on for long, he said he was busy.'

Beverley went quiet and Stephanie could tell she was worried about him.

'Mark doesn't talk much about him. I think he misses him too.'

Beverley got up, walked over to a shelf, and brought back an envelope. Opening it up, she took out a letter and inside was a photo of a baby's scan.

'It's funny that you've mentioned Ricky because this came yesterday.'

'He's having a baby?' Stephanie gasped.

'Yes, isn't it exciting!' Beverley's voice cracked with emotion, 'I'm going to be a grandma.'

'Congratulations,' Stephanie said quietly and put her hand on Beverley's.

'I just wish that they lived closer to us, that's all.'

'Does Mark know?'

Beverley shook her head. 'That's another reason why I asked him here, to show him this.'

'But why didn't Richard tell Mark himself?'

'When Richard left, Mark was angry with him, he was young and adored his big brother… Richard was never very good at keeping in touch, and Mark thought he didn't care. Now, when we do get in touch, Mark refuses to speak to him.'

Stephanie was appalled, 'They should speak to each other, tell each other how they feel.'

Stephanie noticed Mark walking up the path to the kitchen door followed by his dad, they seemed to be getting along.

Mark held the door for Sam. 'I told Stephanie that we'd take her fishing, we could start with the basics here, at the lake.'

Sam looked at Stephanie with a grin, 'No time like the present, I'll go get some rods and bait.'

'Hang on a minute, I didn't say I wanted to go fishing today,' Stephanie said as she looked at Mark, who shrugged.

'We have nothing better to do, we might as well sit by the lake.'

'Ok, but first your mum's got something to show you.'

Stephanie handed the photo back to Beverley and waited. Beverley took it and fiddled with it in her hands thoughtfully.

'It's good news Mark…it's about Ricky… he is going to be a dad.'

She held out the photo and after a stunned silence, Mark took it from her and stared at the scan. Stephanie tried to read his expression and could see a mixture of emotions brewing in his dark eyes. Finally, happiness seemed to win over, and with tears in his eyes, Mark handed it back.

'Wow, I'm going to be an uncle.'

He ran his hand along the stubble on his chin and walked over to sit down at the table. Stephanie stood behind him and put her arms around his shoulders.

'It's time to get back in touch, don't you think? We could face time them, see how they are?' Stephanie said quietly.

Mark nodded, 'Yeah, I suppose so.'

Stephanie looked at Beverley who looked relieved and raised her eyebrows at Sam.

Sam nodded too and said, 'Shall we just ring him? What time is it there anyway?'

Mark looked at his phone. 'It's 6 in the morning, probably better to wait two or three hours.'

'Fine, we've got time for some fishing then.'

Sam walked outside to look in the shed.

22

A FAMILY REUNION

The four of them sat on the settee in the front room, the laptop on the coffee table, waiting for Mark to connect them with his brother. Stephanie hoped that it would go well, she felt nervous for all of them and when Mark sat back, she grabbed his hand.

The screen before them changed and two faces appeared looking just as nervous.

'Hi, hello, how are you?' Everyone spoke at once and laughed.

'Hi, Mum, Dad and Mark, it's so good to see you all,' Richard spoke with his arm around his girlfriend. 'Who'sows this?' he asked pointing towards them smiling.

Mark cleared his throat, 'Hi Rick, Emma, this is Stephanie, my girlfriend. Stephanie, this is my big brother and Emma.'

'Hi, nice to meet you properly,' Stephanie said.

'Wow Mark, you've got so grown up,' Richard said with emotion.

'Yeah, it's been a while,' Mark admitted and looked down.

'Congratulations both of you, I can't believe you're going to have a baby,' Barbara gushed with happiness.

'I know,' Emma said in her American southern accent, 'We're still getting used to it. Y'all got the scan we sent?'

'Yes, we did, it's so clear,' said Beverley excitedly.

Sam added, 'Yes, congratulations both of you. We're really pleased, well over the moon we're going to be grandparents...I can't believe it.'

Everyone laughed, there were tears too, eventually, the conversation flowed as they caught up on each other's news. Mark soon began to relax as well and laughed at Richard who had so many questions for him about his life in London.

'Look, I know we can't catch up in a phone call, so we thought it would be better to come and see you in person,' Richard smiled nervously and held Emma's hand. She lifted her hand to show an engagement ring.

'Oh, my goodness, oh that's wonderful,' Beverley almost screamed.

'We thought it was about time,' Emma laughed.

'Of course, we'd love to see you, when are you coming?'

'We thought we'd come in a couple of months? We need to sort some things out first, you know plane tickets and that,' Richard explained.

'We'll send you some money, don't worry about it,' Sam said quickly, 'and you can stay here of course.'

'Or you can stay at my house,' offered Mark.

'Brilliant, thanks.' Richard looked relieved.

Stephanie watched as the whole family chatted and smiled, it was just what she had been hoping for.

THAT EVENING, STEPHANIE and Mark returned to his house for him to pick up his bags as it was time for him to return to London.

Stephanie sat on his dark blue bed as he packed, she tried not to show how sad she was to see him go.

'Are you coming back next weekend? Remember there's a band at the airfield.'

'Yeah, I'll come back on Friday, hopefully, I won't have any meetings and I can set off early.'

Mark dropped his bag on the floor and sat down next to Stephanie.

'You'll be all right without me, won't you?'

'Yes, why?'

'You know, with those postcards you've been getting, you seemed worried last time I saw you.'

'I haven't had anything since, I told you I'm fine, it was probably a joke. I've got Lucas across the road, he has a trained German Shepherd so I only need to shout and I'm sure they'll hear me.'

'I think it's good that you've got someone like that living close by, you know, to call on if there's trouble. I'm sorry I'm not around…'

He held her hand in his and looked guilty.

Stephanie wanted to say, 'You should be here, I need you!' But instead, she just nodded.

'I'd better go before I get too tired to drive. Come here.'

Mark pulled Stephanie to her feet and he softly kissed her lips. They stood for a while, wrapped in each other's arms.

'I noticed, by the way, that you didn't say anything when I talked about us getting married.'

159

'You noticed, did you?' Stephanie laughed, tears in her eyes.

'Is it such a bad idea?' Mark asked quietly.

'No, not at all.'

'I love you Steph.'

Stephanie closed her eyes, 'I love you too.'

23

MARGARET'S HOUSE

All Monday and Tuesday, Stephanie did nothing but think about the weekend with Mark and how he had said he loved her. Stephanie believed she loved him, she had longed to hear him say those words… and yet, she didn't feel as happy as she thought she should.

While she ate her tea, she gazed out across the field of wheat through the open doors of her dining room and wondered if it was because he wasn't there. How could she feel excited about a life with Mark when he was miles away? She looked across towards his house beyond the field. He should be there, close by when she needed him, not on the other end of a telephone call. She still didn't know how she felt about moving to London, and soon it would be the holidays and she'd agreed to stay with him there. Shouldn't she be excited?

Stephanie sighed and looked at her watch, she'd agreed to meet with the Mystery Club at Margaret's house at six thirty and it was 20 past 6 already. She quickly left her dishes in the sink and went to put on her trainers.

As she walked into the street, she met up with Lucas walking past.

'Hi,' Lucas waved and strolled over, 'Are you going over to Margaret's house? Shall we go together?' he asked.

'Yeah, sure. I was thinking of driving.'

Stephanie opened the door of her Fiesta and stood waiting for a response. He looked at her over the car roof and smiled, 'Yeah fine by me.'

Stephanie started to buckle up her seatbelt and looked across at Lucas who was struggling to fit in the car, his head was touching the roof and he just managed to find the seatbelt and snap it in place.

Stephanie laughed, 'Are you comfortable enough? Would you rather go in your car?'

'No, I'm fine,' Lucas grinned. 'I've been in tighter places.'

Stephanie started the engine and drove down the street, amused by this big guy. His answers always seemed to make her wonder more about him.

'Do you think Margaret's house will offer more clues about the missing jewellery?' Lucas asked, reminding Stephanie to focus on the mystery they were supposed to be solving.

'I hope so. We still don't really know if there was a thief or not. No sign of concrete evidence like footprints or sign of a break-in. Both women are elderly, they could have thought they'd put their jewellery away and just left it somewhere else.'

'I'm always losing my keys, I leave them in a different place every time,' Lucas sympathised as he gazed out of the car window.

'Me too,' Stephanie agreed, 'God help us when we get old then.'

She noticed how Lucas kept glancing in the mirror as she drove, she wondered if he trusted her driving.

She parked the car outside Margaret's house, which was not far from the Village Hall. It was a bungalow with a small tidy garden surrounded by a hedge.

Ben and Rosie were waiting by the gate, Angela and Lisa had already texted to say they couldn't make it.

'They look eager,' Lucas noticed as he undid his seat belt. 'Ben's got his camera round his neck and Rosie has an iPad in her hand.'

'We are very professional,' Stephanie smiled as she stepped out to greet them, she was pleased that her friends were taking this mystery club seriously and it wasn't just a joke to them.

Margaret opened the door at the sound of her doorbell and the group followed her inside.

The narrow hallway was pale green with a flowery carpet. They gathered in the living room where shades of green continued and they stood in front of a marble fireplace. Surprisingly, the curtains were drawn, causing the room to be in semi-darkness.

'Thank you for seeing us,' Stephanie smiled at Margaret who looked up at Lucas nervously. 'I'm Stephanie, and this is Ben, Rosie and Lucas. We hope that we can shed light on your missing earrings.'

'We could do with some light right now,' Lisa whispered behind Stephanie.

'I'm sure they were stolen,' Margaret's eyes grew round, 'I've looked everywhere. What do you think you can do?'

'First of all, if we could ask you some questions, we are looking to see if there is a pattern between all the missing items in Hibaldton.'

'Please sit down,' Margaret nodded and pointed towards the dark green sofas.

Stephanie noticed two green, velvet sofas with tassels at the base and in the corner was a round table full of teddy bears all staring ahead as if hypnotised.

After they had all found a seat, Stephanie began.

'Where did you last see your earrings?'

'I took them off in the bedroom and put them on my dressing table.'

'That's very similar to what Mabel did,' Rosie said, making notes on her iPad. 'Do you wear them a lot?'

Margaret thought and replied, 'Not really, I wore them because we went out to the theatre, my husband and I, bless him, he never liked going to the theatre, but I persuaded him. He wasn't feeling well but he took me all the same.'

She sighed as if remembering a sad occasion and Stephanie noticed how tired she looked.

'Did you see anyone you knew there, from the village or anyone looking at them?'

'Not at the theatre. I popped into the shop here to get some sweets before we went. My husband would never pay theatre prices for sweets. Mrs Cook noticed my earrings and I told her they were diamonds.'

Everyone sat up at that piece of information.

'Was there anyone else in the shop?' Ben asked.

'I can't remember, I think so…I don't know it was a while ago,' Margaret started to get flustered.

Ben changed the subject, 'Have you got a photo of you wearing them so we can see what they look like?'

'I think I can find one, just a minute.'

She walked over to a cabinet which had more teddy bears perched on top and brought out a box full of photographs, eventually, she pulled one out and handed it to Ben.

'Is it ok if I take a picture of this?' Ben asked.

The photo was then handed round for everyone to look at, and they all agreed on how pretty the earrings were.

Rosie complimented her on her collection of teddy bears.

'Thank you, my husband used to buy me one every year for my birthday.'

Stephanie then spoke to Margaret, 'Do you mind if we take a look in your bedroom?'

Margaret looked uneasy as she stood with her back to the fireplace and her face looked pale against her black dress.

She looked down at the carpet and said, 'I suppose it will be all right, it's just that my husband's at rest in there.'

She walked to the door and looked over her shoulder for the others to follow. Stephanie had an eerie feeling being in this house, the hairs on the back of her neck prickled, and Margaret seemed to be acting strangely, waiting nervously for the others to follow. The house seemed so dim and gloomy and far too quiet, making the slow tick-tock of the brass clock on the mantle seem louder than it was.

At the door to the bedroom, the old lady hesitated with her hand on the doorknob, she slowly turned it and carefully pushed the door open. The bedroom was even darker than the hallway and as Margaret stepped inside, the blackness seemed to swallow her up. Ben paused and looked back at the others with a grimace, so Lucas gave him a gentle push and they also disappeared inside into the darkness.

Stephanie heard a small yelp from Ben inside, as she stepped in with Rosie close behind her. The girls bumped into the back of Lucas and they all froze.

It took a few seconds for Stephanie's eyes to grow accustomed to the dark. The first thing Stephanie saw was a pair of black shoes on the bed, and her gaze moved up a pair of legs in a dark grey suit. Margaret's husband was laid out on the bed, his arms across his chest.

'Holy cow,' Rosie whispered, clutching Stephanie's shoulders.

Stephanie tore her gaze away and tried to concentrate on the dressing table, but there was a mirror which framed the body lying on the bed in the darkness. A shaft of light shone through a small gap between the curtains, providing the source of illumination in the room. Stephanie held her breath to avoid breathing in the stuffy air.

Ben reached behind the curtain to open the window wide and he looked outside. Stephanie couldn't tell if he was getting some clean air or looking for clues.

She gulped and tried to speak normally as if it was every day that she visited a recently deceased person in their bedroom to talk about missing jewellery.

'Was it here that you placed your earrings?' she said, her voice sounding a lot squeakier than normal.

'Yes, right there and they're not in my jewellery box, look.'

Margaret opened a dark, velvet box which revealed a few gold and silver items.

Stephanie started to look around the table saying, 'Have you tried moving it, in case they fell behind?' She tried hard to sound normal, willing herself to not look in the mirror.

Lucas started to pull the dressing table away from the wall and Rosie started to help him. Stephanie's eyes were drawn to the grey, lifeless body on the bed and as she looked, she almost saw a twitch of a finger. Was it her imagination? She slowly walked over to the bed and stood staring at his hand. No movement, she must have imagined it. Her eyes moved up to his face, and she noticed how the evening light threw shadows across his cheek, his eyelids were closed and relaxed as if just asleep.

At that moment, his eyes opened, white in the dim light, they glared into Stephanie's. She flinched and a scream flew from her throat in horror.

Margaret's husband jolted upright, and everyone reacted instinctively: Rosie backed into the dressing table, causing bottles to tip over, Ben dived out of the window and disappeared, Stephanie turned to run and fell against Lucas who protectively wrapped his arms around her.

'What on Earth is going on?' A gruff voice shouted, and everyone froze.

'I'm so sorry, Frank. I didn't want to disturb you while you were having your nap. I know you don't like being disturbed when you have a migraine,' Margaret said in a shaky voice.

Lucas turned the light switch on and now Stephanie could see Frank, Margaret's husband sitting on the edge of his bed in a striped shirt, he did not look happy.

'These people have come to find my missing earrings dear.'

'Couldn't you all have waited until I had woken up? Who are you anyway?' he demanded, looking round the room in bewilderment.

Stephanie looked at Frank over her shoulder, still clinging onto Lucas, and then realised with a start that she was holding tightly onto Lucas's T-shirt. She could feel his solid stomach beneath her fists, she opened her hands to lay them flat against his chest, now his heart was beating as fast as hers. They both let go and disentangled themselves from each other awkwardly.

Rosie was the first of them to speak, and she didn't beat about the bush, 'I thought you were dead!'

There was a pause and then the old man burst out laughing, a loud barking laugh.

'Why did you think that?' Margaret asked.

Rosie turned to her still breathing heavily.

'You said…' and she acted out an impression of the old lady, 'my husband…' she looked down towards the carpet and then dramatically raised her hand out in a swooping motion, 'is at rest…'

'Yes, at rest,' Margaret replied motioning towards the bed.

Ben popped his head up outside and leaned in through the open window, he had leaves and rose petals on his head, and the curtain billowing behind him like a cape.

'So, he's not dead then. Thank God for that, I thought we were going to be eaten by a zombie.'

He brushed himself down and then checked his camera hadn't broken in the fall.

'Why did you jump out of the window?' Rosie laughed.

'Well, I don't know, do I? It was a reflex action, you know… life or death.'

'It's a good job we weren't upstairs,' Lucas laughed.

'You kids are crazy, zombies for heaven's sake,' Frank mumbled. 'Who are you anyway?'

Margaret explained, 'This is Stephanie Rhodes, we read about her in the paper. They said that they would help with my missing earrings dear.'

'Not Stephanie, Angel of Death Stephanie? I've heard about you. You're too early my girl, I'm not dead yet despite what you might have sensed.'

Stephanie mumbled, 'I'm not the Angel of Death. I didn't realise people were still calling me that.'

Margaret shook her head in disbelief while everyone laughed and thanked their lucky stars that zombies didn't exist, and Frank was still alive. Stephanie was relieved that they had seen the funny side of it all and after lots of apologies, they finally settled to think about the missing earrings.

Lucas finished moving the dressing table away from the wall, there was no sign of the earrings, but there was something… Rosie reached down and picked up something soft and red- it was a small feather. She held it up and Stephanie regarded it with interest, then put it on the dressing table.

Not long after, the budding detectives went outside to join Ben who was waiting rather grumpily.

'There's a bloody rose tree outside this window,' Ben grumbled holding his arm, and Stephanie could see that he had scratched himself on the thorns. She looked closer at the bush and noticed a small, black piece of material.

'Look, this could be a clue,' she grabbed Ben's arm in excitement, 'You're not wearing black, are you?'

'No, what is it?'

'Take a photo of it then we can take a better look.'

After Ben had taken a picture, Stephanie picked off the material which looked like it had been torn off by the rose thorn. She passed it to Rosie.

'It feels like Lycra,' Rosie said.

'Do you recognise this?' Stephanie asked Margaret who shook her head puzzled. 'Maybe we have found our first clue at last,' Stephanie beamed.

After saying goodbye to Margaret, they hung about to discuss what happened.

Ben began, 'Wow! That was the creepiest house I've ever been in.'

Rosie agreed, 'It would be perfect for Halloween. I think I'm still shaking.'

Ben grabbed Rosie's arm in mock horror. 'In my head, Frank looked like Frankenstein's monster. OMG, I've just realised he's got the same name!'

They laughed and walked up to Stephanie's car.

'Shall we delay our weekly meeting until we have more evidence?' asked Stephanie who had some marking to finish for the next day.

'I've got the Lycra,' Ben said holding it in the air before depositing back into his pocket. 'I'll keep it safe.'

'Are you going to send the photos to Angela for her to investigate?'

'Will do.'

'For now, let's assume they are worth something and hope that another clue shows itself. Who shall we visit next?'

Rosie replied, 'I'll ring Sylvia and Gavin Smith and arrange a time for next week.'

They all agreed and then parted, feeling satisfied with their progress so far.

AT SCHOOL, THE next day, Lisa and friends had roared with laughter when Stephanie told them about Margaret and Frank.

Serina laughed, 'Oh you never can tell what it's like in people's homes can you, that sounded really creepy.'

'Jesus, I would have run out screaming. There would be a human-shaped hole in the front door, and you wouldn't see me for dust,' Lisa laughed. 'What did you do?'

'I pretty much had the same reaction as you, but I turned to run and ran straight into Lucas.'

Stephanie stopped at that point, not sure what else to say, but they noticed from her expression there was more to tell. They all spoke at once, urging her to continue and the other people in the staffroom looked over with interest.

Stephanie leaned forward and hushed them, 'There's nothing to tell,' she insisted, 'it was embarrassing really, I practically pushed him against the wall.'

Stephanie covered her face with her hands for a minute while the others stared at her.

'Go on,' said Tracy. 'What did he do?'

'He put his arms round me…to protect me.'

'Wow, what did he feel like?' Rita asked.

'Hard… what? No not there… his stomach!!! Oh you lot,' Stephanie complained laughing.

'I've got to meet this guy, he sounds hot!' Tracy said.

'It was over in seconds though, and Mark's coming back this Friday,' Stephanie reminded them.

'Don't forget the do at the Skydive,' Tracy said firmly, 'I want you to meet Craig, my current boyfriend.'

They finished their sandwiches while Tracy filled them in on her latest news and soon lunch time was over.

As Stephanie and Lisa walked back to class, Stephanie remembered the clue and couldn't wait to tell Lisa.

'What I didn't say, is we found a clue.'

'Was it parrot footprints?' Lisa asked still sticking with her first theory.

'No, it was a torn piece of fabric- black Lycra… but now you mention it… there was a red feather.'

'You are kidding. You see… maybe the parrot did it after all.'

THE REST OF the week flew by much calmer, and Stephanie started to look forward to seeing Mark again. She did her best to ignore the memory of Lucas standing so close, the feel of his firm, warm body beneath her hands. He acted so calmly at the time of the potential zombie attack, yet his racing heart had told her otherwise.

24

THE SKYDIVE CLUB

Stephanie gave Mark her full attention when he got home Friday night, they had relaxed at Stephanie's house on Saturday, spending it mostly in the garden.

It was the night of the party at Hibaldton Skydive, and Tracy had rung up to make sure that everyone was going to be there.

Mark watched Stephanie as she got ready to go out. She pulled on dark jeans and chose a T-shirt from the drawer.

'I was thinking we could stay at my place and walk from there,' Mark said as he lay back on the bed, his arm behind his head.

Stephanie thought about it, he did live right next to the airfield.

'How long will it take to get there?' she asked as she found her socks.

'About 10 minutes, we could probably get a lift back from someone.'

'Ok, right I'm nearly ready,' Stephanie looked in her jewellery box for a bracelet and Mark stood up to help her to fasten the clasp.

Stephanie looked over towards Lucas's house as they walked towards Mark's car.

'I wonder if anyone has asked Lucas if he wants to go tonight.'

She couldn't help but feel sorry for him as he seemed to be trying to make friends in the village.

'Let's go ask him,' Mark suggested.

As Stephanie locked the front door, Mark waited in the drive messaging on his phone.

They walked across the road, hand in hand, when Mark knocked on Lucas's door. There was a bark from inside.

'That's Bruce,' Stephanie smiled, he's such a cute German Shepherd.

Stephanie could hear Lucas's voice telling Bruce to be quiet and then the door opened.

His body filled the doorway, he was wearing jeans and a black T-shirt.

'Hi Stephanie,' he beamed, rather too enthusiastically Stephanie thought. 'And this must be Mark.'

The men shook hands briefly then Lucas leaned against the door frame with his hand in his pocket.

'What can I do for you?' he asked casually.

Stephanie looked at Mark and then back at Lucas.

'We are going to the Skydive bar at the airfield over there,' Stephanie pointed in the vague direction, 'and wondered if you had heard about it.'

'Yeah, Ben told me about it, I was thinking about going.'

'Oh, good, so we'll see you there?'

'I can give you a lift if you like,' Lucas offered and looked at Mark.

'We have to take the car back to my house anyway,' Mark said.

'Oh yeah, nice car,' Lucas nodded.

'If you follow us, we could drop it off and then carry on with you,' Mark continued.

'Sounds good, I'll just get my wallet.'

Mark and Stephanie walked back to Mark's car and got in to wait for Lucas to follow them.

As THEY WALKED into the bar, Mark spotted some familiar faces and led them over to where Martin and Lisa were sitting.

'What would you like to drink?' Mark asked.

'White wine please,' Stephanie replied.

'Drink?' Mark looked up at Lucas.

'Coke thanks,' Lucas said. 'I'll come with you.'

Stephanie watched as they went up to the bar and Martin went to join them.

The room was a big rectangular space with a bar and a small stage down one side. There was a small square dance floor in front of the stage, and circular bar tables with stools surrounding them filled the floor.

'It's a bit empty yet,' Lisa said looking around. 'I wonder when Tracy and her friends will get here.'

'Maybe the lads she was talking about are over there.'

There was a group of people sitting around a table in the far corner. They looked like they'd been there a while as a pile of bags were on the sofa seat and a few empty glasses were on the table.

'I'm not sure I'd have the nerve to jump out of a plane, I think someone would have to push me out,' Stephanie said.

'It's bad enough jumping off a high board at a swimming pool. Do you remember when we were about sixteen, your dad took us swimming, and we climbed up the highest diving board there? It took ages before I'd dare jump,' Lisa laughed.

'We only jumped because that man was getting annoyed and we couldn't get down the ladder past the queue of people.'

'Hiya,' a voice cried, and Tracy plopped herself next to them with Rita in tow.

'Hi,' Lisa and Stephanie said looking up.

'We were just talking about parachuting, are they skydivers over in the corner?' Stephanie asked.

'Probably, oh yeah that's Craig, the tall one with short hair and the leather jacket. He's so hot tonight.' Tracy almost growled.

They all laughed.

'I need a strong drink. Rita, are you coming?'

Not waiting for an answer, Tracy pulled Rita up and they walked up to the far end of the bar, near where Craig was sitting.

Stephanie's gaze wandered back to Mark where he was still chatting to Lucas and Martin. She noticed Mark clap Lucas on the back and they all burst out laughing, Lisa noticed too.

'They all seem to have hit it off quickly,' she announced.

Stephanie nodded and looked from Lucas to Mark. Lucas was slightly taller and broader, his muscles were bigger but Mark's body was firm and he looked amazing in that black shirt.

'Look at Tracy and Rita, chatting up those guys.' Lisa broke into her thoughts.

Stephanie looked and smiled as Tracy was passed a drink by the man who must be Craig.

A few more people started to enter, and the music went up a notch, so they had to start shouting at each other. Mark and Martin had sat down but Lucas had remained standing. Stephanie couldn't help but keep looking at him, he was standing like a coiled spring. It was funny how sometimes he could seem relaxed and carefree, then other times he acted so tense. At that moment his attention was on a man who was wandering about taking photos.

Ben, Rosie and Angela appeared with drinks in their hands. They pulled some spare stools over to sit with Stephanie and Lisa.

They all said hi and discussed what time the band was starting.

'Lucas is being rather strong and silent over there,' Ben said in Stephanie's ear.

'I know, he seems bothered about that photographer who's coming over here.'

A guy with a moustache in a black bomber jacket weaved his way towards them, stopping now and then to take a picture. A camera hung around his neck. Eventually, he stopped next to their group.

'Is it ok if I take your photos?' he shouted over the noise.

'Why?' Stephanie asked.

He seemed annoyed he had been asked.

'It's to do with the Skydive competition, are you ok with your picture being on the website?'

Stephanie looked up at Lucas and he had stepped closer.

They agreed with the photos, so he started to snap away. They smiled and held up their glasses and pulled faces to make it clear they were having a good time. As he finished, he brushed past Stephanie and a familiar, sweet odour wafted by, like cherries. Stephanie was wondering where she'd smelt that before when she noticed Lucas follow the cameraman through the room and out of the doors. She had a feeling that something wasn't quite right so she decided to follow them.

'Just going to the loo,' Stephanie shouted to Mark, then she quickly got up and weaved her way through the crowd.

Through the glass doors was an entranceway where the toilets were and then the exit to the car park. Lucas and the photographer were nowhere to be seen so Stephanie walked to the exit and peeked out.

The car park was in shadow, it was late but not yet pitch black as the lights from inside the building spilt out through the windows.

Stephanie scanned the car park and her eyes settled on a movement next to some cars. Lucas was standing next to a car, he seemed to be looking at a camera and the photographer was pinned between Lucas and a car. Stephanie watched puzzled as Lucas returned the camera and the man snatched it back, clearly annoyed. Lucas calmly stood aside to let him go and Stephanie heard the camera guy complain but she couldn't hear the words.

Stephanie shot back inside and quickly disappeared into the toilets. Once in the cubicle, Stephanie pondered on what had just happened. Lucas was definitely up to something, was he avoiding having his photo taken?

As Stephanie returned to the corridor, Lucas was standing there leaning against the wall.

'Oh, there you are, it's my round and I was wondering what you'd like,' Lucas asked.

Stephanie looked at his face for some kind of clue to what he was thinking, he was acting as if nothing had happened in the car park. She was nearly going to ask him about it when Lisa appeared.

'Come on the band is playing now and Tracy's trying to get me to dance. I need help.'

Stephanie turned to Lucas, 'Just a glass of orange juice please.'

He raised his eyebrows, 'Are you sure?'

'Yes thanks, I need the energy for dancing.'

Stephanie grabbed Lisa's arm and laughing pulled her onto the dance floor to join Tracy.

'THE BAND ISN'T bad,' Mark said to Stephanie when she'd returned from dancing.

Stephanie took a long drink of her juice and sat down.

'Yeah, they're ok, good music to dance to. Tracy and Craig were starting to dance like they were in Dirty Dancing, so I decided to come and sit this one out.'

She pointed them out to Mark through the crowd on the dance floor.

Stephanie glanced around and smiled at Ben, Rosie and Angela dancing. Rita was talking to one of the skydivers, the one with the camera.

She looked around for Lucas, and there he was standing by the bar talking to someone, he had noticed Stephanie looking and smiled her way.

Tracy came over like a whirlwind to plonk herself down on the seat next to Lisa's.

She leant over to shout, 'They're announcing the winner at the end of this song.'

'How do they work out the winner?' Lisa asked.

'From those who liked their post. You all liked it didn't you?'

'Did you like the post? I shared it a few days ago,' Stephanie asked Mark.

'No,' he shook his head.

'You've got to be in it to win it,' Tracy shouted.

The band finished their song, and everyone clapped and cheered as the dance floor cleared, and the lights went up slightly.

Stephanie looked over at the stage and saw Rita leave the camera guy and quickly walk over.

'Who's that guy you were talking to?' Stephanie asked Rita as she sat down. The camera guy was now talking to a girl in front of the stage as he passed her an envelope.

'He's called Alex, he organised the competition.'

Stephanie recalled that Tracy had thought him slimy, and she smiled as he did kind of look like a seventy's porn star, maybe in an Eastern European movie.

There was a buzz of excitement as the girl stood on the small stage and walked up to the microphone. She had the envelope in her hand.

'Hi everyone and thank you for coming. Are you having a good time?'

The room erupted with cheers and the girl waited for the noise to die down.

'In this envelope is the name of the winner of our skydive competition. Ooh, it's so exciting, isn't it? The winner will be matched up with one of our experienced skydivers sitting over here.'

She pointed to the corner and the group sat there all cheered. Stephanie noticed Alex standing behind them with his arms folded.

The girl opened the envelope and the room fell silent.

'The winner is…' She left a dramatic pause and everyone in the room banged their hands on the tables to create a drum roll.

She had to hold up her hand to stop them and called down the microphone, 'Stephanie Rhodes!'

The room was filled with cheers and clapping. Stephanie's ears were ringing with the shouts of friends and Mark had his mouth open in surprise. Stephanie looked around at Ben and Rosie laughing and congratulating her, Lisa looked surprised and concerned. She put her hand on Stephanie's arm to ask if she was ok. Stephanie looked over at Lucas but couldn't see him at first. Then she realised he was right behind her. Everyone was shouting for Stephanie to go up on the stage, but Lucas put his hands on her shoulders and said into her ear, 'I'll get it for you, stay here.'

Stephanie was relieved she didn't have to get up as she felt a bit faint. There was no way she was going to jump out of an aeroplane. She never usually won anything- typical!

She watched Lucas take the envelope from the girl who looked confused, but then leant over to speak to him and smiled sweetly.

The lights went back down, and music started to play, returning the bar to normal.

Lucas returned and handed the envelope to Stephanie, and they all looked at the certificate.

'Aww, it says you can't give it away.'

Tracy sounded disappointed.

'When is it for?'

'I don't care, I'm not doing it.' Stephanie shook her head as she showed the card to Tracy.

'You shouldn't have entered if you didn't want it,' Tracy said.

'You made me do it!' Stephanie cried.

Mark put the certificate in his back trouser pocket and put his arm around Stephanie.

'You don't have to do it, don't listen to her.'

Stephanie leant over to talk to Tracy.

'You're friends with Craig, you could explain to him that I'm scared of heights and I'm passing the certificate to you. You go in my place.'

'Are you sure you won't change your mind?'

'Positive.'

Tracy dragged Rita up and they walked over to the skydivers.

Stephanie turned to Mark who was talking to Lucas. They both looked like they were having a deep conversation and she wondered what about.

When Mark turned back to her, she said, 'Just my luck that I won, I can't believe it.'

Mark shook his head and put his arm around her again, leaning close he asked, 'Shall we go now?'

Stephanie nodded.

They said goodbye to everyone, Lisa and Martin started to gather their things as well and Stephanie hugged Lisa.

'I'll see you at school Lisa.'

'Yeah. Are you ok? You went as white as a sheet, are you really scared of heights?'

'More like scared of falling.'

Stephanie followed Mark out to the car park, Lucas was right behind them.

They stood next to his car as he unlocked the doors and they both slipped into the back seat. It was a large four-by-four car. Stephanie watched the back of Lucas's head as he started the engine and they smoothly pulled out of the car park. Looking back out of the window, towards the door to the club, she noticed a man step outside for a smoke. With one hand in his pocket and the other holding his vape, he blew out smoke as he watched Lucas's car drive down the road.

LUCAS PULLED HIS car into Mark's drive.

'Thanks for the lift, mate,' Mark said as he opened the car door.

Lucas was already out of the car opening the door for Stephanie.

'Oh thanks,' Stephanie said and smiled at Lucas.

He was too busy looking past her though, so Stephanie joined Mark who opened the front door, and she went inside.

She left Mark and Lucas to have a chat in the driveway and she walked into the kitchen to get a glass of water.

Mark came into the kitchen with a strange look on his face. 'What's the matter?'

'Nothing, I've just remembered that I left my laptop at your house. You go upstairs, I won't be long.'

Mark kissed her on the forehead and went outside. Stephanie heard his Ferrari moving across the gravel and away as she climbed the stairs to bed.

25

POSTCARD NUMBER THREE

The next morning, Stephanie woke up and Mark was still asleep next to her. She quietly slipped out of bed and tiptoed to his trousers to have another look at the winning certificate.

She felt a hard piece of card in the pocket and pulled it out. Out came the envelope along with a postcard.

She frowned and looked at it in her hand. It was a different one from the others, this one had a photo of the sky with a bird soaring high and on the other side the words,

'Can you fly?'

She gasped causing Mark to wake up. He sat up groggily, his chest bare with the sheets pooled around his waist.

'Stephanie?' Mark said and stopped when he saw what she was looking at. 'Christ.'

'Another postcard?' Stephanie asked.

Mark nodded slowly. 'It was on your mat when I opened your door.'

'Were you going to show me it?' Stephanie asked.

She could tell from the look on his face that he wasn't going to.

Stephanie paced up and down the bedroom in her pyjamas, her feet padding into the soft carpet. Finally, she walked over to Mark's side of the bed and sat down on the edge with the creased postcard in her hands.

'I want you to tell me the truth,' she faced him firmly. 'You've kept secrets from me before, talking to detectives without telling me, and it didn't help.'

Mark sighed, 'No because you went ahead and did your investigating anyway.'

'Yes, I did. If you know something that I don't, promise me you will tell me. I can tell something is going on and it's driving me crazy.'

Mark paused and looked like he was thinking. Stephanie pressed him to tell her.

'Promise you won't overreact,' he said softly.

'Why?'

'Just promise.'

'I can't promise anything.'

'Okay, promise you'll listen to what I have to say before you react.'

'I promise, just tell me. Are these postcards threats? Are they from…Sergei?'

She hated saying his name, it flooded her with loathing. She could see his leering face in front of her, with that snake tattoo on his neck.

Mark took her hands in his.

'Don't panic. We don't know if it is or not, but we're worried it might be.'

'Who's we?'

Stephanie took a deep breath and waited for Mark to continue.

'When we were in London, and we told Kate about the postcards, Kate rang me and said she had a plan. She wanted to come up with me this weekend by the way.'

'Kate?'

'Don't worry, she couldn't come anyway because she's still in America.'

Stephanie grew impatient and interrupted him, 'What have the postcards got to do with her?'

When Stephanie didn't say anything, he swallowed and continued, 'You know how her family's loaded, her uncle often hires bodyguards.'

Stephanie continued to look at Mark, who had stopped talking. She stared at him and waited for him to explain further. He swung his legs out from under the covers, pulling on his boxers that were on the floor. He stood up and ruffled his hair with his hand.

'Kate told me that she would send someone who could help us, well you… to look after you while I'm working in London. A bodyguard.'

His voice trailed off and then suddenly everything became clear to Stephanie.

'Oh my god Mark, do you mean Lucas? Lucas is a bodyguard?'

Mark nodded with a worried look on his face. She stood up to face him.

'Lucas is here to …?'

'Protect you, while I'm in London.'

'Oh, for heaven's sake.' Stephanie started to pace up and down again. 'No wonder he's been acting weird. He's in 'security'. He lives opposite my house… did you rent the…?'

'Kate did.'

'Kate did- just wait until I see her. You should have told me.'

'We didn't want to scare you, you'd only just forgotten about Sergei.'

'I have never forgotten about him.'

'You seemed less obsessed, and I didn't want to start it all again.'

'Obsessed? I am not obsessed. I have done my best to put it all behind me.'

Mark walked up to Stephanie and put his hands on her shoulder.

'Look at me,' he said gently. 'I just wanted you to be safe. I'm glad you know about Lucas now – I hope that his being nearby will make you feel safer. And it's working already, it was Lucas who told me someone went to your door last night.'

'How did he know? Has he got a camera pointed at my house?'

Stephanie returned to the bed and got in, she pulled the covers up and hugged her knees.

'I'll go make us a cup of coffee.'

Mark escaped downstairs.

Stephanie tried to breathe slowly. At the back of her mind, she had feared the postcards could be from Sergei, it was the creepy thing he would do. She thought about the pictures of the river, the sea, the boat and now the sky. What was he saying? Did he know she had won the skydiving competition? How could he, it had just happened. Unless all this time he was in the area close by…

Suddenly she remembered the figure lurking in the empty street a few nights ago, the car that nearly ran her over, the vaping man in the car park… was it Sergei?

Stephanie shivered and then she started to think about Lucas and how he acted strangely at the bar. Mark walked in and put a hot mug of coffee into her hands.

'I saw Lucas accosting the photographer in the car park last night,' Stephanie told Mark between sips.

'I know he told me. Lucas wanted to look at the photos he was taking to make sure he was legit.'

'And was he?'

'Apparently,' Mark laughed. 'The guy was pissed off.'

'I'm not surprised… it's not funny Mark, Lucas can't go around the village roughing people up. I thought he was avoiding having his photo taken.'

'Probably he was doing that too.'

'Although… Tracy said that his name is Alex and that he organised the competition.'

It was Mark's turn to pace up and down the bedroom.

'Maybe he's been sending you those postcards.'

'But why? I don't even know him. Do you think he was part of Sergei's gang?'

Stephanie started to panic. She felt a knot getting tighter and tighter in the pit of her stomach. Sergei had to be still alive, and he might not be in Hibaldton, but he was still managing to make sure she hadn't forgotten him.

'I think we should get dressed and go see Lucas,' she decided out loud.

'What now?'

'I want to talk to him and tell him I know.'

'He knows that you know.'

Stephanie looked around the room in horror.

'Does he have cameras or bugs, in here?'

Mark laughed, 'No I texted him.'

Stephanie thumped him on the shoulder. She was mad, and she couldn't wait to tell Lucas what she thought of him too. They just can't put cameras pointing at her house without asking her first. What were they thinking, doing that behind her back?

'And all last night you two knew about each other.'

Mark looked guilty. 'I'm sorry Steph.'

Stephanie's eyes narrowed. 'I can't believe that Lucas has been pretending to be my friend all this time.'

Mark sat on the edge of the bed and replied, 'He is your friend, he told me that he's been enjoying helping you solve that jewellery mystery thing.'

'Is that what you were talking about last night? I suppose he's been spying on me and reporting back to you.'

Stephanie pushed Mark off the bed and swung her legs out.

'Hang on a minute,' Mark complained, 'he's not spying on you.'

Stephanie stood up to face Mark.

'So, what do you call putting cameras up around someone's house and pretending to be someone else?'

'Look Steph, you're taking it the wrong way. He's there to protect you and… he was told to keep it a secret, so don't blame him...I'm sorry, I'm just trying to help you and I keep doing the wrong thing.'

Stephanie took a deep breath to calm down.

'Promise me, Mark, that you will just tell me the truth, I don't need wrapping up in cotton wool.'

STEPHANIE RANG HER mum to say she wouldn't be going to the usual family dinner. She told them she wasn't feeling well which was true. Mark took her home and they had driven in silence.

Stephanie had spent Sunday afternoon in turmoil, deciding when to confront Lucas. She tried to avoid the window and searched the house for listening devices. In films, they were often under tables or above door frames. She ended up giving the house a good top-to-bottom clean until she was exhausted.

As she closed the curtains in her bedroom, she imagined Lucas sitting in the dark with a pair of binoculars. Then she peeped through the curtains, her eyes scanning up and down the street, checking for strange figures.

'I am starting to be obsessed now,' Stephanie told herself, 'It's not that Lucas is watching me, he's watching the house. It's not his fault that he didn't tell me, he was told to keep it a secret.'

She got changed into her pyjamas and stood in front of the mirror to brush her teeth.

'I'll go to bed, and I'll probably laugh about it in the morning.'

26
STAY CALM, ACT MATURE

July is the most hectic time of year in primary school. It's when everyone realises there are only two weeks left to finish everything off, send out reports, and fit in school trips, not to mention Sports Day and Year 6 leaving events.

The week had flown by. Stephanie had driven to school and back every day and had managed to avoid bumping into Lucas or talking to Mark. On the bright side, there had been no sign of Alex the camera guy, or vaping man lurking the streets.

She had received a text from Lucas a few days ago:

'We should talk.'

Stephanie hadn't replied, and yes, there she was moaning about Mark avoiding difficult conversations, but she didn't feel like discussing this with Lucas right now when she was mad at him.

Tonight, was the meeting of the 'Mystery Club' and she realised that she couldn't put off facing Lucas. Stephanie paced up and down her living room while she waited for her friends to pass by on their way to the meeting. She argued with an imaginary Lucas as if he was in the room.

'You put cameras up around my house without me knowing! I don't care if it was for my own good, I should have been asked first. And you are a fake! You pretended to be my friend when all along you were just doing a job... As for you being my bodyguard, it is ridiculous! What are you going to do- follow me everywhere I go? Fight Sergei in the streets?'

She huffed and stopped to look out of the window when she spotted Ben, Angela and Rosie walking past then took a deep breath and went to join them outside her house.

'Stay calm and act mature', she repeated to herself as she crossed the road.

'Hi guys,' Stephanie tried to sound upbeat.

'Hi,' they all chorused.

Ben linked an arm with her to walk to Lucas's door.

'Everything all right? No one tried to run you over recently? I have to say Stephanie love, that I have started to look over my shoulder when I walk down your street.'

'You know Ben, it's not the strangers you have to watch out for, it's the people you know.'

Ben looked at Stephanie puzzled and was about to ask what she meant when Lucas opened the door to let them in.

As they walked in, she heard Lucas say hello to her, but she ignored him. They gathered in the kitchen, Ben stood chatting to Lucas, Bruce was sniffing around them, and Rosie knelt to fuss over the dog.

Stephanie noticed Lucas glancing in her direction, but whenever he did, she looked away and focused on talking to Angela. Lucas placed a bottle of wine in the middle of the table, some glasses and crisps and they all sat down.

'I thought we could all do with a drink,' he said soberly.

'Oh, you read my mind,' Ben said and unscrewed the bottle. 'So, Lisa can't make it then?'

'Just a small one,' Angela said picking up a crisp.

'Not for me thanks,' said Rosie getting out her water bottle.

Stephanie reached out for the largest glass and held it while Ben poured it.

Stephanie explained, 'No, Sophia isn't feeling well so Lisa took her home early from school.'

Lucas picked up the other large glass from the selection and Stephanie watched Ben pour the wine into Lucas's glass.

'I thought you didn't drink when you were *on duty*,' Stephanie couldn't help herself.

Lucas gave a long look at Stephanie as if to say, 'Oh we're doing this are we?' while he took a big drink from his glass.

'Who says I'm on duty?' he responded.

Stephanie took a big drink from her glass.

Ben looked at them with a confused look as he opened up a folder and brought out some photographs.

'I thought we'd get started on our 'clues board'.'

Ben stood up and walked over to the kitchen counter to stick the photos on the whiteboard with round magnets. The whiteboard was still leaning against the wall from the last time they met, and after Ben had finished, it showed photos of Margaret's earrings and Mabel's brooch. Next Ben wrote the victims' names with the blue pen that lay nearby. Bruce had followed Ben and now sank with a deep sigh to lean against Stephanie's legs.

Ben faced everyone and asked, 'We've visited two people so far, so what do we know?' He stood, turning the pen in his hand.

'Yes, let's tell each other what we know, and be honest with each other,' Stephanie said looking at Lucas.

Ben continued, nervously looking at Stephanie. '*Anyway…* we went to see Margaret and apart from me getting scratched to death on a rose tree and almost wetting myself with fright, it was quite successful as we found a clue.'

He lifted the material in the air and tucked it underneath one of the magnets. They all stared at it for a moment as if it could talk.

He continued, 'Next, we have Mabel. A thief could have gained entry by the window or picked her backdoor lock, nothing else seems to have been touched.'

Angela continued, 'I have researched the brooch, and did you know that it's called a cameo brooch because the woman's face is a likeness of Queen Victoria? You'll never believe this, it is possible it could be worth up to four thousand pounds.'

Ben blew a long whistle and Rosie said giddily, 'Oh my goodness, I bet Mabel will be so excited when she finds out.'

'We should tell them both to call the police,' Lucas said.

'The trouble is, Mabel won't be insured because she has no proof she had it or that it was worth that amount,' Angela explained.

'It's a shame she didn't have security cameras when it happened,' Stephanie said, taking another drink of wine.

'Did you do anything about cameras for her Lucas?' Ben asked.

'Yes, I went to see her on Monday and fitted one so she should be able to see if anyone walks up her drive.'

'Well, you're the man for the job.' Stephanie's words were a waterfall of sarcasm that she couldn't hold back. Maybe if she just kept the wine glass up to her lips, she could dam up her mouth.

The others noticed she was in a funny mood, but they carried on as if nothing was happening. Lucas, on the other hand, narrowed his eyes and finished off his wine.

Ben picked up the wine bottle, but it was empty.

'I'm on it,' Lucas had already stood up and was reaching for another bottle from the kitchen counter, he plonked another bottle in its place.

Ben poured them another glass and filled his up as he spoke.

'I bet Mabel was very grateful.'

'More than some people I could mention,' Lucas said looking Stephanie's way as he sat down next to her.

Stephanie ignored him and leant towards Rosie saying, 'So who do you think we should interview next?'

Rosie consulted the notes on her laptop.

'How do you feel about visiting Mr and Mrs Smith next?'

'Who?' Stephanie asked puzzled.

'Gavin and Sylvia Smith.'

'You know who lives in the 'mansion',' Ben explained.

'Ooh, can I go? I'd love to see what their house is like,' Rosie said.

'I'd like to see inside as well,' Angela agreed.

'Me three,' Stephanie added tipsily and then realised that didn't sound right.

'Shall I ring Gavin or Sylvia and arrange a visit? When are we able to go?' Rosie asked.

'I can make it tomorrow, gosh I'm so boring, aren't I?' Ben said, 'I'm never busy.'

'I can do tomorrow,' Angela nodded.

'Me too,' Rosie said.

'Me three,' Stephanie was pleased she'd got it right this time. Bruce looked up at him and she scratched him behind the ear.

'I have nothing better to do,' Lucas said looking at Stephanie.

Stephanie forced herself to focus on the investigation, she really shouldn't have drunk the wine so quickly.

'I have already thought about it,' she said.

Ben asked, 'What do you have in mind?'

'Lucas, our *security expert*, should focus on walking around the property looking at the doors and windows while I talk to Gavin. I thought you three could go with Sylvia upstairs… we need to decide what questions to ask…'

Rosie looked very excited about that.

'Do you think we can see in all the rooms?' Rosie asked keenly.

'I think we should also ask which night the bracelet went missing,' Ben said.

'Yes, and what were they doing? Did they go out or stay in?' Angela suggested.

'If they were in, why was she wearing an expensive bracelet?' Lucas asked.

'Good question,' Angela said. 'Did they have guests and what room did they use?'

Rosie was busy writing this all down on her iPad. 'I think we should record the conversations to save time.'

'Great idea, then we can refer to it later,' Stephanie was getting excited. 'Hey guys, I think we're starting to get the hang of this.'

'Have they got a photograph of the bracelet or of Sylvia wearing it?' Angela asked. 'Have they got photos of the night to see who they were with?' she added, 'It would be a good co-incidence if it was someone who knew Mabel or Margaret.'

They all nodded.

'Maybe they all have a common friend,' Stephanie agreed.

'I could also ask to see camera footage of that night,' Lucas said.

'A big house like that, you'd think they'd have security cameras,' Ben hoped.

'Do you think they could see someone if they snooped in their back garden?' Rosie asked looking pale.

'Probably, why?' Ben said.

'Oh… no reason,' Rosie said uncomfortably.

They all looked at her for a second, thinking it was a strange thing to say.

The talk of cameras in gardens planted a seed into Stephanie's brain, she turned to Lucas quickly which caused Bruce to scamper to his feet and retreat to his dog bed.

'If you were to spy on the Smiths, would you put a camera in their back garden?'

'Probably.' Lucas nodded and then to Stephanie's surprise, his face suddenly flushed, his eyes flew away from Stephanie, and he took another gulp of wine. Stephanie's eyes narrowed as she noticed him look so… guilty about something, she also drank more of her wine.

The drink was starting to affect her, but she didn't care. In fact, she was beginning to feel like she couldn't care less about anything.

'I've got a good idea Lucas, why don't you put up cameras at my house? Oh no, wait, I forgot, I already have plenty.'

'We should talk… about your cameras,' Lucas said seriously.

'Why? Do you think I need more?'

'It sounds like you've had enough.'

'Including the wine,' Ben added quietly,

The others sat looking from Lucas to Stephanie as if watching a tennis match, they were totally confused. Stephanie leaned closer to Lucas and poked her finger into his chest.

'You know what…there are things I need to tell you and you need to tell me, right now.'

Ben, Angela and Rosie were already standing, exchanging looks and getting their things together.

'It's getting late,' Angela said.

'Yes, we'll go now,' Rosie whispered.

'We're walking home together,' Ben said. 'Bye Stephanie love.' He hugged her and whispered for only her to hear, 'I think you should get to bed, and not necessarily on your own if you know what I mean. Lucky girl.'

They thanked Lucas as they walked towards the door. Stephanie overheard Angela talking as they walked down the hall to the front door, 'You could cut the atmosphere with a knife. What's up with those two?'

'Lover's tiff?' Ben replied and then they walked out into the moonlit street.

Stephanie stood up annoyed and took a couple of steps across the kitchen, Lucas stood up to face her. Bruce had been curled up in his dog bed, but when the door opened, he got up excitedly and started to wag his tail.

'I'll be going home as well… all the way… over the road,' Stephanie pointed dramatically.

They stood looking at each other, Bruce's head looked from one to the other wondering who was going to take him outside.

Stephanie pursed her lips. it was annoying that Lucas hadn't said anything to her. This was his chance to apologise for being so secretive and deceitful. She folded her arms, in defiance. If he was just going to stand there, then she could too. Bruce gave up waiting and decided to take himself outside to wee in the garden.

Stephanie noticed a small smile play on Lucas's lips, was he enjoying this feud?

Stephanie threw her arms by her side.

'For goodness sake Lucas, we need to get it out in the open. You know, I know that you know I… know,' Stephanie mumbled, 'But I don't know what you know.'

Lucas looked confused.

'Arrgh.' Stephanie groaned and headed for the door. Bruce came bounding back inside and greeted Stephanie with a wet lick on her hand and rubbed against her legs.

'Goodbye Bruce, at least I can depend on you.'

Stephanie bent over to stroke his soft fur. Lucas walked behind Stephanie and leaning across her closed the door.

'What do you want to know?' he asked quietly.

Stephanie turned around and leant on the door looking up at Lucas. He needed a shave and stubble suited him damn it. Stephanie nearly forgot that she was mad at him.

'I want to be truthful, hell it wasn't my idea to keep it from you. It's a lot easier for me to keep you safe if you work with me,' Lucas said.

'I am mad at you Lucas! I thought you enjoyed being part of the Mystery Club and that you were my friend…'

'I am your friend.'

'But it's a job to you.'

'Ok, I admit it was a job to start with. I agreed to move here and wanted you to meet me so that you knew I was here to help if you needed it. Believe me, when I say that it was very easy to become your friend, I didn't intend to…it just happened.'

There was a long silence between them while Stephanie took in what he had told her. Could she trust him?

'So…what do you want to know Stephanie?' he asked.

'Do you know who I'm scared of?' Stephanie began.

'Yes. I have been told about a Russian man named Sergei who has been missing since he fell in the river… after he kidnapped you.' Lucas's voice went quiet and soft. 'I would like to hear it from your point of view.'

'Do you know what he looks like?'

'I have friends who got hold of his photo and I have personal info on him.'

'Is he here?'

'I don't know. The last place I know he was seen was in Amsterdam last month.'

Stephanie's heart raced, 'So those postcards probably are from him?' she asked.

'It looks like it.'

Stephanie paled.

'I'm taking the threat very seriously Stephanie. He is an extremely violent and deranged man and is wanted for many things, but murder is not one of them. Saying that, people have disappeared who have crossed him. You need to be very careful, he's playing with you.'

Stephanie took a deep breath and asked, 'You don't think your time is being wasted?'

Lucas looked serious and shook his head.

'Not at all.'

'Can you show me how you are…keeping me safe?' Stephanie was starting to tremble. Lucas held out his hand and said softly, 'This way.'

Gently holding Stephanie's hand, he led her upstairs to the spare room.

Stephanie looked around Lucas's office. In front of the window was a desk which had two monitors. Lucas pulled out the chair for Stephanie to sit down then he leaned forward to press a button and the monitors lit up. On the screens, Stephanie could see four camera angles looking at each side of her house. She could see her front garden and door, down the sides of her house and finally the back garden looking towards her patio doors.

'Well, I wasn't wrong when I said I had plenty of cameras… You can't see in my house then, just the outside.'

'Yeah, just the outside.'

Stephanie could see her patio with a round wooden table and two folding chairs. It was dark outside, but the camera still showed all the detail in a spooky monochrome way. She could even see her pyjamas hanging over the table from the time when Mark had stripped her naked. The memory sent a flutter in her stomach, then the realisation – she had been completely naked in front of the camera…in broad daylight! Wait don't panic she thought. She remembered seeing Lucas out for a run, he'd stopped to get his breath back and he was looking at his phone.

She breathed out, so he wouldn't have been here looking at his monitors.

Stephanie stood up, holding onto the back of the chair and Lucas took a step back. She felt like laughing with relief, then she suddenly had a thought.

'How do you watch my house when you're not at home? Like, say if you went for a run?'

Lucas looked uneasy, she could see his throat swallow nervously.

'I look at my phone.'

Stephanie held her breath. 'Did you see me that day, with Mark in the back garden?'

Lucas immediately knew what she was talking about. He nodded slowly, 'I was jogging, and my phone pinged to tell me there was motion detected, and I looked, not realising what I'd be looking at.'

He stopped talking but Stephanie could tell there was something he wasn't saying. His face flushed as it had done downstairs in the kitchen.

'Then you put it away when you realised what you were looking at,' Stephanie prompted.

'Of course… I ran faster to put you…it out of my mind,' Lucas put his hand through his hair and rubbed his jaw, 'I told myself not to look… but…'

'But?' Stephanie whispered. She should have been feeling mad at him, but the thought of him seeing her naked was as hot as hell.

'I couldn't stop myself, I'm sorry.'

Lucas spread out his hands apologetically.

He took a deep breath, the space between them seemed charged with electricity. His eyes wandered slowly down her body then back up again. Stephanie had an image of her taking off her top and Lucas striding over to her, claiming her as his, holding her in his manly hands…

Lucas took a step forward, he pushed the chair under the desk. Their bodies were so close they were almost touching.

He leant forward slowly. Stephanie held her breath, her skin was tingling all over with anticipation and her eyes followed his hand as he unplugged the external hard drive that sat next to the monitor, then he gave it to Stephanie.

'Here, the recording is on here,' he said quietly. 'You keep it in case we need to use any of it. I hope that you will still allow me to protect you.'

Stephanie tried to calm her breathing. With shaky hands, she took the hard drive from Lucas, walked past him down the stairs and he followed.

When she got to the door, she turned to look at Lucas in the hallway.

'It's going to be awkward from now on, isn't it?'

'It doesn't have to be. What can I do to show you I can be trusted?'

He walked towards her slowly causing her to take a step back.

'I don't know. Every time I see you, I'll remember oh you've seen me naked,' Stephanie laughed nervously.

'What if I even things out?' Lucas asked.

'What do you mean?'

Lucas's hands moved to the bottom of his T-shirt. Cautiously he started to lift it, revealing a bit of flesh. When Stephanie didn't protest, he peeled it off, dropping it to the floor. Her eyes went wide when she noticed a tattoo on the left side of his chest, an eagle swooping with its talons open.

'There now you've seen me.'

Stephanie scoffed, 'That's hardly making us even.'

Lucas took a deep breath then unbuttoned his jeans and pulled them down. He smiled nervously and stepped over the trousers and stood in his doorway in spotty boxer shorts, 'What about now?'

'Spotty boxers?' she tried not to giggle.

'What can I say, I secretly like polka dots.'

Stephanie held the hard drive, in front of her mouth in an attempt to hide her growing smile. Her eyes were wide, taking in the taught his wide, firm chest, his muscly stomach, low hanging boxer shorts, the line of dark hair below his belly button, his firm thighs. Her eyes slowly moved back upwards to a long scar on his left side, a small scar on his shoulder, his stubbly chin and finally to a smile that played on his lips.

It was probably the wine effect, but he had started this, and Stephanie was going to take her time and stare with confidence. Just as she thought that Stephanie panicked as his hands moved to the waistband of his underwear.

She shouted, 'That will do… I think we can call us even.'

'Are you sure?'

Stephanie slowly backed away down the drive, 'I think so,' she whispered. 'I'll see you tomorrow.' This last bit was in a squeakier voice than she would have liked.

He stood still in the doorway as Stephanie turned quickly and almost ran across the road. She opened her door breathlessly, took one more look over to Lucas and then shut the door, locking it behind her.

Neither of them had noticed a blue car parked further up the road. In that car, a figure sat in the darkness... watching with interest.

27

RULES

Ast day at school, Stephanie was dying to talk to Lisa about Lucas. She battled with the need to confide in her best friend in revealing Lucas's identity. It was killing her, but she needed time to decide what to do.

After school, Stephanie and Lisa were tidying up when their phones pinged.

'Rosie says we're meeting at the mansion at 7 pm. Are you coming?' Stephanie asked Lisa.

'Of course, I'm not missing seeing inside there. Shall I meet you on the corner?' Stephanie asked.

STEPHANIE WAS WALKING out of her door when she saw Lucas appear from his house. She walked across the road and waited for him to catch up, a smile played on her lips as she remembered the ridiculousness of the night before. It was funny, but the previous night had managed to even things out a bit, although, he still owed her a bit more…something she was too scared to admit. They walked in silence for a while, but Stephanie didn't feel awkward, she felt safe having him there.

206

'I was thinking,' Lucas began nervously, 'that we could make a fresh start.'

Stephanie looked at him briefly and smiled, 'That sounds like a good plan.'

'There also needs to be some rules, it would make both our lives easier.'

'Rules?'

'You should text me if you're planning on going somewhere.'

'What will you do, follow me?'

'I will be discreet, I promise.'

'I can't have you hanging about on street corners,' Stephanie sighed.

'Sometimes I can go with you,' Lucas suggested.

'I go to my mum and dad's every Sunday for lunch,' Stephanie grimaced.

'I like Sunday lunch, and I like mums and dads,' he added after a thought.

'You haven't met mine,' Stephanie rolled her eyes.

'Also, you should stop walking about on your own.'

'I've been driving recently.'

'Good.'

Stephanie sighed with frustration.

'We don't know what he has planned. Until we know more, you need to be careful, and if you don't want me following you everywhere you go, then you need to follow my rules.'

'Anything else?'

'It would be a good idea if I showed you some basic self-defence.'

'What if I've already learnt self-defence?'

'Have you?'

'I know how to use a fire extinguisher.'

Lucas raised his eyebrows at Stephanie. 'To put out a fire?'

'No, to hit someone across the face.'

Lucas laughed, 'And I believe you don't mean that as a joke. What if there isn't a heavy object at hand?'

Stephanie sighed, 'I suppose I could do with some lessons.'

Lucas smiled.

'Lesson one can start today. If you're faced with an attacker, don't try to kick him or do anything clever. If you can't get away from him, go for his eyes.'

'His eyes?'

'Yes. Stick your thumbs right in his eyes. He'll let go of you then.'

'Eww!'

28

THE SMITH'S HOUSE

S tephanie and Lucas arrived at the corner of the Old Mill where Lisa was waiting.

'Hi,' Lisa said smiling at them both.

'Hi,' Stephanie said. 'You looking forward to seeing inside the mansion?'

'I was just thinking, with the gates at the front, I bet their security must be high,' Lisa said as they walked on.

'I'm surprised they've had anything stolen,' Stephanie agreed. 'Is it likely that there is a professional jewel thief in Hibaldton?'

'It's a small inconspicuous village, just the place I'd hide out in if I were a jewel thief,' Lucas pointed out.

Lisa eyed him suspiciously… 'Which I'm not,' he added quickly.

Angela, Rosie and Ben were waiting outside the gate. The 'mansion' was set back from the road. Through the huge iron gate, Stephanie looked down the tarmacked drive towards the impressive facade. Four columns stood like soldiers guarding the front door and above was a large leaded window. Stephanie watched as Rosie pressed the intercom and spoke to Gavin, there was a click as the gate slowly opened to allow them in.

'It's like Fort Knox here,' Angela remarked.

Stephanie noticed Lucas looking around at their security with interest.

Inside, Sylvia welcomed them into the reception room which was the first room on the right. The group stood in awe gazing at the high ceilings and plush furniture.

'You have a beautiful home,' Ben gushed, 'so tasteful.'

'Thank you,' Sylvia smiled, and Gavin came to stand next to her.

'Would you like to sit down or look around?'

'Look around,' Rosie said probably with too much enthusiasm.

Sylvia laughed, 'Is there anywhere, in particular, you'd like to see?'

'If you don't mind, I'd like us to split up to be as quick as possible. We don't want to take up too much of your time.' Stephanie attempted to make them look professional.

'What do you suggest?' Gavin asked.

'Lucas will look outside. Will he be able to walk all around the property?'

'Err, yes that should be possible,' Gavin said looking at his wife.

'If you could show me and Lisa around downstairs Gavin, Angela and Rosie could go upstairs with you Sylvia.'

Alone with Gavin, the room seemed much bigger. They stood in front of the fireplace and Stephanie pressed 'record' on her phone.

'Is that necessary?' Gavin sounded nervous.

'Oh, it's just so I don't have to take notes,' Stephanie said casually.

Gavin nodded and waited for her to continue.

'When did you say the bracelet went missing?'

Gavin thought about it and was vague.

'It was a couple of nights before the council meeting, I think.'

'Okay and what was the occasion?'

'What do you mean?'

'Did you go out for a meal or were you at home?'

'We stayed at home.'

'Just the two of you?'

Gavin started to get impatient, 'Yes just the two of us. How is this helping?'

Stephanie continued with her line of questioning.

'Can I see the rooms you were in?'

'That's more like it,' Gavin grumbled and walked out of the room.

Stephanie had the feeling that they had interrupted something and couldn't wait to get it over with. She exchanged looks with Lisa and then followed him across the hallway, through a door into a large open room. It had huge French doors which were open, inviting you onto a patio with a wrought iron table and chairs. The room had a wide television at the end with a couple of sofas facing it. They walked over to that end of the room. Gavin pointed to one of the sofas and walked over, his eyes searching the floor around it.

'We were watching TV, and Sylvia was sitting there.'

'Here?' Lisa put her hands on the back of the sofa.

'Yes, then we went upstairs to bed and that is where she usually takes off her bracelet.'

'Could she have dropped it here?' Lisa asked looking at the seat.

'Well, she said that she'd had a look…'

He sat on the sofa and put his hand down the side… and brought out a glittering, diamond bracelet.

'Oh, my goodness, it's here!' he announced shocked.

Stephanie and Lisa looked at him surprised.

'Are you sure that's not another bracelet?' Stephanie asked hopefully.

Gavin laughed, 'My wife loves her jewellery, but I know which bracelet went missing.'

'Still, we should ask her just to be sure,' Stephanie said disappointed that the investigation was over so soon.

Lucas appeared at the patio doors, he walked in to see Stephanie looking disappointed and Gavin holding up the bracelet.

'I must apologise. At the meeting, you were talking about all these thefts, and I must have jumped to conclusions. Did you find that lady's brooch?'

'Mabel? No, we didn't.'

'Well, hopefully, it will turn up as ours did. Cameo brooches are very common though, I'm sure she'll be able to replace it,' Gavin said hopefully.

'Lucas wanted to talk to you about your security, I'll just go get the others, Lisa, you coming?' Stephanie looked at Lucas and he nodded.

Stephanie and Lisa walked out of the room and turned towards the staircase. They started to walk up the stairs and talked quietly.

'That was a waste of time,' Lisa mumbled.

'Hmm, a bit convenient,' Stephanie whispered. 'I wonder if we have a chance to do a bit of snooping.'

'What? Stephanie, what are you doing?'

Stephanie texted Ben, 'Keep Sylvia occupied.'

They reached the landing and listened for the others. Ben popped his head out of a room and put his thumb up, then disappeared again. They heard his voice exclaim, 'Oh a bath! I've always wanted one of those.'

'But you have a bath,' Angela's voice could be heard as Stephanie and Lisa crept along the corridor.

'Not a roll-top bath though. Tell me, Sylvia, would you recommend one?'

Before Lisa could argue, Stephanie pulled her into the next room, and they found themselves in the master bedroom.

'Oh, this isn't good,' Lisa whispered nervously peering around the door up the hallway. 'We've already found the bracelet, we'll get into trouble.'

'I just want a peek, they'll never know.'

Stephanie looked about the room, it was bling city.

'Wow,' she gasped.

She walked around letting her fingers dance over the glass and rose gold furniture with crystal-looking drawer knobs. The bed was huge covered in a white bedspread, the thick carpet a blush pink, and a crystal chandelier hung above the bed.

'That's an accident waiting to happen,' Stephanie said.

Stephanie opened a drawer next to the bed. There was a man's watch which had a gold strap, a pen and some mints. Stephanie thought that was probably Gavin's side of the bed. She quickly walked to the other side.

Lisa was getting anxious. 'Hurry up they're going to come out any minute.'

'We'll be fine. If I know Ben, he's probably discussing hair products and giving her some advice.'

She opened the top drawer: glasses, lipstick, a vibrator and a blindfold. Stephanie pulled a face, that was an image she didn't want to see. She took out the vibrator to show Lisa and turned it on. It buzzed louder than expected and when Stephanie tried to turn it off, it just got faster until the bottom flew off and a battery flew out knocking a photo frame over.

'Shit,' Stephanie whispered as she tried to catch the frame before it fell onto the carpet.

As she picked it up, the back came open and it revealed a second photo inside. It looked like a holiday photo with Gavin and Sylvia sipping cocktails onboard a fancy yacht.

'Wow Lisa, look at this. This yacht must be expensive, there's a helipad up there and look at the size of the pool.'

'There's a sign on the boat with a name on, Viktor? What's that attached to the side?'

'That thing with the yellow roof? A speed boat, I think.'

'Well, if it's Sylvia and Gavin's boat then I'm surprised they live here,' Stephanie whispered.

'Maybe it belongs to a friend.'

'Friends in high places.'

Stephanie quickly put everything back as it was and then noticed Lisa had discovered a walk-in wardrobe. Stephanie walked over to see rows of clothes all arranged in colour order.

'I always thought about what type of person arranges their clothes like this,' Stephanie said, 'I wonder…'

'Probably a psychopath,' Lisa said nervously looking towards the door.

Stephanie took a step closer to the black clothes section where there must have been at least ten different black cocktail dresses. Just as she pulled out a drawer full of lycra sports leggings and tops, frustratingly, Lisa pushed the drawer closed.

'Quick, someone's coming.'

Lisa pulled her away as they heard Angela's voice outside the room.

Stephanie and Lisa rushed to the bedroom doorway just in time to see the others walk out.

'Oh, there you are,' Stephanie shouted as casually as she could. 'We've just come to tell you that we've found your bracelet.'

Sylvia's eyes narrowed for a brief second looking towards her bedroom and then she smiled, 'Really? That's fabulous, let's go downstairs then.'

They followed her back down to where Gavin and Lucas were discussing the sensors on the patio doors.

Gavin turned round, 'Oh darling look, it was here all along.'

He held up the bracelet and gave it to Sylvia, she looked so relieved.

'You are all amazing, thank you so much. What brilliant detectives you are, you should go professional.'

'Your husband was the one who found it straight away,' Lisa said bluntly.

Sylvia frowned and looked across at Gavin, 'I'm so sorry that we wasted your time. Gavin will see you out.'

Gavin started to walk out of the room, and they all followed him to the front door.

'I hope that you will visit again,' Sylvia flashed a grin towards Lucas and held out her hand. 'It's a shame *we* didn't get to talk.'

Lucas smiled and held it for a second. Stephanie grinned, 'I bet she'd eat him alive,' she thought.

They left Sylvia and walked to the huge front door.

Rosie looked at Gavin. 'Maybe next time you have a cocktail party you could invite us? I have a dress that I bought, and I haven't had a chance to wear it yet.'

Gavin opened the door to let them out and smiled at Rosie.

'Cocktail parties? We haven't had one of those for ages. If we do, you'll be the first to get an invite. Goodbye, everyone and thanks again.'

He held Rosie's hand and kissed it.

'Thank *you* for showing us your lovely home,' Rosie blushed.

They all walked down the drive into the growing darkness.

'Shall we regroup at the pub?' Ben suggested.

29

YOU KNOW WHERE I AM

Inside The Old Mill, the group sat at the table in front of the window.

They huddled together to discuss the night.

'That was a disappointment,' Ben huffed.

'I'm not surprised there wasn't a break-in, their house is as secure as a prison,' Lucas said sipping his coca cola.

'Wasn't the house a dream though,' Rosie breathed.

'The whole thing was fishy if you ask me,' said Angela, 'and why do they need so much security anyway, what do they have in there…the crown jewels?'

'I couldn't believe it when he pulled out the bracelet. What a waste of time,' Stephanie sighed and sat back.

'I know. You'd have thought they would have got their cleaner to look for them, I presume they have a cleaner,' Lisa thought aloud and picked up her glass of lemonade.

Ben agreed, 'Can you imagine cleaning all those rooms?'

Stephanie nodded. 'Did you see all the glass furniture in her bedroom, and it was all spotless.'

Lisa added, 'I can't imagine Sylvia bending down with rubber gloves on.'

Ben chuckled, 'I bet she does it for Gavin.'

Lucas laughed out loud.

'I did find a vibrator on Sylvia's side of the bed.'

'And you turned it on and it flew off and exploded everywhere!'

Everyone fell about laughing at that. When Stephanie could talk she defended herself.

'I didn't, it just turned on by itself!'

Lucas looked at Stephanie and shook his head with a grin.

They all had a drink in silence for a minute.

Stephanie sighed and asked, 'Was there anything you noticed when you were with Sylvia?'

'Just how amazing her house is!' Rosie sighed.

Ben nodded, 'You have to admit it, that girl has good taste. There was something weird though -- I saw a blue feather on the windowsill and a red one on the bedroom floor, I don't know if it's important, but it's odd,' Ben said.

'"That is odd because there was a feather in Margaret's bedroom too,' Stephanie recalled.

Lisa gasped, 'Did it look like a parrot's feather?'

'I'm not sure what a parrot's feather looks like. Why a parrot?' Ben asked, puzzled.

'It's a strange theory but… what if someone trained a parrot to fly in and steal jewellery?'

They all sat in silence for a minute to take it in, and then together they laughed and shook their heads.

'Interestingly, we have found feathers at everyone's house though,' Lisa pouted.

'Not everyone's,' Ben pointed out and laughed, 'but let's not rule your theory out.'

'Who shall we visit next?' Angela asked.

Rosie took the iPad and looked at her notes.

'Next, we could visit the couple who lost their watch.'

They all sighed. 'It's not looking good, is it?' Lisa said deflated. 'An old lady who has probably misplaced her earring, a rich, bored couple who like to play games with us and a kid who probably flushed the watch down the loo.'

'We might as well finish the investigation. Let's visit the couple with the watch, shall we?' Stephanie tried to lift their spirits.

'I'll give them a ring and organise a visit. Shall we try for next week?'

On the way home, Stephanie walked next to Lisa and Lucas walked behind as the path was narrow.

'Have you heard anything from Mark?' Lisa asked in a low voice.

'Nope,' Stephanie replied. 'He always does this.'

'Does what?'

'Avoids important conversations, it's really annoying.'

'What is he avoiding?' Lisa asked.

Stephanie remembered that she hadn't told her about Lucas or the worry that Sergei was threatening her. Maybe she should warn Lisa as she was with her a lot of the time, he could be a threat to her too.

'I need to tell you something,' Stephanie began.

She started to tell Lisa all about the postcards, and then how she had recently discovered from Mark that he and Kate had hired Lucas as a bodyguard. By now, they had stopped at the corner of Lisa's road, Lisa's eyes were wide and her mouth was open in surprise.

Finally, she said, 'And you're only just telling me this?' She looked from Stephanie to Lucas.

'Like I said, I've only just found out. Lucas was told not to tell me in case I panicked, I was so mad with Mark when he told me.'

'I can't believe that Mark's gone off to London and left you when you're worried for your life… and he hires a bodyguard?'

She looked at Lucas who had stood there awkwardly with his hands in his pockets.

'Technically, it was Kate who hired him,' Stephanie mumbled.

Lucas shrugged and smiled, 'It's difficult to say no to Kate, have you met her?'

The women laughed and nodded. They both knew how forceful Kate could be from her visit in the Spring.

'Do you know Kate well?' asked Lucas.

'We don't know her that well, we only met her once when she came to visit Mark. She is a character that's for sure, I wasn't sure I liked her to begin with, but when you get used to her, you realise that she is very generous and caring.'

Lucas nodded, 'Yeah, that sounds just like my sister.'

'Your sister!' Lisa and Stephanie both shouted in surprise.

'I'd just gone to stay with my parents after finishing a job in Scotland and Kate came round for a meal. She told us what happened to you, it was some story. And you're right, she is one of the most caring people I know, I couldn't refuse her.'

'I can't believe you're Kate's brother,' Stephanie said shaking her head.

'Wow, I wonder what the next surprise will be,' Lisa laughed.

'Well, it's not so bad being stuck with Lucas, as we have our own bodyguard, we might as well walk you home Lisa.'

They walked further down the road and Lisa walked on the other side of Lucas.

'It would be useful to know where you live Lisa, just in case.'

'Can I borrow him, Stephanie?' Lisa laughed.

'Sure, anytime,' Stephanie replied cheekily.

'Hey, I'm not here for your entertainment,' he protested.

'I'm planning a hen do for my sister, you don't happen to be free in a couple of months by any chance?'

Lucas laughed, 'What did you have in mind?'

'Tell us what talents you have to offer Lucas?' Stephanie teased.

'Now you two are making me nervous,' Lucas grinned. 'Where did you say your house was?'

Stephanie couldn't stop laughing after they said goodbye to Lisa.

'I'm sorry Lucas, but the look on your face was priceless.'

Lucas laughed and shook his head. 'When women get together… no man is safe.'

'Seriously though, I'm glad that Lisa knows. She's my best friend and if I'm in danger, there's a good chance she may be too.'

'Don't worry, I'll do my best to keep you both safe. So, Mark's not in your good books at the moment then?'

Stephanie sighed and pressed her lips together.

'No, he's not. I don't like being manipulated. You know, I've only just realised that ever since we got together, he's been doing that. I was forever wondering if I could trust him and feeling guilty about it.'

'How long have you two been together?'

'Since January.'

'Not long then,' he said.

'No not really, but we knew each other at school.'

They reached Stephanie's house and Stephanie unlocked the door.

'I…' Lucas seemed to be searching for the right thing to say. 'You take my breath away Stephanie, every day I get to know you, I see how intelligent and perceptive you are… and beautiful.'

Stephanie stood in the doorway. This was the last thing she expected him to say.

Lucas grinned at her, and he lowered his gaze to his feet. Stephanie didn't know what to say, her stomach was tied in knots.

Lucas took a step backwards and put his hands in his pockets.

'We make a good team you and me. I'd better go see how Bruce's doing, he's probably thinking about eating the sofa.'

'Oh no, you'd better go see. See you tomorrow.'

'Yeah, you know where I am if you need me.'

Lucas turned and walked across the road back to his house. Stephanie closed the door and leaned against it. She was in trouble.

As if on autopilot, she walked up the stairs to her bedroom and got ready for bed. She needed to see Mark, her mind was in a whirl, she couldn't think straight with the memory of Lucas's surprisingly nervous smile. Did she make him nervous?

'This is ridiculous,' Stephanie said aloud.

She found her phone and looked at the time, it was only 10:30. She rang Mark. It rang for a while and then went to voice mail.

'Oh, answer it, Mark, I need to hear your voice,' Stephanie almost cried.

She tried again and then he answered. He sounded like he was outside and there were voices in the background.

'Hi, Stephanie?' Mark answered.

'Hi, where are you?' Stephanie asked.

'I've just popped out for a drink with some mates from work, you met them last time.'

'Oh, you mean John, Laura and Tammy?' Stephanie remembered.

'Yeah, and a couple of others.'

A woman's voice in the background was giggling.

'Who's that?' Stephanie asked.

'Nobody, there's some drunk people walking about, you know what it's like in Soho. Are you all right?' he sounded worried.

'Yes, I'm fine. I just wanted to talk to you, I miss you.'

'Do you want me to come home tomorrow?'

'Do you want to come home tomorrow?' Stephanie threw back at him.

'Well, I just wondered if you'd calmed down. The last time we spoke you were mad at me.'

'With good reason! You hired somebody to spy on me, without my knowledge, installed cameras around my house and made me think I was paranoid for no reason.'

'God Stephanie, you're blowing it all out of proportion.' Mark sounded annoyed.

At the moment everything she said seemed to lead to an argument.

'I can't speak to you while you're outside a bar. Ring me tomorrow.'

'Are you coming Mark?' a woman's voice called in the background.

'I'll speak to you tomorrow then,' Mark replied. 'Are you sure you're all right?'

'Yeah, I'm fine, bye.' Stephanie said and then hung up.

30

A NOISE IN THE NIGHT

Stephanie tossed and turned in the darkness, the air was stifling and sticky. She rolled out of bed to open the window and stood for a while to enjoy the open air. Looking across the road, she could see that Lucas's light was on, the streetlight bathed the road in a pale glow, casting eerie shadows. The church bells chimed 2 o'clock which surprised Stephanie as she didn't think she'd slept much. Her eyes felt swollen from crying, she missed Mark and was hurt that he was out having fun when he should be miserable, missing her. She looked over at Lucas's bedroom window again, what a hypocrite she was. She had no right to be angry with Mark, how would he feel if he knew the thoughts she'd been having about another man?

Stephanie crawled sleepily back into bed when there was a crashing noise, it came from the back garden. Stephanie sat up, suddenly wide awake and listened, but all she could hear was her own heart pounding. The night was so still, it was probably a cat knocking something over, would Lucas notice if someone was in her garden? What if he was asleep?

Stephanie fumbled in the dark for her phone and messaged Lucas.

'Are you awake?'

'Yes. You ok?'

'I heard a noise I'm scared.'

She sent the message without thinking and now she regretted it. She was such a wimp, but when she heard a knock at the door, she was glad Lucas had come.

Stephanie ran down the stairs and called through the door, 'Who is it?'

'Lucas.'

Stephanie opened the door and felt a flood of relief when she saw him standing there, Bruce by his side.

Once inside, Lucas locked the door and they walked into the front room. Stephanie turned the light on dimly and wrung her hands nervously.

'I'm so sorry, I was awake and heard a noise.'

'It's ok, that's what I'm here for. Stay inside and lock the door.'

Stephanie stood rooted to the spot, nervously biting her nails whilst listening for sounds of a fight or a chase... nothing. After agonising minutes there was a soft tap at the door.

'It's Lucas, everything is fine, you can open the door.'

As he entered her house, Stephanie rushed up to him and buried her face against his warm chest. She held onto the material of his T-shirt with her eyes closed until her breathing calmed down.

Lucas stroked her hair and calmly soothed her.

'Bruce has been round the house and didn't sense anything. I found a broken plant pot.'

He leaned back so he could look at her face, and then his brow furrowed when he saw her puffy eyes.

'Are you all right on your own tonight?' he asked concerned.

Stephanie shook her head and then shrugged. She couldn't speak because she thought she might cry again.

'I've got an idea. You take Bruce up to bed, I'll sleep down here.'

'Oh, you don't have to really,' Stephanie felt awful that she had disturbed him at all.

'I mean it, stop arguing and go back upstairs. I'll see you in the morning. Bruce, with Stephanie.'

Stephanie was too tired to argue. She walked towards the door and patted her leg for Bruce to follow.

'Go on,' Lucas ordered his dog.

Bruce ran upstairs and Stephanie followed. She turned in the doorway. 'Thanks,' she whispered to Lucas.

'See, Bruce wants to protect you, just like I do,' Lucas said softly.

Stephanie climbed up the stairs and into bed, she pulled up the covers, patting the bed for Bruce to join her. With Bruce's warm, protective body next to hers, she fell fast asleep.

IN THE MORNING, Stephanie awoke with the feeling of something in the bed next to her. There was a weight on top of the covers, she put out her hand to stroke the soft fur of the German Shepherd and felt the lick of his tongue. She opened her eyes and laughed, 'You know what Bruce, I realise that I don't need a man, I just need a dog.'

He whimpered and crawled a little closer so that his cold, wet nose was in her face. She giggled and pushed him away.

'Hey Bruce, that's enough.'

There were footsteps on the stairs and Bruce leapt off the bed towards the door, his tail banging excitedly against the wardrobe. The door opened slowly, and Lucas stood there nervously.

'Hello sleepy head, I hope you don't mind, I heard you and wondered if you wanted some breakfast. Has Bruce been well-behaved?'

He bent down to stroke Bruce behind the ears.

'Amazing. I slept like a log thank you,' Stephanie smiled.

'You can borrow him anytime.'

Bruce started whimpering and ran downstairs.

'I'd better let him out into the garden,' Lucas said. 'I've made some pancakes if you'd like some.'

'Pancakes, wow. I'll be right down.'

Lucas disappeared and Stephanie jumped out of bed to get ready. She looked at the time, it was 8 o'clock and Friday. Oh, how she wished it was Saturday and didn't have to go to work.

In record time she was downstairs to find pancakes and coffee out on the table.

'Thanks a lot, Lucas.'

'No problem. It's nice to make pancakes for a change, there's no point when there's only one of you.'

They both sat down and helped themselves.

'Did you sleep ok on the settee?'

'Yeah, I managed to get a few hours of sleep.'

'I feel awful, you could have slept in the spare room.'

'No, I preferred to sleep downstairs, you know in case someone was trying to get in. I looked at the camera footage…'

Lucas showed Stephanie his phone and played back the video.

'A figure could be seen walking through the back garden and then tripping over the plant pot. The person was wearing a puffer jacket with a hood and, dark trousers, the face couldn't be seen clearly. Stephanie stared in shock. 'I thought it would just have been a cat.'

'If it is, it's a huge cat that walks on two legs.'

'Can you tell if it's a man or a woman?'

'It's difficult to tell, I'll have to open it on my PC to get a better look.'

'Who an earth can it be?' Stephanie moaned. 'I don't think it's Sergei, he's much bigger than that. You know, I almost wish he would come to get me, and then it would be over one way or another.'

'I'll have a look when I get home.'

Stephanie finished her pancake, drank her coffee and stood up with a sigh.

'I have to go to work.'

'Would you like me to drive you?' Lucas asked, also standing up.

Stephanie looked at him in his crumpled grey T-shirt, dark blue, baggy jogging bottoms and bare feet. She bit her lip, she loved the way he seemed to be so relaxed in her house, she could get used to this.

'I think people would start talking…' She started to feel guilty again and pushed those intoxicating thoughts aside.

'I have your door key, I can tidy up and let myself out if that's ok.'

'Yeah, that's great thanks,' Stephanie called over her shoulder as she dashed upstairs.

❧ ✿ ❧

AT LUNCHTIME, LISA cornered Stephanie before she left the classroom.

'What is going on Stephanie?' Lisa asked firmly.

'Nothing, why?'

'Because you look tired and seem a million miles away, even when Kevin threw up on the carpet.'

'Don't judge me, promise.'

Lisa stared at Stephanie, waiting for her response.

'Last night, I woke up and heard a crashing noise in the garden. I was scared so I texted Lucas. Before you say anything, it's the first time I've texted him.'

'Did he go round?'

'Within seconds, and you know it was the best sleep I've had in ages.'

Lisa's eyes grew round.

'You two didn't…'

Stephanie laughed. 'He slept downstairs and Bruce slept on my bed.'

Lisa laughed and shook her head. 'I think you got that the wrong way round.'

'Lucas was the perfect gentleman. Seriously though, he did tell me before I went to bed, that Bruce wants to protect me like he does.'

'Oh, my god. I'm feeling tingly all over,' Lisa gasped.

Stephanie laughed and then grew more serious. She sat on the edge of a table and explained, 'There was someone in my garden last night.'

Lisa stopped laughing, 'Are you being serious?'

'Unfortunately, yes. Lucas showed me the video from my camera, but you can't see who it is.'

'Was it… you know who?'

Stephanie shook her head, 'I don't think so.'

'Is it the jewellery thief? Maybe that's the person we're searching for.'

'I hadn't thought about that… but I don't think so. Whoever it was stumbled over a flowerpot, they seemed too clumsy.'

'At least you have Lucas to look after you. You like him, don't you?'

'Maybe… but he's getting paid, so he's not doing it cos he wants to, is he?'

'What about Mark?' Lisa asked carefully.

Stephanie sighed and shrugged.

'I rang Mark when I got home. He was busy having fun in Soho, and I could hear a woman in the background. It sounded like Tammy, a woman he works with.'

'Did he say who he was with?'

'Yes, he said he was with a group of work friends, and then we had a bit of an argument.'

Lisa put her arm on Stephanie's shoulder.

'It's hard when you are not seeing each other. Is he coming back this weekend?'

Stephanie shrugged. 'Come on. Let's get some lunch,' Lisa said.

On the way to the staffroom, Lisa continued, 'Why don't you come over to our house tonight? We could get a takeout.'

'You sure Martin won't mind?'

'Of course not. You might as well come round straight after school.'

'Yeah, ok that would be great thanks.'

'What about Lucas?'

231

'He knows where you live if we need him. To be honest, I'm beginning to think that those postcards are just to get under my skin. If Sergei was going to kidnap me or do something, he would have done it by now wouldn't he?'

31

PIZZA NIGHT

Lisa's daughters, Phoebe and Sofia were so excited to have Stephanie at their house. They played board games in the front room until Martin got home. Snakes and Ladders, Ludo, Uno, they all came out of the cupboard.

'Dad's home,' Sofia shouted at the sound of the door.

Martin walked in and dropped his bag in the hallway.

'Hello pumpkin,' he shouted as Sofia jumped up and clung to him like a monkey.

Martin limped into the front room, by then with both daughters hanging off him.

'Hi Stephanie,' he said as he tipped Sofia upside down and deposited her onto the chair, and then picked Phoebe up. 'This is what I have to put up with every day I come home,' he laughed.

Lisa came in from the kitchen with take-out menus.

'What do you fancy? Chinese, pizza or a curry?'

'Pizza,' shouted Phoebe and Sofia.

Stephanie's phone rang, it was Mark. Stephanie took it into the kitchen.

'Hi,' she answered.

'Hi, I'm at your house, where are you?'

Stephanie was surprised, she had no idea he was coming home.

'I'm at Lisa's, we're just ordering pizza. Do you want to come over?'

'Ok, I'll walk over. See you in a bit.'

Stephanie stood for a moment and took a deep breath after she had hung up. She felt so annoyed, why couldn't they communicate with each other? Stephanie realised with sadness, that she wasn't sure she wanted him there, right now.

Mark arrived and to Martin's delight, Sofia and Phoebe jumped on Mark so that they ended up in a heap in the middle of the room. Eventually Lisa rescued him with shouts of, 'Milkshake!' in the kitchen. They ran off leaving Mark to sit up, exhausted.

Martin and Stephanie laughed while he stood up on shaky legs and then plopped down on the settee next to Stephanie.

'Thanks for the help,' he sighed and leaned his head back with closed eyes.

'You looked like you had it all under control,' Stephanie said.

'Now you know how it feels for me every day,' Martin said without sympathy.

'You need to train them better,' Mark said opening his eyes and then looking at Stephanie properly for the first time.

'When's the pizza coming, I'm starving.'

'It should be here in about half an hour, we ordered a variety so there should be something for everyone,' Martin said.

'You should have said you were coming,' Stephanie added.

'I thought I told you I was.'

'No, we haven't spoken properly all week,' Stephanie pointed out.

Martin probably felt a bit awkward so he did the only thing he could think of in a situation like this and asked, 'Beer anyone?'

Mark jumped up, 'Yes please, I'll help.'

Stephanie was left sitting on her own, until Lisa came in with a bottle of wine. She poured them both a glass.

'I'd better only have one, I'm driving remember,' Stephanie said with a sigh.

'Why didn't you walk?'

'My bodyguard's instructions.'

'So, Mark, he's just going for the 'there's nothing wrong' routine?'

'Yep.'

Stephanie took a sip of her wine and listened to the men laughing in the kitchen.

'I can't pretend everything's fine when it's not... Maybe it is as far as he's concerned,' Stephanie wondered. 'Do you think I'm being unreasonable to expect him to tell me when he's setting off?'

'No, I don't, that's what you do when you're in a serious relationship.'

Stephanie looked at Lisa thoughtfully, 'Why does that word 'serious' sound so ominous?'

'Maybe neither of you is ready for that yet?'

'How do you know when you're ready?'

Lisa thought about it for a while.

'I think it's when you feel completely at home with someone. There's no pretence, you can be yourself- you're lovers but also best friends.'

'I don't know why we can't have that. It's not just Mark's fault, it's mine too. There's something that stops me from opening up completely to him.'

'If you two are meant to be together, it will happen. You can't force it,' Lisa said wisely. 'Maybe it's because you both can see a future together, that you both find it a bit scary.'

Stephanie laughed, 'We've only been together a short while, I think we are taking it too seriously.'

THE DOORBELL RANG and soon they were all sat around the kitchen table devouring the pizza. Stephanie sat quietly listening to Martin telling them about his day. He was working on the installation of fibre in the area and had been accosted in the street by some residents complaining about all the road works.

Lisa recalled what had happened at school particularly how Kevin had been sick, it was so smelly in the heat of the room that everyone had to go outside for some fresh air while Lisa cleaned it up. Stephanie apologised but pointed out that she had ended up running round the playground with the class three times. Plus, she would have thrown up if she had had to clean it up.

Mark told them about how he had spent all day on the computer watching the stock market and keeping an eye on his clients' investments. Tammy had apparently brought everyone in their corner of the office doughnuts, and she'd spilt jam all down her blouse. Stephanie didn't find it funny, great his story had to be about an attractive girl he worked with every day. She imagined him watching her as she dabbed at the jam sexily while he licked his lips…

'Is your office one big room or is it small?' Lisa asked.

'It's a big room, people sit at desks that have dividers up, so you feel like you're in detention.'

'Haha like when you were put in detention at school for putting a whoopie cushion on the geography teacher's chair,' Martin remembered.

'Haha yeah, she had no sense of humour,' Mark replied reaching for another slice of pizza.

'Can we do that?' Phoebe asked with interest.

'Not unless it's on Miss Rhode's chair,' Lisa replied.

'Oh no you don't young lady, and you two had better stop giving her ideas,' Stephanie wagged her finger at everyone.

'Isn't it the school holidays soon?' Martin asked Lisa.

'Yeah, I told you we break up next week. Next Saturday is the Garden Club show remember. You need to choose which roses to pick.'

'I didn't realise you were into gardening,' Mark said.

'Yeah, come on I'll show you round our garden.'

Martin and Mark disappeared outside, leaving Lisa and Stephanie to chat.

After a while they returned and opened the fridge for another beer.

'Someone at work was talking about the parachute jump in two weeks, are you still doing it Steph?' Martin asked.

Stephanie looked at Mark, 'You rang them to cancel it didn't you?'

Mark nodded. 'Yes, I did. The woman I spoke to was very understanding, she said it wasn't a problem.'

'Oh phew,' Stephanie said with relief, 'thanks.'

'We see them jumping out every weekend, it looks safe enough,' Martin said.

'You do it then,' Stephanie shot back.

THE NIGHT CONTINUED after the young girls had gone to bed, when it was midnight, Stephanie and Mark thought they'd better go as Lisa and Martin were nearly asleep.

They said goodbye, walked into the warm night air and got into Stephanie's car. On the drive back Stephanie was quiet, she was thinking about her conversation with Lisa earlier on.

'Are you still in a mood with me?' Mark asked.

'I'm not in a mood. Why is it my fault?' Stephanie felt herself getting annoyed again.

'I'm sorry. Let me start again. I'm sorry I said you were overreacting, and I realise now that I should have talked to you about Lucas and the cameras… I just didn't want you to worry.'

'I see… but we both need to communicate better.'

Mark put his hand on her knee as they drove down Field View.

'Are you tired?' Mark asked.

Stephanie pulled in outside her house.

'No, I'm thinking about our relationship.'

'What do you mean?'

Stephanie turned to look at him.

'Are we in a serious relationship?'

'Why do you have to use the word serious?' Mark asked.

'It was a word Lisa used and… It made me realise that we haven't had this conversation.'

They were quiet for a while.

'We talked about getting married the other day.'

'It wasn't a proper conversation.'

Stephanie opened the car door and got out.

'Do you want a serious relationship?' Mark asked as they reached the door.

'All I know is that what we're doing at the moment isn't enough for me anymore. I want us to be together more…'

'You'll be coming to stay with me in London soon, you break up next week, don't you?' Mark pointed out.

'What am I going to do every day though while you're out at work?' Stephanie asked.

'I don't understand what you want Stephanie,' Mark sounded tired. 'I'm going home.'

He walked over to his car which he'd left at Stephanie's house.

'Are you all right driving?' Stephanie asked.

'Yeah, I only had a few beers.'

He stood looking at Stephanie.

'I'll come round tomorrow at lunch time, and we can talk then.'

Stephanie nodded and watched him get into his car and drive away.

Just as she was about to put her key in the lock, she heard a bark. She turned around to see Bruce trotting over the road, his tail wagging excitedly.

Stephanie laughed, 'Hello Bruce, isn't it past your bedtime?' She sat on the step and wrapped her arms around his warm, soft neck, and he leant his head on her shoulder.

Stephanie looked up to see Lucas saunter over.

'Sorry, I just let him out for a last tinkle, and he was off when he saw you.'

'Haha, that's ok, I needed a hug anyway.'

'Do you want to borrow him again tonight?'

Stephanie shook her head and stood up.

'No, but thanks anyway. I'm fine. Goodnight Lucas.'

She opened her door and stepped inside. Lucas called Bruce and waved goodnight.

32

IF YOU'RE MEANT TO BE TOGETHER

It was Saturday morning and Stephanie opened her patio doors to allow the air into the stuffy kitchen. Birds were singing outside, and the sun was shining brightly with hardly a cloud in the sky. It should have been a perfect day. Stephanie made a drink of tea and sat by the open doors in thought.

There was a knock at the door, Stephanie walked to the window to see Mark standing there. She let him in with a forced smile and led him to the kitchen where she made him a coffee.

'I've just been to see mum and dad,' Mark said.

'How are they? I have been meaning to pop in to see them, but I've been busy.'

'They're fine, Dad hasn't thrown the computer out yet, so that's good news.'

'Any news from Richard?' she asked as she passed him his mug.

'Yeah, Emma's doing well, and they've bought a ticket to come over in October.'

'That's great.'

It should have been good news, but Stephanie felt like her stomach was tied in knots. She stood by the open patio doors holding her hot mug, letting the warmth of the drink comfort her. The sound of bird song floated in the morning air.

'Can't you come back here for a few weeks again, and do your London work from home again?'

Mark rubbed his chin and looked at Stephanie.

'If I asked you to move to London, would you?'

Stephanie looked at him but couldn't meet his eyes. She turned to stare across the field behind her garden, towards Mark's house which nestled between lush trees in the distance.

'I don't think I'd be happy in London, I like living near my family and friends,' she heard herself saying, and then frowned for not thinking it through.

'You asked me if I wanted us to have a serious relationship. I do Steph. The thought of coming home to you every day makes me feel happy, I can see us being really good together, but I don't think I want to live here, not yet anyway. There's so much you can do in a big city, everything's on your doorstep.'

She needed time to think. It was one thing to stay for the holiday, but to commit to living there permanently… what did she want?

'So, you want me to move in with you in London?' she eventually said, sitting at the table and placed her mug down.

Mark sat down and inched his chair closer to Stephanie so that his legs were on either side of hers.

'I'd like you to try it over the summer and see how you feel.'

'I can do that,' Stephanie said slowly, 'but I need to finish the investigation into the missing jewellery first.'

Mark gave a frustrated sigh and scraped his chair back noisily as he stood up. He walked out onto the patio and stood staring across the golden field. It was a surprise how annoyed he seemed. Stephanie watched him wondering what was wrong. She ached to wrap her arms around him and tell him that she'd go to London, but the jewellery case was important to her, and she had to see it through.

Stephanie slowly stood up, as if he was a bird that she might scare away if she moved too quickly. She took a step to join him, and they stood in silence for a while.

The breeze cheekily danced through the field. The wheat leaned forward as if to listen in on their conversation and then swayed away whispering about them. Stephanie closed her eyes to listen and feel the warm breeze on her face before she spoke.

'I'm in the middle of something that means a lot to me, there are people that need help, and I can't just…'

'So it means more to you than being with me?' Mark's steely voice made Stephanie open her eyes.

'Of course not. I was just going to say…'

'I think we should have a break Steph. I think our timing's wrong again.'

Stephanie felt numb. 'I think you may be right.'

Mark turned to look at her.

'Right… I'll go then.'

He walked back into the house towards the front door.

Stephanie wanted to run after him, but she was frozen to the spot. She remembered what Lisa had told her, 'They couldn't force it, if they were meant to be together, then it would happen.'

Stephanie watched his car drive away again for the second time with tears in her eyes. She took a deep breath in and out, she had a yearning to go see her mum and eat a full tub of ice-cream -she'd buy it on the way there.

'WHAT'S WRONG WITH Stephanie?' Malcolm asked as if his daughter couldn't hear him.

'I'm right here dad,' Stephanie said with a mouth full of chocolate chip ice cream.

'She's just having an emotional day,' Barbara loudly whispered.

'Women's troubles? Say no more, I'm off out anyway for a walk so you two can have a good talk. Bye Munchkin.'

He kissed Stephanie on her forehead and went to get his coat.

'So, you said Mark wants you to move to London? You know we don't mind if you say yes, don't worry about us. We just want you to be happy.'

'But I like living around here, I don't want to live in London. It's noisy and scary and I don't know anyone there. I'd have to get a new job, it's more expensive…'

Stephanie started to feel like she was going to have a panic attack.

'Just take one thing at a time. There's plenty of parks and quiet spaces in London, you two could live in the suburbs where its quieter.'

'I suppose so,' Stephanie said eating more ice cream.

'You could join a club to meet friends and Mark will introduce you to people.'

'His work friends seemed friendly,' Stephanie agreed.

'As for a new job, you could be a supply teacher for a while until you get settled.'

Grandma Bettie entered the room, she sat quietly on the other side of Stephanie.

When they'd finished talking, Grandma Bettie advised, 'Go with your gut Stephanie dear. Whatever path you choose, it should make you feel happy.'

'Thanks grandma,' Stephanie said. 'Thanks mum.'

She tried to fight back the tears, but they spilled out down her cheeks and as she spoke, her words came out as sobs.

'But I think it… it's too… late anyway. He's fed up w… with me.'

She leant her head on her mum's shoulder while Barbara stroked her hair soothingly.

'He's not fed up with you love, he's just impatient. Men are always impatient, but he loves you, so he'll wait. And when work is finished, and you go down to London, you'll have a good holiday down there and everything will become clear.'

When Stephanie's breathing calmed down, she asked slowly, 'What if I don't like it in London?'

'Then you'll come back.'

Grandma Bettie added, 'Change is a good thing Stephanie, you can't let your worries hold you back.'

'Mum, can I stay for the weekend?'

'Your room is always there. Erm, just don't go up yet though because all my knitting is on your bed.'

'Your mum's turned it into a craft room. She's been making Christmas cards and knitting snowmen,' Grandma Bettie whispered as if it were a secret.

'What are you going to do with all the snowmen?' Stephanie asked intrigued.

'I'm going to sell them at the Rigby Christmas Fair and the money will go to charity.'

Stephanie thought about it. 'But it's only June, how many are you going to knit?'

'I think I've already knitted fifty…'

'Or… it could go towards a new washing machine because yours keeps going funny.'

Barbara looked at Bettie. 'It is going to charity.' Barbara turned to her daughter, 'The washing machine is fine, it's just that grandma keeps putting dishwasher tablets in.'

Stephanie sat up to look at her grandma.

'It frightens me that thing. The last time I used it, I opened the door and there was foam everywhere.'

Barbara shook her head. 'I keep telling her to not use the machines. Malcolm went to get his clothes out the other day, and he pulled out two forks, a broken plate and a wig. He thought next door's cat had somehow climbed inside.'

Grandma Bettie cackled impishly, 'He was getting a spade to bury the cat when he saw the real cat jump over the fence.'

Stephanie and Barbara laughed at the image of Malcom looking from the cat to the sopping wet ginger wig sat on the grass.

'He should have gone to Specsavers,' Grandma Bettie said and winked. 'Like in the advert.'

Stephanie couldn't stop laughing, she wiped back more tears to ask, 'Where did the wig come from?'

'It's mine,' Grandma Bettie answered. 'I bought it from Oxfam but it's a bit big so I thought if I washed it, it might shrink.'

'So, you put it in with the cutlery?'

'Oh, I don't remember…' Was all Bettie could say, her hands in the air.

Stephanie was beginning to feel much better as she sat in between her mum and grandma, and they settled down to watch TV. She suddenly thought about Lucas so she texted him so he wouldn't worry. 'Staying at mum and dad's this weekend.'

33

MAGDALENA

Monday, after work, Stephanie found herself leaving early yet didn't feel like going home. She texted Lucas to tell him that she was driving to Mabel's, she needed to get her casserole dish back anyway.

He texted back to say hello from him and ask if her camera was working ok, which Stephanie thought was sweet of him.

When Stephanie arrived at Mabel's house, she found her sat on a bench in her front garden stroking a dog. Now this was surprising, as for ages Mabel had been complaining about dogs in the village, particularly a certain dog leaving a mess on her drive. Stephanie walked towards her with a questioning smile on her face.

'Hello Mabel, I see you've made a friend.'

'Oh, its Stephanie, yes we have become pals I think.'

Stephanie sat on the bench and reached out to stroke the cute, brown Spaniel.

'Any idea where he's from?' Stephanie asked feeling for its collar.

'He lives next door. The little scamp has been escaping through the hedge and he's been going to the toilet on my drive. The mystery was solved after your young man, Lucas, set up the camera.' Mabel laughed.

Stephanie was going to correct her to say he wasn't *her* young man, when she remembered what Lucas had said.

'By the way, Lucas was asking about your camera, so it's still working then?'

'Yes, it's amazing. When I found out about Pippa here, I went next door to tell them. Now Ann next door pops round sometimes and brings Pippa with her. I thought she'd mended the gap in the hedge.'

'I came round to see how you are and to tell you about the investigation,' Stephanie said.

Mabel stood up. 'Let's go inside then, would you like a cup of tea?'

They left the Spaniel to find its way back through the hedge, then they went into the kitchen.

To Stephanie's surprise another lady was there cleaning the floor. She was short and plump with jet black hair tied up tightly into a bun.

'This is Magdalena, she cleans for me once a month, I don't know what I'd do without her.'

Stephanie said hello and said, 'I didn't know you worked for Mabel, how long have you been working here?'

Magdalena stood with the mop in her hands. 'Abouta threea years I think,' she said with an Italian accent.

Mabel agreed, 'I forgot to tell you about Magdalena. When the brooch went missing, she was a dear and helped me look for it.'

'I've a never seen it,' Magdalena said defensively, 'I don't a know what it looks like.'

'Didn't we give you the photo of you wearing it?' Stephanie reminded Mabel.

They walked into the front room and Mabel got out her photo album and took out the photograph for Magdalena to see. She stared at it for a long time and then said, 'I'ma sure I've a sin one just like it, but I can't rememba where.'

'If you remember, please give me a ring.'

Stephanie wrote down her number on a piece of paper and gave it to Magdalena.

'I'm sorry we don't have much to go on at the moment Mabel. We shall be talking to some more people tomorrow,' Stephanie said looking at her phone.

'Well, I'm very grateful that you're looking into it for me.'

Stephanie walked back into the kitchen with Mabel and watched her boil the kettle. Magdalena apologised once more as she squeezed past Stephanie in the tiny kitchen. She picked up a white plastic tub from the kitchen table which held an assortment of bottles, sprays and cloths, but the item which immediately caught Stephanie's eye was a rainbow-coloured feather duster lying on the table. Stephanie watched with interest as Magdalena picked it up and casually gave the table a dust as she walked out of the room, leaving a red feather behind which floated like an autumn leaf to the floor. Stephanie hardly heard Mabel talking to her as thoughts were rushing to her brain. Feathers in all the houses where things had gone missing, did this mean that Magdalena was the common factor in all of this? Could she be the thief?

Stephanie sat with Mabel at the table and sipped her tea, she had to be careful as Magdalena was only in the next room, so she asked as casually as she could, 'I was only thinking the other day about getting a cleaner, do you think Magdalena has time for another house?'

'I'm not sure, I know she cleans a few houses in the village so she might be fully booked. You could ask her.'

'Did she give you references when she started?'

'Yes, do you know Margaret Mason?'

'Is she the lady who was at the council meeting who lost her earrings?'

'Yes, that's the one, and Magdalena cleans for Mrs Grayling at the vicarage too. Oh Magdalena!' Mabel shouted, making Stephanie jump.

The tiny lady came rushing in to see what the matter was.

'There you are, Stephanie wants to know if you can clean her house.'

Stephanie looked up and opened her mouth, not sure what to say.

'Too busy, too busy,' Magdalena said shaking her head, 'I have a too much cleaning, sorry.'

'Er, I was really asking for Sylvia Smith. Do you know her?'

'Yes, yes, I clean for her. Such a biga house and she is so fussy, but…' Magdalena sighed dramatically and threw her arms up in a typically Italian way, 'she pays good.' Then she hurried out as if she had to be somewhere soon and didn't want to be late.

Stephanie stayed for a while longer and then thought about her casserole dish. She was going to ask for it back, but she decided it would be an excuse to return and visit Mabel again sometime.

ON THE WAY home she texted Lucas to tell him she was on her way home and was he going to meet up with the Mystery Club the next day.

'Of course, best club ever.'

Stephanie laughed, and she smiled as she couldn't wait to tell the group what she had just discovered.

34

SANDRA AND MIKE'S HOUSE

Stephanie was looking forward to the Mystery Club after school the next day. They'd planned to visit Sandra and Mike Davies about their missing watch. Rosie had spoken to them on the phone and this time she checked that the watch was still missing before they got there.

LUCAS HAD TEXTED Stephanie that he'd call for her on the way past and they walked up together. On the way, Stephanie told Lucas about Magdalena, they agreed that she was their best suspect so far.

'That explains the feathers then,' Lucas laughed.

'Yes, I think so. I must admit, there was a moment when I started to believe in the trained parrot theory because I couldn't think where the feathers had come from. Lisa's going to be disappointed.'

As they walked up Church Street, Stephanie kept an eye open for a blue car, the trouble was that nearly every car seemed to be blue that day. She felt safe with Lucas though and for a brief moment, when his arm brushed hers, she thought he was going to hold her hand. She stole a glance at him and told herself that he was her bodyguard and nothing else. He was there to do a job, and she should be thinking about her future life in London…

INSIDE SANDRA AND Mike's house, the Mystery Club gathered in the front room, Stephanie, Lucas, Ben and Angela were the only ones who could make it.

Stephanie looked at Sandra and Mike, they were a little younger than Stephanie so probably early twenties, their little boy was busy playing with his train track in the corner by the TV. He was a cute, chubby boy with neatly combed hair wearing blue, denim dungarees.

'That's Toby,' Mike said.

'Hello Toby,' they all said.

He looked up briefly, then continued to play with his train making choo-choo noises.

Stephanie smiled, 'He's so cute, he makes me almost want to have a baby.'

Sandra chuckled, 'He's not always this good, you should be here at bedtime.'

'Is it likely that he hid your watch?' Angela got to the point.

Mike shrugged, 'Anything is possible with Toby, he gets up to all sorts of mischief.'

Sandra nodded, 'Once I wheeled his pushchair outside to the car, and when I collapsed it, a pile of cutlery poured out onto the road. He must have emptied the whole drawer into the basket under his seat.'

Mike chuckled, 'He does like shiny things, but he's never moved the watch before. We've looked everywhere but we can't find it.'

'You have a lovely house,' Stephanie wandered about the room.

Sandra smiled, 'Thank you, I'm afraid it's a bit of a mess at the moment, we've only just got in.'

Stephanie gazed about, looking for a sign of a feather, a clue that Magdalena had been. 'I think it looks really tidy, if I had a child, they'd be toys everywhere.'

'To be honest, we do have a cleaner. It's a bit of a luxury but she's such a help.'

Stephanie couldn't believe her luck. 'Who is it? I was thinking of getting one myself.'

'Magdalena, I can give you her card if you like.'

Sandra walked across the carpeted room to open a drawer in the sideboard and passed Stephanie a small card.

'Bingo,' Stephanie thought and popped it into her handbag.

Ben turned to Mike, 'Tell us where you were when you last wore the watch?'

Mike walked to a coffee table next to an armchair by the French windows.

'I definitely remember taking it off and putting it on the table.'

'Yes, I remember him doing that,' Sandra agreed.

'Is it ok if Lucas and Ben look at your security and have a wander around the outside?'

'No problem, I'll go round with them If you like,' Mike led the way and the men walked off to leave the women to talk.

'Tell us about the watch, did you say it belongs to your husband?' Stephanie asked.

'Yeah, it was left to him by his grandad, he's so upset about it,' Sandra said.

'Do you have a photo of it?' Angela asked.

'I think so.'

She walked over to the bookshelf and then over to the windowsill and brought to them a framed photo.

'Will this do? You can see him wearing it.'

Stephanie and Angela looked at the family photo. The three of them looked so happy, Mike was carrying Toby and luckily, the watch could be clearly seen. It had a large round face with a gold strap.

'May I take a photo of this? I'll zoom in on the watch.' Angela reached into her bag to get her iPad.

'Be my guest,' said Sandra holding up the frame.

Stephanie looked at the watch, she was sure it looked like the watch she had seen in Gavin's bedside drawer. She couldn't remember the exact features, but it had a similar gold strap, the kind made up of separate links so the size can be adjusted.

'It looks expensive, is it insured?'

'We kept talking about getting it valued, we're not sure if it's worth anything. Do you think it is?'

Angela finished taking the photo, 'I'll do some research for you and let you know, then you can decide if you should tell the police. Do you have any idea how old it is?' Angela pressed record on her iPad.

'His grandad told him that he bought it with his first proper wage, I'm guessing in the 1950s.'

'When was the last time you remember him wearing it?' Stephanie asked.

'It was a couple of days after the Summer Fair, which we enjoyed by the way, loved your singing,' Sandra said this to Stephanie and that embarrassing memory came flooding back.

'Oh, gosh, that was a complete accident that I ended up singing. I only went on the stage to…' Stephanie noticed Angela giving her a funny look, 'Anyway…do you remember anyone noticing Mike's watch at the fair? Maybe they complimented him or asked for the time?'

'Not really, Mike might remember.'

'Did he wear it on Monday?'

Sandra thought about it. 'That Monday he had to catch a train to Leeds for a meeting, so he wore his watch that day.'

They paused and couldn't think of any more questions to ask so Angela stopped the recording and looked over at the men outside. 'Shall we go see if Mike and Lucas have finished?'

'I'll go see.' Sandra walked over to the French windows and opened them.

'I found out yesterday that Magdalena is the cleaner at all the houses we've been to,' Stephanie whispered to Angela when Sandra was out of earshot.

'Really? Shall we ask if they suspect her?'

'I don't want to make them suspect her in case it's not her.'

Stephanie turned to the men as they appeared in the room, 'Did you notice anything?'

Ben began talking and went through what might have happened. 'Mike took off his watch and left it on the table, there's a movement sensor in the front room.'

He pointed to the corner of the ceiling next to the French doors. 'Lucas says it is possible that it could have been taken with a long grabbing stick.'

Lucas nodded, 'The French doors open outwards and may not set off the alarm as there isn't a sensor on the doors. Shall we try it?'

They all stepped outside the patio doors, into the warm summer evening and closed them again. They waited while Mike turned on the alarm with his phone and Lucas slowly opened one of the doors - Silence.

'Let's use this stick I found, it might reach the table,' Lucas picked up a long branch slowly reaching the stick into the room and placing the end of it on the table, the alarm still wasn't triggered.

'I can't believe it,' Sandra said.

'We definitely should get door sensors,' Mike agreed. 'Thanks a lot for showing us that.'

Stephanie thought to herself, if it was Magdalena, why would she steal the watch from outside when she could take it easily from inside the house?

'Did you notice that the doors had been opened?'

'I don't think so, did you honey?' Mike looked towards his wife.

Sandra thought about it, 'I don't remember noticing the doors were unlocked.'

Toby toddled over to his mum, and she picked him up with a huff.

'Ooh, he's heavy. I think he'll probably be getting hungry.'

'We should go,' Ben suggested, and they all agreed.

As they walked down the side of the house towards the drive, Stephanie decided to mention Magdalena again. She took out her card and looked at it as she walked next to Sandra.

'I wonder what days she's available?' Stephanie said as if thinking out loud.

'I don't know, but she cleans our house every Tuesday morning,' Sandra answered.

'Thanks, I'll maybe ask her. Would you recommend her?'

'Yes, she does a good job and is usually punctual… except for today that is…'

'Was she late this morning?'

'She didn't turn up at all,' Sandra shrugged.

BACK IN THE street, Stephanie couldn't wait to tell them about Magdalena.

'The feather duster…that's why there were feathers in the other houses,' Ben laughed.

'Not from a trained parrot then,' Lucas added.

'Lisa will be disappointed,' Ben said.

'I wonder why Magdalena didn't turn up?' Angela spoke as she put away her iPad into her shoulder bag.

Stephanie shrugged, 'Maybe she's busy selling all the stolen goods… although, you'd think she'd be worried that the police would suspect her.'

'There's a reason for her fingerprints being in all the houses so I suppose it's difficult to prove she did it,' Ben shrugged.

'If word gets around, she'll lose her customers,' Stephanie bit her lip in thought. 'I don't think she's our thief you know.'

Ben replied, 'If she's been stealing expensive stuff, then she might not need a cleaning job anymore… We should go visit her and look around her house, but not tonight because I'm going out for a meal. Can we discuss it at the meeting?'

'Yeah, ok see you tomorrow.'

'Bye guys. Are you walking my way Ange?' Ben asked.

Angela nodded and they parted ways.

Stephanie reached into her pocket to pull out Magdalena's card and she looked at the address.

'Are you thinking of going to see her?' Lucas smiled.

'No time like the present… d'you wanna come?'

'Where you go, I go, remember?' Lucas laughed, 'Where does she live?'

35

MAGDALENA'S HOUSE

They stopped outside the fish and chip shop as Stephanie looked up the road.

'I think it's up there, opposite the Memorial Club.'

They turned the corner and walked up the road. Gentle music floated out the window of the clubhouse, and through the thin blinds, silhouettes of dancing figures waltzed and twirled.

'I bet my grandma's probably dancing in there tonight, she has more fun than me.'

'And visiting possible jewel thieves in the night isn't fun?'

Stephanie giggled, 'You've got to admit, it's not what most people would call a good night out.'

'Well, we're not most people.'

They stopped outside Magdalena's house, which was practically opposite the club, and gazed about for a sign that she was home. Down the side of the house, a light was on illuminating an open window, Lucas pointed to it, and they walked slowly up the drive to the front door.

'Have you got a plan?' Lucas whispered as they stood on the doorstep.

Stephanie chewed her lip and stared up at Lucas for inspiration.

'I could ask her if she could clean my house again, she said she was busy when I asked before but maybe she would do it for more money.'

Lucas nodded and he rang the doorbell. They waited but there was no answer.

'Maybe she's in the bathroom.'

Stephanie stepped back and looked up at the open window, listening out for the sound of running water from a shower or a bath. Down the dark driveway, a campervan was parked in front of the garage directly below the open window. Lucas followed Stephanie's gaze and put his hand on her shoulder.

'I know what you're thinking, and it's a bad idea.'

'But if we could get inside, we could…'

'Get arrested for breaking and entering, and possibly for stealing *everyone's* jewellery.'

'We wouldn't be breaking in if the window is wide open,' Stephanie whispered back as she quickly walked towards the window. 'If you could help me up onto this van, I can be in and out in no time.'

Lucas caught Stephanie up and they both stood looking up at the bathroom, the window was wide open, swinging freely.

'It's odd the way the window is open like that,' Stephanie squinted into the darkness that was gathering around them. 'Maybe we should try the front door, it might be unlocked.'

'I'll go see. Don't try to climb onto that van when I'm gone.'

Stephanie peered inside the van while Lucas disappeared around the front of the house. Stephanie reached into her back pocket for her phone and turned on the torch to get a better look.

The camper was quite cute Stephanie thought. It had curtains at the side windows, a small kitchen and a sofa that probably turned into a bed. It was tempting on these warm summer nights, Stephanie thought, to spend a weekend camping under the stars.

As she walked down the side of the van, her foot caught on something on the ground. Shining her phone downwards, Stephanie stepped back expecting it to be a bag but as she bent nearer, and reached out to touch it, she realised to her horror that it was hard, hairy and… she screamed as the hair parted revealing a ghostly face. It was Magdalena!

'Lucas!' Stephanie backed away so fast that she banged her back into the wall and tripped over her foot in her desperation to get away. Her hands and feet scrabbled in gravel as she attempted to get up until strong hands grasped her arms and pulled her up.

'What's wrong?'

Stephanie's breath came out in gasps, 'Magdalena, she's lying next to the van.'

Lucas took the phone from her hand and carefully walked over to the body with Stephanie close behind. Maybe it was a doll or a cat or something, Stephanie hoped. Unfortunately, it was a person who looked like Magdalena. Her legs were at an odd angle, half under the van. Lucas shone the torch around, illuminating blood smeared down the side of the van, the roof was dented as if something heavy had landed on it.

'Come on Stephanie, let's go back to the front of the house and call the police.'

IT WASN'T LONG before five police cars and an ambulance were parked outside. Blue lights flashed and lit up the buildings like a disco and people emerged from their houses to see the cause. The pensioners came out from the Memorial Club shielding their eyes and squinting to get a better look, and Stephanie saw her grandma was amongst the crowd.

'Oh no, that's my Grandma Bettie,' Stephanie groaned and tried to hide behind Lucas who was talking to PC Brown.

'Let's get this straight,' the policeman summed up with his notebook and pen in his hand. He was middle-aged and spoke like a stereotypical policeman. Stephanie was almost waiting for him to say, 'Hello hello.'

'You both came to the house to question Magdalena about the missing jewellery, saw the open window and then discovered her body.'

'Yes, we tried ringing the bell but there was no answer, I looked in the front room window but there was no sign of anyone,' Lucas added.

PCSO Manning appeared at their side. 'Hello again Stephanie, keeping us busy again I see.'

Stephanie grimaced at the sarcasm.

'We found out that she cleans for three of the people who have had their jewellery stolen,' Stephanie explained.

'And instead of contacting the police, you decided to pay her a visit?' PC Brown commented disapprovingly.

'Erm, well… I thought that…' Stephanie faltered.

'It's a good thing that we did come, otherwise, it would have been hours, maybe longer before her body was discovered,' Lucas pointed out.

Men in white overalls had begun to erect a tent over the driveway and a line of police were having trouble keeping people back. A few voices could be heard demanding to know what was going on and then a familiar voice piped up.

'That's my granddaughter over there, hey Stephanie, Stephanie it's me. Get your hands off me.'

Grandma Bettie was waving madly to get Stephanie's attention and at the mention of Stephanie's name, the other elderly people were buzzing with excitement.

'I bet there's been another murder.'

'It's the Angel of Death.'

'She tried to push me down the stairs.'

'Don't be ridiculous Alfred.'

'Who's turn is it this time?'

'She came to *my* house the other day.'

'I thought you weren't looking very well.'

Stephanie started to get annoyed at being called the Angel of Death and wanted to get out of there, thankfully the policewoman had the same idea.

'I think we'd better get you home Stephanie, did you drive?'

'No, we walked, can you drive us?'

PCSO Manning looked for approval from PC Brown and he nodded before adding. 'But don't go far.'

'This way.'

She opened the back door of the police car for Stephanie and Lucas to get in and the crowd of pensioners started to boo.

'Get off my granddaughter, she's innocent. What happened to innocent until proven guilty,' shouted Betty at the top of her voice.

Stephanie sighed and thought about her mum and dad finding out about it from her grandma, so she stopped and shouted across the road over the top of the police car, 'It's ok grandma, they're just taking us home, I'm not being arrested.'

Then for everyone else's benefit, 'and I'm not the Angel of Death by the way!'

Stephanie turned to PCSO Manning who was beginning to look concerned there was going to be a riot. 'Can we take my grandma home?'

PCSO Manning walked over to the officer who was trying to hold Bettie back, he looked relieved to let her go, and Bettie came trotting over to the car, opened the door and got in next to Lucas. Stephanie sighed and got in.

'I'll go with you to the police station, don't worry Stephanie I know a good lawyer, he's 86 though, but he still has all his marbles.'

'Grandma, you're not listening, there's nothing to worry about.'

'Put your seat belts on,' instructed PCSO Manning trying not to laugh as she started the engine.

As the car slowly pushed through the crowd of waving pensioners, Bettie waved back and showed the peace sign with her fingers through the window.

'Fascists.'

'Grandma, we're not being arrested. PCSO Manning is just taking us home.'

'She's taking you home? So, they don't think you killed someone? Did you find a body? What's going on?'

'We found Magdalena in the driveway, under her campervan.'

'Magdalena? The cleaner?'

Lucas leaned forward to give the policewoman directions while Stephanie talked to her grandma.

'Yes, did you know her?'

'She used to clean for a friend of mine, but she stopped because she got a better offer, that new big house that's been built.'

'Sylvia and Gavin Smith?' Stephanie asked.

'I think their name was Smith. In my day, people used to pretend to be called Smith if they were hiding something.'

Stephanie laughed, 'You might be on to something there.'

'What were you doing at Magdalena's? Do you think she's been stealing from people? Alma did lose things, she lost her wedding ring. I bet it was Magdalena.'

PCSO Manning looked at Bettie through the mirror as she drove. 'Now don't start spreading rumours, we don't know any facts yet,' she warned.

'Yes grandma, you mustn't say anything to anyone. We don't know what happened.'

'Maybe she killed herself because you were starting to investigate, and she thought she was going to get caught.'

Stephanie looked horrified at her grandma.

'Don't say such a thing, it wasn't because of me.'

'No, no dear, of course not.'

The police car pulled up outside Stephanie's house and PCSO Manning opened the doors for them to get out.

'Thanks a lot for taking us home.'

'The crowd were getting angry back there,' she laughed.

'They do like a rumpus,' Bettie nodded, 'some of them were at the protest against building that biochemical plant down the road you know. It still got built, but they had to wait for someone to break the concrete off George, and they wouldn't do it without a doctor present because of his pacemaker.'

She turned to the policewoman, 'Would you take me home too please my dear? With the shock of dead bodies and nearly getting arrested, I feel faint all of a sudden.'

She rolled her eyes and smiled, 'Get back in then.'

Grandma Bettie winked at Stephanie, grinned at Lucas as if noticing him for the first time, and then got back into the police car. Stephanie had a feeling that Bettie would be grilling her for information about Lucas later.

Lucas followed Stephanie into her house and watched as she put the kettle on.

'Are you ok?' he asked, noticing that she'd gone quiet.

'I think so… I don't know really.'

Stephanie reached into the fridge to get out some milk and opened the cupboard for two mugs.

She paused to ask, 'Do you ever get used to finding dead bodies?'

'Me personally, or people in general?'

'Have you seen many bodies?'

Then it was Lucas's turn to go quiet. Stephanie poured out the tea, stirred in the milk and they carried their drinks to the front room.

'The answer is, no you never get used to it, but you learn to distance yourself. Of course, if it's someone you were best buddies with then…' he sighed and drank his tea.

'I expect you have come across some scary things, being in the forces, where did you serve?'

'Afghanistan mainly, Libya, that general area.'

Stephanie put her hand gently on his which lay on his thigh. He held her hand for a minute then reached up and put his arm around her shoulders so she could lean against him. They sat, in silence for a while, sipping tea, and watching TV.

Stephanie was glad Lucas was there and she had the feeling that Lucas needed some comfort too.

36

A PLAN IS HATCHED

It was finally the last day of term. Lisa had spent that week pulling the displays off the walls and re-backing with clean paper ready for September. The children were so excited and happy to finally be able to choose any activity they wanted, which meant for most of them, playing on the laptops all day.

Towards the end of the day, Stephanie's desk was buried under presents, thank you cards, handmade cards and drawings. It had been a lovely class and she was going to miss them.

Home time came and she couldn't wait to put everything in her car and go to the Mystery Club that evening.

THE MYSTERY CLUB sat around the kitchen table, Bruce didn't bother getting out of his dog bed.

'Bruce looks tired,' Rosie said.

'We've just come back from a run,' Lucas explained.

Angela was the first person to speak about the police.

'I heard there were police cars up North Street last night round the corner from Mike and Sandra's, it wasn't anything to do with you was it, Stephanie?'

'Why do you think it has anything to do with me?'
Stephanie pretended to look hurt but then admitted, 'Ok, yes, it
was us, Lucas and me.'

After everyone stopped talking, Stephanie explained from
the beginning.

'After we left you, we decided to pay Magdalena a visit.'

'Hang on, I thought we were going together?' Ben grumbled.

'I know, I'm sorry. When we parted, I just couldn't wait.'

Angela said, 'It's a good job you did though.'

Ben agreed and announced dramatically, 'I need to update
the whiteboard.'

He walked over to the board, which was leaning on the
worktop, he added Magdalena's name with an arrow joining up
to all the people apart from the Smiths.

'You can join her up to the Smiths too. According to my
Grandma Bettie, she cleaned at their house as well.'

'But she didn't steal Sylvia's bracelet, it was down the seat of
the sofa,' Rosie interrupted.

'That's true,' said Ben sitting down.

There was a pause while they all thought, Ben tapped the
pen on the table. 'Go on then.'

Stephanie continued to tell them the details of
finding her body.

'We don't understand yet why Magdalena died,' Lucas said
looking at Stephanie.

'That's true. Did she commit suicide… or was she
murdered?'

Rosie looked shocked, 'Who would murder her and why?'

'Maybe someone who suspected her of stealing their stuff? If we could work it out then someone else could.' Ben picked out a crisp from a bowl in the middle of the table.

Rosie leaned forward. 'They could have gone inside to accuse her of stealing, then there was a fight.'

'In the bathroom?' Stephanie asked, thinking it seemed an unlikely place.

'Maybe she ran into the bathroom to lock herself in, but they forced open the door and then threw her out of the window.'

Rosie seemed happy with her version of events.

Lisa who was quietly sipping her wine, laughed, nearly spitting out her drink.

'So, do you think the murderer is Mabel, Margaret or Sandra or Mike? Or maybe it was Mr and Mrs Smith, even though she didn't steal from them.'

Rosie was rather put out, 'I don't know when you put it that way… it's a better theory than a trained parrot anyway.'

Stephanie backed up Lisa as she pointed out that the feathers were an important clue that led them to Magdalena's house in the first place.'

They all sighed and thought again. Lucas got up to open another bottle of wine.

'Maybe there's another person she has stolen from, who we don't know about.'

'How are we going to find that out?' Stephanie groaned.

'Maybe she didn't steal anything,' Angela said slowly, 'but she knew who had.'

'And the real thief murdered her!' Stephanie sat up straight, the hairs on her arms stood on end and she shivered. 'You know, that theory feels right to me. Magdalena was so popular in the village if she had taken anything, it would have ruined her reputation.'

'So, the question we should be asking is, what did she find out?'

'Tell us again Stephanie what happened when you met her at Mabel's.'

Stephanie thought back, 'She was cleaning in the kitchen and Mabel told me she had helped her look for her brooch. Magdalena said that she couldn't help much because she didn't know what it looked like, so…' Stephanie got more excited as she remembered, she felt it was important, 'Mabel got out the photograph Ben took of her wearing it.'

Ben smiled, 'So she didn't know what it looked like. Do you think she was telling the truth?'

Stephanie nodded. 'I think so because when she looked at the photo, she admitted that she'd seen it somewhere before. She said that she couldn't remember but…there was something in her expression. I'm sure she did remember.'

'So, who was it?' Lisa asked in frustration.

'Ooh, I've just remembered, would you like to see the video I took?' Angela asked.

'Video?' Stephanie asked, surprised.

Angela got out the iPad from her bag. 'I completely forgot that I'd taken it when we were at The Smith's. Rosie and Ben were being so enthusiastic about the house, that I don't think she noticed me videoing. I was looking through my photos last night when I saw it.'

'Ooh, let's see,' Stephanie said, and they all leaned in to look.

Sylvia was in the bedroom talking about the bracelet and how her husband had bought it for their anniversary. She sat on the bed and acted out taking the bracelet off and putting it on the side table, next to the photo frame.

Angela paused the video. 'And we all know that she lost it down the side of the settee.'

Rosie defended her, 'She probably thought she'd taken it off in the bedroom.'

The video continued and Angela could be heard asking her why she had worn such an expensive bracelet that night.

'We had just finished having a cocktail party, for a small group of old friends and I always like to look my best,' Sylvia smiled.

Rosie huffed so Angela paused the video again. 'He said they hadn't had a cocktail party for ages.'

'Either he's lying to not hurt your feelings Rosie, or she's lying,' Ben said.

'Why make it up though?' Stephanie said puzzled.

'Don't you think it's odd that Sylvia didn't seem surprised when Gavin found her bracelet? Lisa and I told her we'd found it when we were outside her bedroom, and she automatically assumed it was downstairs.'

'That's true, she did,' said Lisa, nodding.

'I think they were embarrassed when they realised it hadn't been stolen, so they carried on with the act of talking to us. They obviously didn't come up with a story that matched, did they?' Ben laughed.

'Did you see the size of their wardrobe? Did you get a look in there?'

'No, she didn't show us in there, she said it was just clothes.'

'That must be where she keeps her jewellery though, her dressing table didn't look like it had a drawer. Let me see the video again.'

They watched as the iPad scanned the bedroom.

'Why are you so interested in her jewellery?' Ben asked.

Stephanie shrugged, 'It's just the first thing Mabel did was show us where she keeps her jewellery. I don't know, there's something odd about them. They look like they're loaded with money, they live in this huge house and yet choose to build it in Hibaldton. It doesn't make sense to me. Also…I've just remembered that Gavin knew it was a cameo brooch. How did he know that?'

Lucas looked at Stephanie – and Stephanie stared back.

'The Smiths,' they shouted at the same time.

'What?' the others asked.

'Magdalena accused them of stealing it,' said Stephanie, her eyes wide.

'Oh, do you think Sylvia or Gavin could really murder someone?' Rosie said appalled.

'I've known people to murder for less,' Lucas said quietly.

'I bet poor Magdalena tried to blackmail them,' Ben suggested, 'I could just imagine Sylvia popping around for a visit and asking to use the toilet. He put on a posh accent and said, 'Oh Magdalena, I'm sorry I can't close your window, could you just lean out and do it yourself? I'll hold you so you don't fall.' Then… 'Oops, a daisy.''

They were all silent, Lucas got up to put out some biscuits.

'How are we going to prove it?' Stephanie eventually asked quickly grabbing a jammy dodger.

'Couldn't Lucas, our technical expert, put a bug in the house and we could listen in?' Ben suggested.

Lucas munched on a chocolate digestive.

'I could, but it's unlikely we'd catch them confessing. Plus, you can't break into someone's house and plant a listening device; it's frowned upon.'

'We need to catch them in the act,' Stephanie said, 'we need bait.'

'Good thinking,' Angela agreed, 'something they can't refuse.'

'What like an antique?' Rosie asked.

Lucas handed out the mugs of tea and said, 'Has anyone got any expensive jewellery?'

Everyone looked disappointed, then Stephanie said, 'My Grandma Bettie does have a ring. She's always told us it's worth a lot of money as it belonged to her grandmother.'

'What does it look like?' Angela asked.

'It's gold with a large ruby. I remember asking to see it when I was little. I'll ask if I can borrow it, but we need a good plan. She'd never forgive me if I lost it.'

37

GRANDMA'S RING

Stephanie stood in her parents' kitchen the next day. She made a pot of tea and carried it into the front room for her mum and Grandma Bettie.

'I'm glad you're here Stephanie,' Bettie said, 'you can take me back to Hibaldton when you go back. Can you drop me off at the Memorial Club?'

'No problem,' replied Stephanie. She had been thinking of how to get her grandma alone and this sounded like the perfect opportunity to discuss the ring. Stephanie didn't like keeping things from her family, but she knew they would be worried, and Grandma Bettie had always been more adventurous. She was hoping her grandma would be excited about the plan.

AN HOUR LATER, Stephanie was driving her grandma back to Hibaldton. She wasted no time filling her in on the jewellery thefts and what the group had uncovered. For once, Grandma Bettie listened intently without uttering a word apart from the occasional 'Ooh.' and 'Oh dear.'

Eventually, Stephanie reached the Memorial Club and parked the car. She turned in her seat to face her grandma.

'That's why we need your ring grandma, I promise you that I won't let anything happen to it.'

Grandma Bettie grinned from ear to ear and put her shaking hand on Stephanie's.

'My dear, I am so proud of my gutsy, brave granddaughter, who do you think you remind me of?'

'You?' Stephanie smiled, tears in her eyes.

Bettie patted her hand and nodded.

'Pick me up at 1 o'clock, and I'll get it for you.'

'Step 1- achieved,' she texted the group.

That afternoon, Stephanie sat in her front room, the ring looked breathtaking as she turned her hand this way and that to catch the light. The golden band hugged her centre finger. Twinkling diamonds peeped along the shoulder of the ring and encircled the centre stone, which was a single, perfect ruby.

It wasn't long before Lucas came round to see for himself.

'Wow,' Lucas gasped as he looked at the ring. 'If there was something to get the Smith's attention, that would be it. How much is it worth?'

'I'm not sure. Grandma told us that her mum got it valued at a jeweller about fifty years ago and it was £1,000 then. It's a Georgian ring apparently. Isn't it beautiful?' Stephanie whispered.

'We had better not lose this ring,' Lucas said slowly.

By 6 o'clock, the whole gang was there.

'Wow, I need to research this ring,' said Angela looking at her phone, 'Georgian did you say?'

278

'Where does your grandma keep it, Stephanie?' Rosie asked wide-eyed.

'I hope she has it insured, crikey Stephanie, I hope you know what you're doing,' Lisa warned.

'Geez, there's a ring like it on here and it's selling for wait for it… thirty-four thousand pounds.'

Stephanie started to feel faint.

'Really, that much? Let me have a look?' She grabbed Angela's phone. 'When this is over, we should get this valued and insured.'

'Where does your grandma keep it?' Ben asked intrigued.

'In her jewellery box next to her false teeth. Oh God, I remember now that I borrowed it one night when I was a teenager. Do you remember I wore it when I dressed up as Morticia from the Adams Family one Halloween?'

'That was this ring? Crap, it's a good job you didn't lose it,' Lisa said.

'Let's go over the plan again then,' said Lucas.

'This Saturday is the Garden Club show,' Angela said.

Rosie continued, 'I am on the committee, and will ask Sylvia if she would like to be a judge. Hopefully, she will say yes.'

'That will guarantee she sees the ring,' Ben nodded.

Lisa joined in nervously, 'She will judge the roses and I will wear the ring as I stand next to Martin…Are you sure Stephanie? I don't think you should trust me with it.'

'You will be fine Lisa. Here, try it on.'

Stephanie took off the ring and placed it on Lisa's finger.

'It's a little tight, but that's good so it won't fall off,' Lisa said feeling a bit better.

'Good. Then we will discuss the ring after the exhibition, in front of the Smiths, and you will ask me about getting it valued. I will say that I have a friend who works at the jeweller in Rigby, and you give it to me,' Stephanie said taking a deep breath.

'Don't forget Stephanie to say you'll take it on Monday morning so if she's going to steal it, it will be this weekend.'

'Lucas and I will be waiting. What an Earth can go wrong?'

Stephanie looked around the group, but no one looked convinced.

'The worst thing that can happen is she doesn't take the bait,' Ben said. 'We have nothing to lose.'

38

GARDEN SHOW

Stephanie got ready early for the Garden show. She wore her jeans and her blouse that had little roses on. She also had daisy earrings that she thought she might as well wear. Stephanie looked in the mirror. 'This is going to work. We are going to catch the Smiths in the act and get Mabel's brooch back. And not lose grandma's ring,' she added to her reflection before moving away.

'Can we drive there?' she texted Lucas. 'I haven't had breakfast yet.'

'Pancakes?' Lucas answered.

Stephanie replied with a hungry face emoji and grabbed her things as quickly as she could.

When she was ready, she walked across the road and tried his front door, it was unlocked so she walked into the most delicious smell… coffee and pancakes.

Lucas grinned as he put them on the table.

'Did you plan this?' Stephanie asked putting a piece of pancake into her mouth hungrily.

'I think I know you quite well now, well your stomach anyway,' Lucas laughed.

'What else can you cook?' Stephanie asked as she sat down and chose which topping to use.

Lucas joined her.

'Pancakes, buns, biscuits,' he laughed. 'I used to bake with my gran.'

Stephanie looked surprised and drank her coffee. Every time he told her something about himself, it surprised her. There were so many things she was interested to know but now wasn't the time. They had a show to go to.

THE VILLAGE COMMITTEE and Parish Council were there getting everything ready. The main room was full of tables covered in crisp white tablecloths. People had started to enter with their garden produce and were positioning them for display. One side of the room was for vegetables and the other for flowers.

Stephanie had the job of organising the judges, so she nervously waited for them to arrive to tell them where they would be meeting.

Lucas was helping to put out tables and chairs in the next room for refreshments.

In walked Mabel Moor, she was a judge every year and knew where to go.

'Hello Mabel,' Stephanie smiled. 'How are you?'

'A bit shaky after hearing about Magdalena but Ann next door says she thinks she knows a nice lady who can help me out once a month.'

'That's good news.'

Stephanie greeted the next groups of people then finally Sylvia and Gavin arrived. Stephanie was impressed with the effort they had gone to, they looked like they were dressed for the Chelsea Flower Show. In fact, Sylvia's hat barely fitted through the narrow door.

'You look amazing,' Stephanie said with a fake smile.

It was true though. Gavin was wearing an off-white suit with a carnation on the lapel. Sylvia had a floaty dress in different shades of green with a low neckline which stopped at a pink rose brooch.

'I love your brooch,' Stephanie finished.

'Thank you, my dear, it's Harry Winston,' Sylvia purred. 'Where would you like me?'

'Please go through to the room on the left, where Rosie will explain what you will be doing.'

They walked into the building and Stephanie breathed a sigh of relief and wondered who Harry Winston was.

'Step 2 accomplished,' she thought.

Lisa and Martin arrived looking flustered. Martin was busy spraying his roses and went through to get them out of the sun as quickly as possible. Lisa leaned close to Stephanie with panic in her voice.

'I can't get it off.'

Stephanie looked at her hand and the ring was there, but her finger did look a little swollen.

'I slept with it on my hand, I was so scared to lose it, and I think my fingers swelled up in the night. It was so hot.'

'Have you tried putting your hand in cold water?' Stephanie suggested.

Lisa lifted a bag of ice.

'I just bought this from the shop.'

All the judges had arrived, so Stephanie went with Lisa into the kitchen to look at the ring. Ben soon joined them.

'What an Earth are you to up to?' he whispered.

Stephanie was putting water into the washing-up bowl and she was just about to pour in the ice.

'Lisa's fingers have swollen, and she can't get the ring off,' Stephanie whispered back.

'Have you tried butter?' Ben asked.

'Yes, it was the first thing I tried, well after soap then lube,' Lisa hissed.

'Lube?' Stephanie and Ben said together.

'I was in the bedroom, I just used what I could find.'

'How about lotion, hand cream, massage oil…'

'Okay Ben, stop listing products and help,' Stephanie said.

'I suppose it is slippery but normally it's for getting into tight things, not out of.'

'Ben!'

Lisa stood with her hand in the water complaining that it was going numb. Stephanie tried to twist the ring around while Ben looked on.

There was a cough behind them, Ben turned around, elbowing Stephanie in the ribs and tried to shield them as Stephanie's mum stood there.

'*Mrs Rhodes*, what can I do for you?' Ben said loudly.

'I was just wondering where Stephanie was,' she said. 'Can I help?'

'Mum? I didn't know you were coming,' Stephanie said.

'Just washing up, the plates were a bit dusty,' Ben said.

Stephanie looked up and grabbed a plate holding it for her mum to see and then lifted the washing up bottle. Flashing a toothy grin, she proceeded to squirt the green liquid into the water.

Lisa put the plate on the draining board, green soap sliding down it.

'Everything's taken care of,' Ben told Barbara. 'You are always helping out, go and enjoy the show. Have you seen the roses?'

Ben walked Barbara away back into the main room.

'Got it,' Stephanie said and held the soapy ring in her hand.

'Don't drop it,' Lisa said and started to rub her hand.

'Has the swelling gone down?' Stephanie asked.

'I think so, give me the ring.'

She pushed it carefully onto her finger on her other hand.

'I'll be fine, it's not for long anyway. Come on let's go see how Martin is getting on.'

'Don't let my mum see the ring,' Stephanie warned.

They wandered into the exhibition area and over to Martin who was inspecting the other roses.

'There's a torn petal there, and that one has a pale colour don't you think?' he asked Lisa.

Lisa nodded, 'I think yours are the best.'

'You're not just saying that?'

'No really, what do you think Stephanie?'

'Yours are definitely the best,' Stephanie nodded.

'Which ones are mine?' Martin asked with raised eyebrows.

Stephanie looked at the roses. There were eight vases, she tried to remember the colour of Martin's roses when he came in. Her eyes narrowed in concentration, they were yellow she was sure of it. There was only one yellow display. She looked at Lisa and Lisa's eyes were signalling right and up. Stephanie pointed confidently to the yellow flowers.

'Those are absolutely the best by far.'

Martin looked suspicious, and then smiled, 'Thank you, I think so too.'

Stephanie and Lisa breathed a sigh of relief, but it was short-lived as Sylvia floated up to them.

'These roses are beautiful,' she announced to everyone standing around the table.

She looked at her clipboard and began ticking off the list of things she was looking for. As her attention moved from one display to another, Stephanie and Lisa waited for their turn to talk to the judge.

Stephanie could see Lisa was sweating, she looked at her hand and hoped the ring didn't slip off.

Finally, Sylvia turned to them.

'And whose gorgeous roses are these?'

Before Lisa could say anything, Martin put his hand up.

'Guilty as charged,' he said with a nervous chuckle.

Sylvia looked Martin up and down and turned on her charm.

Lisa and Stephanie watched in amazement as Martin blushed as he explained how he grew his roses to perfection. Lisa's eyebrow lifted when Sylvia asked him if he would help her with her rose garden.

'We would love to help you, wouldn't we darling.'

Lisa wrapped her arms possessively around his shoulders and flashed the ring in front of her face.

Stephanie saw Sylvia's eyes focus on the ruby and her pupils grew wide.

'Gotcha,' Stephanie thought to herself. 'Step 3.'

THEY STOOD IN the field waiting for their category to be announced. The judges sat on chairs and each one took it in turns to approach the microphone. Soon it was Sylvia's turn to announce the winner of the rose category.

'And first place goes to… Martin Croft for his gorgeously perfect, yellow Golden Celebration Rose.'

Everyone clapped and Martin walked up to receive his prize. Lisa looked so proud of him and gave him a big hug when he returned. He had won a gift voucher for the garden centre for one hundred pounds.

Lisa, Stephanie and Martin stayed together and waited for Sylvia to approach. Unfortunately, Stephanie saw her mum and grandma walking over.

'Oh no, mum's coming, she'll see the ring,' Stephanie said.

Stephanie watched her mum stop to talk to someone and caught her grandma's eye. Stephanie held Lisa's hand up so Grandma Bettie could see the ring, and then she shook her head and hands vigorously, hoping her grandma would understand.

Just then, Gavin and Sylvia came over to congratulate Martin once more.

'By the way, your ring is exquisite,' she said. 'May I?'

She held out her hand for Lisa to show her.

Stephanie tore her eyes from Sylvia to check where her mum was, if she saw the ring then it was all over. To her relief, Stephanie was in time to see her grandma clutching her chest, staggering about. Barbara looked shocked and was holding her up by her armpits. They were still quite far away across the field, Stephanie turned back to concentrate on the ring.

'Come on Sylvia dear, we must go,' Gavin said.

'I was just wondering, where did you find this beauty?'

Lisa said casually, 'It was passed down to me by my grandmother and before that, it belonged to her grandmother. It's Georgian by the way.'

Lisa deserved an award for her acting skills.

Stephanie looked back towards her grandma to see her mum fanning her with a leaflet, people had started to gather around, and someone was carrying out a chair.

Lisa took her hand from Sylvia's grasp and turned to Stephanie as if forgetting that Sylvia and Gavin were there.

'Stephanie, do you think your friend will be able to value it for me?'

'Yes, as we discussed, if you give it to me now, I'll take it Monday morning. It could be a few days though.'

'Oh, but I haven't got my ring box, what's your address again?'

Stephanie told her address and Lisa promised to pop by later that day. When Stephanie looked up, the Smiths were walking away.

'Did she hear my address?' Stephanie asked.

Martin nodded, 'Yes I noticed she looked interested.'

'One more step to go. Well done, Lisa, you did great.' Stephanie gave her a giant hug.

Over Lisa's shoulder, Stephanie watched Grandma Bettie as someone brought her a glass of water, she was starting to worry that her grandma might not have been acting.

'Quick, give me back the ring.'

Stephanie put it in her ring box, in her bag then she rushed over to her mum and grandma.

'Grandma, are you all right?' Stephanie asked loudly.

When Grandma Bettie saw Stephanie, she miraculously improved.

'Much better now, thank you that water was just what I needed,' Bettie said returning the glass to the young lady.

Bettie winked at Stephanie and then turned to Barbara, 'Can you take me home?'

Stephanie was impressed. Her grandma never ceased to amaze her.

39

TO CATCH A THIEF

That night, Stephanie sat on her bed and watched Lucas. He reached up to fix a camera in the corner of the bedroom, his T-shirt rose to reveal his rock-hard, back. She realised she was staring and thinking how she would love to press up against him and stroke her hands around his back until they would settle on his stomach and…then she realised he was looking at her.

'Everything ok?' Lucas asked as he finished fitting the camera.

'What do you mean?'

'Are you nervous?'

'Of course, I am,' she confessed, but secretly more scared about spending the night with Lucas than with a cat- burglar.

Lucas sat on the end of the bed to see the camera footage.

'When this is all over, we can go to the beach and relax.'

'You know, I'm not much of a sun worshipper, but the thought of lying on the beach and doing nothing all day sounds like heaven.'

Lucas seemed happy with the camera angle. He walked to the window and ducking down, he placed something on the windowsill.

'What's that?' Stephanie asked.

'Microphone,' Lucas replied, 'it's very sensitive so it should pick up everything.'

'Hopefully, I can get her or him to confess. Hang on…what if it isn't Mr or Mrs Smith? What if they hire someone else to do their dirty work?'

Stephanie suddenly felt panic rising inside her. The Smiths didn't seem that scary to her, she felt like she could handle them, she hadn't considered someone else.

'Don't worry, I'm here, remember.'

Lucas sat next to Stephanie and looked at her seriously.

'Are you sure you want to be here? I can handle this on my own.'

'No chance. If the thief believes he can escape, he'll tell me everything- that's what happened before.'

Stephanie remembered the last time someone confessed to a murder, it was a memory she'd rather forget.

'All right, you win. When they come, I'll hide in the ensuite,' Lucas said.

'Should we have a safe word?' Stephanie suddenly thought.

Lucas grinned, 'Shouldn't we discuss that after all this is over?'

Stephanie looked blank then felt herself go red, 'Not that kind of safe word, a signal and you know it.'

Lucas chuckled, 'Just shout Lucas, let's not make it complicated.'

They looked at each other, Stephanie bit her lip and noticed Lucas's eyes look at her mouth. He lifted his hand to her face, and ever so gently brushed his thumb across her bottom lip.

'Don't worry Stephanie, I won't let anything happen to you.'

Stephanie felt hot and bothered. God Lucas was so gorgeous and sexy and sitting so close… she had to focus on the task ahead. She sprang up off the bed.

'Right, I'll close all the curtains, so no one knows you're here, we'll bring up some snacks and then I guess it's a waiting game.'

Lucas nodded. The window was open, warm air drifted in from the empty street below as Stephanie leaned out to breathe in some fresh air. There was no sign of anyone in the street, music floated across the road from someone's garden but apart from that there was silence. She closed the curtains and made sure the jewellery box was far enough from the window, so the burglar would have to climb into the bedroom to get to it. Lucas then followed Stephanie downstairs and waited for the curtains to be closed before joining her in the kitchen.

'Be calm Stephanie, if they come tonight, it won't be 'til the early hours when they're sure no one's around.'

'My head knows that but tell it to my blood pressure.'

Lucas picked up a tray and started to look in her cupboards.

'Let's stock up on lots of sugar, what goodies have you got hidden away?'

'Oh, you're in for a treat,' Stephanie said and soon there was a heap of junk food to take upstairs. They walked upstairs, Stephanie holding a big bottle of pop, water and glasses followed by Lucas carrying the tray of food.

'This feels like a girl's sleepover,' Stephanie giggled.

'Please tell me we get to have a pillow fight,' Lucas said behind her.

Stephanie put the drinks on the floor next to the bed.

'Not this time, this is a serious stakeout,' she stared at him firmly.

Lucas put the tray on the bed and returned the serious look.

'Not this time? So, we can do it next time then?'

Stephanie shook her head, she couldn't help but return the tease.

She sighed, 'I should get ready for bed. It will look suspicious if I'm dressed.'

'Uhuh,' Lucas looked over to the tray and started to move the bags about to look for something to eat, Stephanie wondered if he was feeling a bit nervous himself.

She grabbed a T-shirt and shorts from a drawer and slipped into the ensuite to get changed. She suddenly felt giddy, it was the first time they had spent this long together, alone, and she had to admit it felt good. Hesitating, hand on the door handle, she took a deep, calming breath and willed herself to act normal. She reminded herself that this wasn't a romantic evening, it was a stakeout and a possibly dangerous situation. This wasn't the time to feel flirtatious, although his aftershave did smell delicious. Anyway, she had to remember that he was being paid to be there- by her boyfriend nonetheless…maybe ex-boyfriend… she was so confused right now, she'd been so busy lately, she hadn't had time to think about Mark. For a moment, the thought of Mark made her heart lurch but then she remembered how little he seemed to be missing her.

'Get a grip,' she whispered to herself opening the door.

She walked around to the foot of the bed, leaned over the tray, and chose a pack of popcorn before walking around to the window side of the double bed.

'Pour me a drink will you?' she asked as casually as she could.

'Water or cola?'

He leaned over to get the bottle from the floor.

'Water please.'

Lucas passed her a glass of water and filled one for himself. They were quiet for a while as Stephanie found something to watch on the TV.

'Indiana Jones?' she suggested.

'Uhuh, is there Temple of Doom? That's my favourite.'

'That's mine too,' said Stephanie searching the TV.

'I love the bit when Indiana Jones is facing the Arab with the big knife,' Lucas said.

Stephanie laughed, 'And Indi gets out his gun and just shoots him.'

They both settled down to watch the film. Lucas was as focused as a soldier on night watch Stephanie noticed. He sat stiffly, alert and was careful not to let their bodies touch.

At the start of the film, when Indiana Jones broke through a giant spider's web, Stephanie laughed. 'How big must that spider be?'

'Urgh, I hate spiders,' Lucas said.

Then they both reached out to each other in horror when dozens of small, creepy tarantulas covered a man's back and Indiana brushed them off with his whip. Lucas shivered dramatically in disgust and Stephanie laughed in surprise and changed position, so she was sitting with one leg folded under her.

'I didn't think you were scared of anything muscle man.'

'*I* never said I wasn't scared of anything.'

'So, if I were trapped in a cave and you came to my rescue but had to walk through a nest full of spiders, what would you do?'

'Oh, I'd definitely… decide that you are a resourceful young lady who can look after herself… and then run.'

Stephanie hit him with a pillow and continued to watch the film pretending to be annoyed, and then they both laughed out loud when the huge boulder appeared to chase after Indiana Jones out of the cave.

Stephanie offered popcorn to Lucas who took some, they sat munching as they watched the film and Stephanie noticed they were sitting closer to each other on top of the bed, shoulders touching. Now and then she sneaked a sideways look at him and was glad that she wasn't alone on her adventure this time. She glanced at the bedside clock which read 21:12, she wondered if she were a burglar, what time would she choose to enter a house? Her hand moved into the bag, not realising Lucas's hand was already in there, and as their hands touched, a shiver trembled up her arm. They both quickly pulled their hands out and continued to watch the film.

At the end of the film, Lucas turned and said, 'You do realise that Indiana Jones did not affect the outcome of the film, don't you?'

'What d'you mean?'

'The Nazis would have found the Arc of the Covenant without his help, and they would have still died when they opened it.'

'I suppose so, but if Indy hadn't been there, then the Arc wouldn't have been put where no one could find it.'

'Apart from the US government and that's worrying.'

Stephanie yawned, 'Actually now you mention it, if it weren't for Indiana Jones, they might not have discovered it at all.'

Stephanie yawned again, tiredness was taking over, and it wasn't long before she closed her eyes to listen to the TV and then fell asleep almost sitting up, her head leaning on Lucas's chest. He had carefully put his arm around her to make it more comfortable and was watching TV quietly when his phone alerted him to movement. He looked and saw it was 2:35 am and movement was at the front of the house.

He watched a dark figure walk to the side gate and then reappear in the back garden. It appeared to be searching in all the places cameras or sensors would normally be. Of course, Lucas had been careful not to put his in the usual places. The slim, hooded figure retraced its steps back to the front. It wasn't the preferred place, but the easiest to execute- the thief could see the window was open.

Lucas gave Stephanie a gentle shake.

'W…what?' Stephanie said sleepily.

'Step 4, action time,' he said.

Stephanie sat up, wide awake.

'Lie down and I'll get ready.'

Lucas slid off the bed and quietly crept into the ensuite, leaving the door open slightly.

Stephanie pulled the covers up to her chin and tried to steady her breathing. She heard a slight movement on the roof below her window.

The only reason she knew the window was opening, was that the breeze was a little stronger on her face. A chink of light fed into the dark bedroom as the curtain was slowly peeled back.

Stephanie breathed slowly and steadily, mimicking what she thought was the sound of her asleep. Of course, she didn't know what she sounded like asleep, she threw in a snort for good measure.

She thought she'd blown it when the figure froze, but then cautiously stretched with one fluid movement and lightly stepped onto the carpet.

'Was this person human?' Stephanie thought it made hardly any sound at all, like a ghost. Stephanie peeped over the covers, her heart felt like it was beating hard enough for the intruder to hear. Stephanie waited, it was so difficult, but she had to wait, wait until she heard the click of her jewellery box open.

When the music started playing, Stephanie leapt out of bed, turned the light on and stood in between the cat burglar and the window.

Stephanie was expecting the figure to pounce with claws out, or flee to the door, but instead, an arm pulled down the hood and Sylvia shook out her hair with a sly smile.

'She is a cool cat,' Stephanie thought.

Sylvia looked around, at Stephanie and then at the box with the revolving ballerina.

'Swan Lake, a favourite of mine, how appropriate.'

Then she traced her fingers over the rings, then stopped-her face, this time was murderous.

'Where is the ruby ring?'

Her voice was like ice.

'Sorry to disappoint Mrs Smith… if that's your real name.'

Sylvia laughed and it sounded so shrill it made Stephanie jump.

'Of course, it's not my real name. Do you think I'd allow myself to be named Smith?'

'Well…technically that's what you did,' Stephanie began until Sylvia took a step forward.

Stephanie stood her ground and said confidently, 'Tell me where Mabel's brooch is, you thief.'

'Thief? I'm not a petty criminal, what I do darling is an art form. Weren't you impressed how I got in without you noticing?'

'You are very agile, for your age, I must admit.'

Sylvia's eyes narrowed dangerously. 'How dare you. I have studied ballet and acrobatics with the best!'

'Where is Mabel's brooch?'

Stephanie needed a confession. Lucas was messaging the gang right now, she needed proof.

'You don't believe that catching me is going to get your friend's brooch back, do you?' she purred.

'Because you've sold it already?'

'It so happens I collect beautiful works of art, so no. It's been added to my collection and there's nothing you can do to prove it.'

'And I suppose that's what you said to Magdalena?'

At the mention of Magdalena's name, Sylvia's demeanour changed. The playful panther became a hunter. Suddenly Stephanie noticed a glint of a steel knife as Sylvia crouched, ready to pounce. Stephanie leant backwards against the windowsill. She could feel the night air behind her, she wanted to shout for Lucas, but she hadn't had the confession she needed. All this time, the tinkly music was still playing, it had now changed to "You Are My Sunshine".

'So that's how you killed her, with a knife?' Stephanie whispered.

'You're an inquisitive thing, aren't you?'

Then she laughed, so sure of herself.

'All I did was corner her against the window. She even leant out, wondering if she could escape…It was convenient that the van was there to break her… neck. Maybe I did give her a *little* push.'

Her laugh sent Stephanie's blood cold.

'Why did you kill her? Did she try to blackmail you?'

'Of course, she did. Is that what you want? Money?'

'You could have given her some, you have plenty of it, what's a few thousand pounds to you?'

Sylvia was so close now that Stephanie could see the streetlight reflected in her eyes.

Sylvia whispered in Stephanie's ear, 'But that's the problem with blackmailers, they never stop -- until you stop them.'

Stephanie put her hand on the sill to feel for an object, she was sure there was a glass paperweight somewhere.

'One push and it will be over Stephanie, just like Magdalena.'

Suddenly Stephanie felt her legs being lifted in the air. Stephanie spread her arms across the windowsill and screamed, 'Lucas!'

Her legs wrapped around Sylvia's shoulders pushing her back.

Stephanie's bottom was now on the windowsill, her back, half out of the window. Stephanie pushed against the window frame with her right hand and held Sylvia's hand, which held the knife, in her other. This hell cat was stronger than she looked, their arms trembled as they pushed against each other.

To Stephanie's relief, Lucas appeared taking hold of Sylvia's hand, he bent it behind her back and the knife dropped to the carpet. Stephanie seized the chance to climb off the windowsill with shaky legs as Lucas attempted to get hold of Sylvia's other arm.

Without warning, Sylvia ran up the wall and flipped in the air, flying over the top of Lucas's back to the tune of "We'll Meet Again". Before he could react, she kicked him in the back of his knee causing him to collapse onto the floor, and when Stephanie lent over, Sylvia used her as a springboard to escape out of the window, knocking Stephanie over onto Lucas.

They both scrambled to their feet and looked out of the window in time to see the black shape of Sylvia run across the front garden. Sylvia stopped on the path, she threw back her head and laughed at them confidently. With one swift movement, she darted into the road.

SMACK!

A small dark car hit her as it screeched to a halt, sending her bouncing over its roof, onto the boot and she landed in a rose bush in the garden opposite, feet in the air.

Stephanie and Lucas looked at each other and then raced downstairs, out into the dimly lit street.

They arrived on the road to see the passenger door of the car open and out jumped Angela, ready for action.

Angela swung her arm and an extendable baton sprung out with a dramatic "SHLICK!" as she turned around. She stood poised, knees bent with her baton in the air and shouted, 'Come on then!'

'Is that a stab vest your wearing?" Stephanie gasped.

'Always be prepared. Did we get one of them? Where are they?'

They looked over towards the rose bush where a pair of legs were still sticking up in the air, Lucas ran over to check on Sylvia.

'What's going on out there?' one of the neighbours shouted from his bedroom window.

'It's ok Richard, the police are on their way,' Stephanie called. 'I hope,' she added quietly.

Ben poked his head out of the car window. His face looked green. 'Is it safe to come out?'

'I think so Ben,' said Stephanie as she walked over to open his door.

As Ben stepped out, Stephanie roared with laughter.

'What are you wearing?'

She looked him up and down, taking in his lilac, silk pyjamas and fluffy slippers.

'I know I look an idiot, but I didn't want Simon to know what I was doing so I had to pretend it was a normal night.'

'You look like that every night?'

Angela rolled her eyes. 'As soon as we got the signal, Ben raced over to pick me up. We had a different idea of what to wear.'

'Have you got something on your face?'

Stephanie reached out to touch his cheek. Ben leant away from her and said, 'It's an avocado face pack. To be honest, I didn't think our thief would show up. I decided to put on the face pack because I was trying to stay awake. Did I hit something?'

'You just caught the thief.'

'What? Is that what I hit? I didn't see anything.'

'Yes, it was Sylvia dressed like a cat burglar. Don't worry, she's alive. Look.'

301

Three police cars appeared as Lucas led a dazed Sylvia into the road and he handed her over to the police. It wasn't long before Lisa and Rosie appeared and soon the neighbours were coming out to see what was going on.

THE MYSTERY CLUB stood talking to PC Brown as he looked at the evidence in his hands- a hard drive with video footage and a knife in a plastic bag.

'Are there police at her house? Her husband might be hiding the evidence?' Stephanie asked desperately.

She didn't want to have gone through all of this to lose Mabel's precious brooch or the other jewellery.

'Yes, don't worry, her husband is being questioned right now. You know, when you rang me and told me your plan, I was dead against it. However, it does seem to have worked and I must admit I am impressed. But don't tell anyone I said that -- and don't make a habit of this, by the way.'

Eventually, Stephanie and Lucas watched the police cars drive away and waved goodbye to Lisa, Ben and Angela.

Stephanie felt such relief, she looked at Lucas and they both stood and stared at each other for a while, their grins getting wider and wider. Stephanie jumped up and down with her hands on his shoulders.

'We did it, we did it, I can't believe it,' Stephanie cried and laughed.

Lucas swung her around and laughed.

'You were incredible. I desperately wanted to jump out, I was watching on my phone and when she turned on you -- I don't know how I stopped myself. But how you got her to confess to the murder was pure genius.'

Stephanie laughed, 'I'm an expert at getting confessions, I'm a teacher remember.'

Lucas laughed and lifted Stephanie and let her down again. Then they kissed.

Stephanie broke away, breathing hard. What were they doing?

Lucas looked at Stephanie with panic in his eyes and let go of Stephanie's waist.

He took a deep breath and said quickly, 'I'll go take down the cameras.'

Stephanie stood, in shock on the driveway, lips still tingling from the passionate, impulsive embrace, but did it mean anything?

Quickly, she walked upstairs to find him dismantling the camera from the corner of the ceiling, her breathing was so fast and unsteady that she had difficulty speaking.

'That was easier than I thought it would be,' she finally said walking into the bedroom.

Lucas walked around, collecting wires and equipment. 'You think it was easy to escape from being stabbed and thrown out of a window?' he laughed and stopped to put his hand through his hair. Shaking his head, he looked at Stephanie for a minute then gathered everything up in his arms and strode towards the door.

'Are you going?' she asked, stunned. Was he just going to leave her after they had just kissed without talking about it?

In the doorway, Luca turned to say, 'I shouldn't have let it happen, it's all my fault.'

Stephanie's eyes narrowed, 'What do you mean it's your fault? I make my own decisions you know, and I wanted it to happen.'

'But… it was reckless and stupid. I need to take these back before I drop them and… I should let Bruce out.'

Stephanie followed him out and watched him run downstairs. She stood, anger rising in her chest.

'You think it's reckless and stupid to kiss me? What, are you afraid you won't get paid? Worried you'll lose your job because don't worry, you can leave…I don't need you anyway.'

She turned with a huff and stormed back into the bedroom, her face burning and tears threatening to form. How could he act so caring and then be so cold and mean?

A noise on the stairs made her turn and Lucas burst through the door.

'I wasn't talking about us kissing, I was talking about putting you in danger.'

He held her shoulders in a tight grip until she looked him in the face a tear spilt down her cheek.

'Kissing you is something I've wanted to do since I met you, and…' he brushed the tear from her cheek, 'I've been trying so hard to not show it… and when you pulled away, I thought you regretted it.'

'No, I loved it.'

'Really?'

'Really.'

'What about Mark?'

Stephanie paused, not knowing what to say.

Lucas replied for her, 'I don't think we should do this now. I'm supposed to be looking after you, my sister will kill me and so will Mark probably. We've become close friends and I care about you. Do you understand? I want you to be sure that it's me you want.'

Stephanie nodded, she knew that her body wanted him right then and there even more. He looked so worried that he'd upset her.

'My ego is a little bruised, I don't usually jump on men when they enter my bedroom you know.'

Lucas raised his eyebrows in the dim light.

'Not that men enter my bedroom frequently, you know what I mean.'

Lucas laughed softly, 'Look, it's taking all my willpower to be good, so we'd better stop talking and I think I should go. I'll see you tomorrow?'

He slowly let go and backed towards the door again.

'I'll ring you in the morning?'

Stephanie listened to him running downstairs and she heard the front door close and lock behind him.

'How did he even get a key to her house?' Stephanie thought and then shrugged with a smile.

40

GOOSE, GOOSE, GOOSE, GUN

Late morning, Stephanie awoke to find her phone buzzing, she answered it to hear Lucas's voice.

'Good morning.'

'Good morning, what time is it? Oh heck, it's 11:15 and Sunday. My parents. I need to call them and tell them I'm not going for Sunday Lunch.'

'You can still go,' Lucas said.

'I'd rather we did something together, like go to the beach. I feel like I need to do something after everything that's happened. Can you believe that we caught Sylvia last night?'

'This morning you mean.' Lucas laughed, 'The beach sounds perfect, we'll take Bruce, he'll love it. How about I go and let you get ready, and I'll pick you up in an hour?'

AFTER RINGING HER mum and jumping in the shower, Stephanie quickly pulled on a pair of shorts and a T-shirt. She brushed her hair and decided to tie it back into a tight ponytail in case it was breezy on the coast. She looked in the mirror and decided that she didn't need any makeup, the sun had brought out a healthy glow to her skin along with a few cute freckles. She smiled as she dabbed a little sun cream onto her cheekbones and nose, she felt so alive after the previous night, and she wasn't quite sure if it was catching the crazy Smiths or spending the night with Lucas that had her pulse racing.

Suddenly she thought of Lisa and the others, how were they feeling this morning?

Stephanie quickly grabbed her phone and a jacket from the wardrobe and dialled Lisa on her way down the stairs.

'Hi Lisa, how are you?'

'Relieved that we're all still alive.'

'I can't believe we did it, Lisa, our plan worked.'

'You were amazing, Lucas had us connected at the time, we heard every word when you were talking to Sylvia. She sounded like she was going to kill you.'

Stephanie popped some bread into the toaster and opened the fridge for some butter.

'She had a good try. I was half hanging out the window with my legs wrapped around her neck when Lucas grabbed her off me.'

'What would you have done if he wasn't there?' Lisa sounded worried. 'I'm sorry I got there so late.'

'You missed the best bit. When Ben ran her over, she flew in the air over his car. She did say she was a trained acrobat, but for a moment, I was worried he'd killed her.'

'Ben would never have forgiven himself.'

' Hey, I'm just getting some breakfast and then guess what?'

'I know, you're going for a picnic.'

Stephanie looked at her phone in surprise, 'How did you know… have you talked to Lucas?'

Lisa laughed, 'No, Ben. He sounded so excited just now. He rang Lucas and now he's ringing the gang and apparently, we're all meeting up for a celebration picnic at the boating lake.'

Stephanie sighed and smiled, 'Great, how are you getting there?'

'You're not disappointed it's not just you and Lucas?'

'Don't be silly, it's going to be fun. Shall I make some sandwiches?'

'If you like, I was going to bring some sausage rolls and crisps. Ben's taking me Rosie and Angela in his car. Lucas said he'd take you and Bruce.'

'Well, I'm glad you've told me what's going on.' Stephanie rolled her eyes and laughed, 'See you soon.'

As she filled some bread with ham and squirted on some mayo, Stephanie admitted to herself that she was slightly disappointed that it wasn't going to be just her and Lucas, but it was going to be fun going out with the Mystery Club. They had all become close this summer, it was funny how these jewellery thefts had brought them all together, and Stephanie realised that she was also sad that it had now been solved.

Stephanie packed everything into a cool bag with a large bottle of water, she walked into the front room and looked around to make sure she had everything. Her grandma's ring! Stephanie rushed to the drawer where she'd hidden it, she needed to make sure it was returned before anything happened. They could drop it off on the way.

AN HOUR LATER, they were all sat on the flat stretch of grass, picnic rugs spread out, the sun shining down on them in a brilliant blue sky a few metres from a boating lake. The beach was a five-minute walk behind them.

Rosie handed out paper plates as Ben started to open up the food boxes. Lucas threw a ball for Bruce to chase but he seemed more interested in following the geese about, so they called him back. Bruce walked around the group, wagging his tail, sniffing at the food being brought out.

'If you're really good, there might be something here for you boy,' Stephanie said giving him a stroke down his back. His fur was hot and he was already panting so Lucas poured out some water into a bowl for him.

Stephanie poured herself some water into a plastic cup as Ben asked, 'Do you think what we did will reach the news, or shall I contact a reporter?'

Stephanie looked up in surprise, nearly pouring water over Rosie's leg.

'We don't want it to be in the news, do we?'

'Why not, it will be good publicity for our Mystery Club,' Ben replied excitedly.

Angela and Rosie nodded. 'It has been fun, don't you think?' Rosie said pushing her glasses further up her nose.

Lucas lay on his side with his head propped up with his hand, he raised his eyebrows questioningly at Stephanie and smiled.

'What do you think Lucas?' Stephanie asked.

He sat up and moved his cap to shield his eyes from the glare of the sun.

'I think you all work well as a team, and you have a talent for helping people…'

Ben interrupted him, 'We could hire ourselves out, you know like private detectives.'

They all laughed apart from Lucas who was starting to look serious, and Stephanie guessed what he was thinking so she added, 'Nothing scary though, just missing cats that kind of thing.'

Ben bit into his sandwich, 'After last night, who knows…'

Stephanie hadn't missed that Lucas hadn't seemed to include himself in the description, she held out a sandwich for him and the others and opened a large bag of crisps in the middle.

'We need to ring Mabel and the others to let them know who stole their jewellery,' Lisa said.

'The police will get in touch, but they might not get their items back straight away,' Ben added.

'They might need them for evidence. It could take ages for the case to be taken to court,' Angela said with a moan.

'Do you think we'll have to give evidence?'

'Hopefully, you won't need to. They have all the video and audio evidence,' Lucas told them then added, 'I know some people who will take care of it for us.'

They all looked at Lucas and finally, Angela asked, 'Who are you, Lucas?'

'What d'you mean?'

'You know -- your job is to do with security, and you know people who can talk to the police.'

'It's like you're a spy or something,' Ben joked.

Stephanie looked down, not sure how much he was going to divulge, and she felt uncomfortable keeping secrets from her friends. She glanced at Lisa who looked back.

Lucas laughed calmly, 'You know, I could tell you but then I'd have to kill you afterwards.'

'So Lisa, what's Martin and the girls doing today?' Stephanie changed the conversation as quickly as she could.

'Oh, they're going swimming and then to Blyton for an ice cream,' Lisa replied but was watching Lucas carefully.

Stephanie laughed, 'You enjoy the peace while you can. It's so nice round here, I don't know why I don't visit more often.'

'We come here a lot with the girls, they love playing in the sand pit.'

Rosie handed out some hard-boiled eggs and salad.

'Oh, I didn't bring any forks, sorry we'll have to eat it with our fingers.'

They sat there, enjoying the food and chatting about everything that had happened recently. They all had been chatting for about an hour before Stephanie looked around to take in the view around them.

She looked around at a few other people sitting and eating like them. A man and woman were throwing a frisbee with their son, a couple walked across the field towards the beach with their dog following behind. On her right side, the lake shimmered as it reflected the sun. A couple rowed a boat around the duck island and Stephanie noticed a group of young men had got their boat stuck in the shallow end. They all watched with amusement as one of the men got out and waded in the water to push the boat away from the bank until it was free again. He struggled to get back into the boat so he climbed onto the path and walked alongside as the others rowed as fast as they could laughing at him to jump back on board.

'That's going to end in disaster,' Lucas said in Stephanie's ear. She jumped as she didn't realise how close he'd leaned towards her so that she could feel the warmth of his breath.

She laughed, 'It will be interesting to see what happens next.'

It wasn't long before the man made up his mind to leap into the boat, but he misjudged the distance and splashed into the lake and grabbed the side of the boat in panic which nearly sent them all overboard. Their shouts and laughter sang out into the air causing everyone to look at them and laugh. Ducks and geese took to the air and skidded across the water in surprise, finally calming down to return to normal, but staying away from the inexperienced sailors.

'I like the way the ducks are giving those men the evil eye,' laughed Lisa.

Angela agreed, 'They are not amused. Look he's climbing back onto the path again. Oh no, he's soaking wet.'

'I fancy going for a paddle,' Ben announced.

'What in the lake?' Stephanie asked.

'No, in the sea. Anyone else fancy a walk to the beach?'

Bruce, who had been lying down, perked up at the mention of a walk and got up to join Ben.

'Well, that's two of us. Anyone else?'

Stephanie groaned, 'I'm shattered, I don't feel like exercise at the moment.'

Angela and Rosie started to pack things away.

'I could do with stretching my legs,' Lisa said yawning.

'You lot go, and I'll stay here with Steph,' Lucas said lying on his back and lazily tilting his cap over his eyes.

'Can we take Bruce with us?' Rosie asked standing up.

'Sure, you can let him off his lead when you get to the beach if you want, he won't go far.'

It wasn't long before they had all left except for Stephanie and Lucas. Stephanie lay on her front next to him, and closed her eyes, enjoying the closeness of his body next to hers. She listened to the occasional quack of a duck and the giggling of children playing in the distance.

'Relaxing isn't it,' Lucas's voice was soft near her ear, and as she turned onto her side to face him, he did the same.

They looked at each other in silence for a few moments. Stephanie noticed flecks of yellow in his blue eyes and a freckle near the corner of his mouth.

'Did you know that you have a cute dimple when you smile?' Stephanie whispered.

'I don't think I've smiled as much as I have recently.'

Lucas grinned as if remembering something funny.

'What?' Stephanie asked.

'Nothing, I'm just remembering when you screamed when you realised that man on the bed wasn't dead.' Lucas started to laugh out loud, and Stephanie joined in.

'We have had some laughs, haven't we?' Stephanie asked.

'And some frights.'

'It's mostly been fun, wouldn't you say?'

Lucas paused thoughtfully and smiled, 'It has – I'm glad, you know, that I came up here. I never thought I'd get so attached.'

'Our little Mystery Club has meant a lot to me too.'

Lucas shifted position so he was laying on his front and picked a blade of grass and twiddled with it absent mindedly.

He spoke in a low voice. 'With all the fuss of mystery solving, we never really got to talk properly.'

'About what?'

Stephanie copied his position and wondered where this conversation would lead.

'I told you that Kate is my sister, but I didn't tell you that I know Mark. I don't really know him well, but we've met a few times, at parties and he's been to my dad's house. Did Mark tell you?'

Stephanie briefly stiffened at the mention of Mark's name but then curiosity took over.

'So, when Kate asked you to be my bodyguard, did Mark know it was going to be you?'

'Yes, but you should know that he only agreed because he knew it was me. He knew I could be trusted and then I…'

Lucas sat up, obviously finding it difficult to find the right words. Stephanie mirrored him again and he turned to face her.

'I really like you, I'm sure you've picked up on that.'

He laughed nervously then continued, 'But there's been so many reasons why I couldn't act on it.'

Stephanie thought about what he said and partly understood. They sat and watched the geese glide past on the lake.

She hugged her knees and asked carefully, 'So, are you saying that we can't be more than friends right now?'

Lucas took his time to reply. 'Is it true that you're going to stay with Mark in the summer holiday?'

Stephanie wasn't expecting that and she didn't know what to say. Truthfully she answered, 'That was the plan, but lately we've been arguing and I'm not sure anymore.

Closing her eyes, she tilted her face up to the sun, needing to be comforted by its distant but warm embrace. He was right, she needed to see Mark to sort out this mess.

Lucas decided to change the mood with a question. 'Do you fancy a boat ride?'

Stephanie laughed, 'You saw what happened to those men. You know me, we'll probably end up in the lake.'

Lucas stood up and held out his hand towards Stephanie.

'I'm an expert rower, I won't let anything bad happen. Trust me.'

Stephanie sighed. 'Fine,' she conceded allowing him to pull her to her feet.

'See, I told you that I'm an expert rower.'

Stephanie relaxed back in the boat and dangled her hand in the cool water of the lake. It was slightly cooler on the water, under the shade of the trees that grew on the island. Stephanie peered through the branches and could make out some duck houses in the centre with a few white ducks lazing in the heat of the afternoon.

Stephanie sighed as she watched Lucas pull back slowly on the oars. He grinned at her, and she realised that she'd not seen him this happy before. Even when they were laughing in the pub, or walking through the village, he always seemed to have his guard up, always scanning around for danger like a guard dog, alert and protective.

'Okay, now it's your turn.'

He handed over the oars.

'Oh, I don't think it's a good idea, Lucas, we'll crash and burn.'

He laughed and leaned back, 'I have every confidence in you Steph, you got it.'

Stephanie lowered the oars in the water and slowly pulled back.

'That's it, lean back, then lift the oars out of the water, tilt them when they're in the air and then twist and back in again.'

Stephanie laughed as they moved backwards, she was glad they were the only ones on the lake so she couldn't crash into anyone.

'Luckily the ducks are clever enough to stay out of our way. Right, I'm going to turn us around now.'

Stephanie lifted one oar out and slowly inched the boat around in an anti-clockwise direction.

'So far so good,' she was starting to impress herself.

She looked up at Lucas to see how many marks out of ten he'd give her, when she noticed his face was serious again. He was staring behind her with a frown, and she was just about to ask him what he was looking at when…

'Get down!' Lucas shouted at her as he leaned forward to grab the oars.

Stephanie was pulled forward into the boat, her head turned expecting to see them about to crash into the bank, but they were far from the side. What she did glimpse, however, was a man standing at the end of the lake pointing something in their direction. Before she had time to recognise what it was, a cracking sound rang out across the lake, it echoed around them causing confusion as birds flapped into the air. Feathered wings flew close to Stephanie's head, she lifted her arm to shield her face and looked up at Lucas as he pulled back on the oars to power them away across the swirling water.

She couldn't help but look over her shoulder to see where the figure had gone.

'Stay low! Damn, we'll have to get onto the island.'

Lucas quickly tried to steer the boat into the middle while another shot hit the water next to them. Stephanie heard shouts from people as they dashed away to safety.

Another shot was followed by a grunt from Lucas, and he slumped forward.

'Stephanie, we're not going to make it. We're going to have to go in.'

'What?' Stephanie shouted. 'In the water?'

'One, two, three. Trust me…'

With that, Stephanie felt the boat tip over as Lucas rocked it and they both fell into the dark water. Stephanie was a good swimmer, but she felt herself panic, not knowing how deep the lake was. It felt cold compared to the summer air, her eyes closed she kicked her legs and felt for the boat with her hands. A strong arm grabbed her around her waist and pulled her upward, her face broke through the surface, but it was dark and muffled as she opened her eyes. They were under the capsized boat.

'You can put your feet down,' Lucas said, and Stephanie realised that it wasn't as deep as she feared.

Another shot was fired. It hit the bottom of the boat but didn't go through. They both flinched.

'I'm not sure if this boat is thick enough, we need to get out.'

Stephanie looked at him, her eyes went wide as she noticed the water was dark around him.

'Your shoulder! You've been hit!'

'I'm all right. You need to swim under water and get onto the island.'

'He'll see us.'

'He'll follow the boat. I know what I'm doing, just do what I say.'

'I can't!' Stephanie spluttered as water splashed into her mouth.

'You can do it. Look at me.'

Stephanie looked into his eyes and saw calm and confidence, he knew what he was doing, she had to trust him.

'When I say go, I want you to dive under and swim for the island. Get yourself across the other side, then swim over to the other end of the lake. When you get out, run for the car. Here, take the keys.'

He lifted up the car keys for her to grab.

'Don't think, just do it... now GO!'

Stephanie took a deep breath and forced herself to open her eyes under the water. They didn't sting as she expected them to. She could see the roots and bank of the island in the murky depths as she pushed down as far as she could. Her hands grasped the plants and when her lungs felt like they were about to burst, she pulled herself up, face hidden amongst the tall leaves and searched the lake for Lucas. She could see the capsized boat approaching the bank towards the shooter, who had run around the path and was now nearer to them. Was Lucas crazy? He was heading straight for him. At least the man was saving his bullets, he was standing looking around the boat uneasily, waiting for someone to come out.

Stephanie wasn't sure what to do. If she climbed onto the island, would he see her? Would he start shooting again? She looked around and noticed that all the people had vanished. She watched through the reeds as the man touched the boat with his foot. He looked unsure now if there was anyone there underneath. Stephanie was beginning to think that Lucas had swum off, when she saw his hand reach out of the water and grab the man by his ankle. He toppled over and tumbled into the lake, hitting the boat on his way in.

Stephanie didn't wait to see what happened next. She hauled herself onto the island and ran into the middle before daring to look to see what was happening.

She heard splashing and another shot fire before her eyes focused on the two men fighting in the lake. Lucas had hold of the man's arm, forcing his hand back to let go of the gun which dropped into the water. As the man looked towards where the gun had disappeared, Lucas thumped his face and then dragged him to the side.

Stephanie, her heart pounding in her chest, remembered what Lucas had told her. She staggered on wobbly legs to the other side of the island to discover a man and woman cowering in their boat. They screamed as Stephanie appeared above them and moved apart as she climbed in between them.

'Don't just sit there!' Stephanie ordered. 'Row!'

She pointed in the direction of the bank, and without arguing, the frightened man grabbed the oars to propel the boat to the side as fast as if it had a motor.

'Thanks,' Stephanie said wearily, as she climbed out in soaking clothes and left them sitting there gawping.

She ran, ran across the path, over the grass, through a garrison of brown and white geese. They rose up and spread their wings as she ran past. Stephanie squealed as they flapped and honked at her. It wasn't until she reached the corner that she looked back hoping to see Lucas following her. She couldn't see him, she knew that she didn't have to worry about the gun

319

anymore, but he had been shot. She whirled around, not sure what to do. If she got to the car, could she drive it nearby for him to get in? The path looked wide enough to get a car down. The people who owned the café had a van parked next to it.

With determination, Stephanie turned towards the car park and ran as fast as she could to where she thought the car was parked. It was difficult to run in wet clothes, she squeezed water from her ponytail as she went. She remembered they had parked the car near to the path. As she ran, she looked about to see if there was anyone who could call the police. Where were the police anyway? Surely someone must have called them. Sure enough, she could hear sirens in the distance. She slowed down next to a white van to look and saw police cars entering the carpark but they were far from her. She turned back towards the lake to see if she could see Lucas, he was running towards her and shouting something.

Without warning, something hard banged against her face, she closed her eyes. She felt her arm being pulled back and then her hair was yanked that made her scream out.

'Shut up!' A steely voice hissed in her ear.

Stephanie looked around as much as she could, to see a gun pointing in front of her towards Lucas.

'Let her go,' Lucas shouted.

'Do you think I've come here just to let her go?' the man screamed viciously.

'Who are you? What do you want?' Stephanie cried.

He slightly let go of her so she could turn to see him. His back was to the van, and he leered at her, quickly looking back to check on Lucas.

'Stay where you are, or I'll blow her pretty face off now.'

Stephanie looked at his familiar face, the dark hair and moustache. She gulped as she recognised him from the Skydive party in Hibaldton.

'You remember me then?'

'Alex.'

He looked visibly shocked that she knew his name.

'What do you want with me?' Stephanie demanded, more annoyed now than scared. She tried to relax in his hold, so that he wouldn't panic. He looked as nervous as hell, sweat was trickling down his face.

'Nothing personal. I've just got a job to do.'

'Why here?'

'You are a tricky person to get alone Stephanie Rhodes. Have you not realised that I've been following you around?'

'No, you've been following me?'

He looked annoyed, 'I've been standing on street corners, and didn't you see me sitting in the car?'

Stephanie realised that he was the 'vaping man', but she wouldn't let him have the satisfaction of knowing he's got to her.

'Erm, where was that?'

Lucas must have moved closer because Alex tightened his grip on Stephanie's arm so that she flinched, his gun shaking as he pointed it.

'I nearly ran you over for fuck's sake! I wish I had now. I've had to follow you for weeks and I'm sick of it. I was going to frighten you in the parachute jump, but you didn't even turn up.'

'I don't do parachute jumps.'

'I'm fed-up screwing around, and I'm sick of your boyfriend over there. Thanks to my new boss… I don't have to put up with it anymore.'

'Your new boss?'

Stephanie was intrigued, she hoped that he would give the usual confession before trying to kill her.

'Sergei?'

They could hear shouting by the lake and Alex knew his time was running out.

'Sergei wanted me to kidnap you, but guess what? My new boss wants you -- dead.'

He threw Stephanie in front of him between him and Lucas.

'I'll just have to kill two birds with one stone.'

He pulled the trigger, and the gun went off. It was so loud, Stephanie thought her ear had been blown off. She jumped back with her hands to her ears and staggered back. Just as he turned to aim the gun at her, a brown shape jumped onto the roof of the van and leapt onto his head bringing them both with a thud onto the ground.

Bruce growled as his teeth gripped the man's hand forcing him to let go, and he screamed in pain under the dog's body.

'Arghh! Get him off me!'

'Good boy Bruce, hold on.'

Lucas arrived by her side, but then sagged to the ground next to her. She could see he was bleeding heavily so Stephanie pressed her hands onto Lucas's shoulder where a dark blood stain was spreading across his T-shirt. Lisa and Angela knelt on the tarmac next to her, passing her bandages while Rosie rummaged in her first-aid bag for anything else that would help. Lucas was drifting in and out of consciousness.

'Lucas! Please, Lucas, try to stay awake,' Stephanie sobbed. 'The ambulance is coming.' She could hear the sirens in the distance.

The police and ambulance soon arrived, Ben stood waving his arms. 'Don't worry Steph, everything is going to be all right.'

'Who was the man who shot at you?' Angela started to ask. 'What's going on?'

Lisa replied for Stephanie, 'I'll explain later. There's a lot to fill you in on.'

STEPHANIE SAT ON the ground, in shock, as paramedics and police swarmed around her. She could feel the reassuring weight of Bruce standing next to her, his body leaning against her shoulder. She watched as a paramedic checked Alex over.

Alex was on his knees, his hands handcuffed behind his back with two policemen standing over him. In the distance, Stephanie noticed the other man was caught and was being placed into a police car.

'Who is your new boss?' Stephanie asked Alex, she tried not to show how scared she was.

At first, he didn't answer, he just smirked at her. Then as the policemen started to lead him away, he stopped, looked over his shoulder and said, 'You know my boss.'

Stephanie replied, 'Sergei?'

He smiled slowly. 'No. Sergei still wants you, but there's someone more powerful than him who wants you out of the way.'

'Who? What d'you mean?' Stephanie shouted.

But he just laughed and allowed himself to be led away.

41

A LOUSY BODYGUARD

Stephanie sat in a hospital bed, waiting to hear if Lucas was going to be okay. The bullet had grazed her arm, and she had been treated for shock. She held her arm, it stung like crazy. Her hand was still shaking, the nurses had given her an extra blanket to stop her from shivering. Lisa sat in the room with her as they waited for news about Lucas.

'Where are the others?' Stephanie asked.

'They're waiting outside with Bruce. The nurses wouldn't let Bruce in the hospital, and they said you could only have one visitor.'

'Did you tell them that Bruce is a hero?'

'Ben did, he also said that he was your emotional support animal, but they still wouldn't let him in.'

Stephanie smiled at the thought of Ben arguing with the nurses and then she remembered Lucas.

'Do you think Lucas is going to be all right? He lost loads of blood in the lake.'

Lisa inched her chair closer to Stephanie and held her hand.

'I don't know what would have happened if Bruce hadn't had heard the shots.'

'Where were you?'

'We were on the beach. Ben threw a piece of driftwood for Bruce to chase, when suddenly Bruce stopped with his ears pricked and that was it. He flew towards the lake, we didn't even know why. We chased after him and as we got closer to the lake, we knew something bad had happened because some people were crying and running away. When I saw a capsized boat, and you were nowhere to be seen, I thought you'd drowned.'

'Lucas turned it over so we could hide inside it. Someone was shooting at us, I was so scared! Lucas made me cross the island and run to the car while he fought him off.'

Stephanie started to cry, and her best friend stood up to hug her.

A nurse came in the room and tried to reassure them that Lucas was going to be ok.

'He's just gone into surgery to remove the bullet. Don't worry, he's lost a lot of blood, but they'll give him a transfusion and he'll be fine. He looks strong. The doctor will be in soon and he will explain things in more detail.'

After the nurse left, two policemen entered to question them about what had happened.

AFTER THEY HAD gone, Stephanie was exhausted. She sat back against the pillows and turned to Lisa.

'I'm sorry you've been brought into all of this.'

'Don't be silly, it's not your fault,' Lisa insisted.

'I don't know.'

'Was it Sergei?' Lisa asked.

Stephanie shook her head.

'It was Alex, the camera guy from the Skydive club.'

Lisa frowned, 'Are you sure? What was he doing with a gun? Oh no, and he organised that competition!'

'I can't go on like this,' Stephanie rubbed her forehead. 'One minute I'm scared, the next I feel I'm being paranoid, and now I'm terrified. That's the kind of snake Sergei is, he said he liked to play games.'

'But you said it wasn't Sergei.'

'From what Alex said, Sergei has been getting him to follow me around and scare me.'

Lisa stared at her friend, things starting to drop into place.

'Was it Alex who tried to run you over?'

Stephanie nodded. 'Sergei is obviously still alive but too scared to come back, so he's been getting Alex to do his dirty work for him.'

'The police have got Alex now, so he'll confess, won't he? Then there'll be evidence against Sergei,' Lisa said hopefully.

Lisa started to pace the room angrily. 'You need to get hold of that detective you met before, he needs to know about all of this. They should be doing something, what *are* they doing?'

Martin walked through the door and Lisa ran into his arms.

'Nothing happened to me, it's Stephanie and Lucas,' Lisa began.

'Are you ok?' Martin asked Stephanie after giving his wife a loving kiss on the forehead. 'I saw Ben and the others outside and they told me what had happened.'

'Are they still there?'

'Yeah they've been talking to the police, and they asked me to tell you that they're going home now.'

'That's good, there's no point staying, and you may as well take Lisa home.'

'I'm not leaving you here,' Lisa argued as a doctor entered the room.

'You can see him now. The bullet was successfully removed and luckily it missed major organs. He has lost a lot of blood, so he's had to have a transfusion, but he should feel better in a few days.'

Stephanie started to get off the bed. 'Will you wait until I get back?'

STEPHANIE STOOD AT the end of the white, metal hospital bed, and with shaking legs she slowly walked around to stand next to Lucas. He was asleep, his pale face turned to the side, his arm lay on top of the covers connected to a drip. Stephanie trembled as she looked at the machine next to the bed and watched as each drip of saline inched down the tube into his body.

The nurse told her he was sleeping because of the drugs he'd been given, and Stephanie asked if she could stay.

'If I were you, I would go home and get some rest.'

When Stephanie shook her head the nurse continued, 'He'll sleep until the morning, and you could come back with some clean clothes for him.'

Stephanie gave Lucas a gentle kiss, picked up a bag with his blood-soaked clothes and returned home with Martin and Lisa.

THE FIRST THING Stephanie did when she got back, was to ring Ben who brought Bruce round. By then, Stephanie had found Lucas's keys and was already in his house looking for some clean clothes. Once Bruce was home, she didn't need to search for the dog food as Bruce headed straight for the cupboard, his tail wagging against the door.

'He must have been hungry,' Ben said. 'I was going to give him some of our dinner but then you rang. How is Lucas?'

'The bullet's out and he just needs to rest. I'll go see him in the morning.'

As Bruce devoured his food, they gathered up some more things and Ben helped to carry them across to her house.

'Are you sure you're going to be all right? I can ring Simon and tell him I'm stopping with you, or you can crash at our house.'

'I'm fine Ben, really. Bruce will look after me and Alex is in custody.'

Ben shook his head. 'I can't believe all this has happened, but at least you can feel safe now – Stephanie -- what are you not telling me?'

Stephanie imagined Ben's reaction if she told him that someone else had ordered her to be killed -- and it was someone she knew. He would freak out. She decided against it for now.

Stephanie turned Ben to face the door and smiled, 'I will be fine, I promise. Go home and get some rest, I know I'm going to be asleep as soon as my head hits the pillow.'

Before going to bed, Stephanie found Detective Jackson's number.

After an hour of discussing everything that had happened, she then decided to ring Lucas's sister, Kate. She explained as much as she could and reassured her that Lucas was doing okay at the hospital in Grimsby.

Lastly, she rang Mark. He wanted to rush over, but she managed to persuade him not to. She was fine, she was just worried about Lucas.

He didn't ask why they had gone to the seaside together. He told her he was sorry he wasn't with her and thank God Lucas had been.

EARLY IN THE morning, Stephanie got out of bed, it was as if she were on autopilot. She went through the motions of getting dressed, even her bandaged arm hardly hurt. It was like she was in a dream, she had to force herself to move her arms and legs, to feed Bruce and let him into the garden. As he slowly walked around the grass, she stared at nothing until his tongue licked her hand to remind her to get going again.

'You are my hero, Bruce.'

She said giving him a hug around his neck. She knelt next to him, rubbing the fur behind his ear. He always seemed to like that, he lifted his chin and panted with his eyes closed and listened to her talking.

'I'm going to leave you here, while I go back to the hospital to get Lucas. You'll be ok for a while, won't you?'

Bruce barked a quick bark in answer as Stephanie stood up to go.

AT THE HOSPITAL, she rushed up to the room she had last seen Lucas, but there was someone else there. Confused she went up to the nurse's station and they informed her he'd been moved into a private room.

Stephanie walked into the room and with relief she saw Lucas sat up eating breakfast.

'Hi,' Stephanie said trying not to cry.

'Hi,' Lucas smiled.

'Nice room.'

'Yeah, Kate rang up and suddenly I'm being wheeled in here.'

'How are you?'

She sat next to him and searched his face for a sign that he really was okay.

'I feel stronger and I'm stiff but honestly, I'm going to be fine.'

Stephanie kissed him with relief and thanked him for saving her life.

'I never really thought that you'd have to risk your life for me.'

Lucas looked grim. 'I'm sorry I wasn't prepared, I was enjoying myself too much. I am a lousy bodyguard.'

Stephanie kissed him again.

'You're a perfect bodyguard, you literally took a bullet for me.'

Lucas noticed the bandage on her arm, and he frowned.

'Did you get hit?'

He reached out for her hand and gently took it in his as she sat on the edge of his bed.

'Shit Stephanie, I didn't know you had been hurt, why didn't someone tell me?'

'I'm fine, it was just a graze, you had enough to worry about.'

Lucas grimaced at the memory of what had happened.

'I knew him from somewhere,' Lucas said.

'It was Alex, the camera guy and the vaping man.'

Stephanie told Lucas some of what Alex had said in her ear when he was holding her.

'So he *was* acting for Sergei.'

Stephanie nodded.

'I noticed he was standing with the skydivers when the results of the competition were being called,' Stephanie recalled.

'I got a list of names of the skydivers, that night we went to the club. I should have done a background check on them. I'll ask a friend to do it for me. I'm angry at myself for not doing it sooner. Skydivers are well known for travelling around the world, those people could be from anywhere,' Lucas spoke grimly and closed his tired eyes.

'Bruce was such a hero, did you see him jump onto the van and knock him down?'

Lucas grinned, 'I bet Brucie boy took a chunk out of him, where is he by the way?'

'He's fine, he's at my house. I spoke to Detective, Jackson and he wants to meet us when you get out,' Stephanie told him.

'I think I'll be out in a couple of days. I need to be fit and well, there's so much to do.'

42

STEPPING INTO A SPY FILM

S tephanie waited for Lucas to return home. He had insisted on driving his car back and then they had spent the morning together waiting for Detective Jackson.

Stephanie fussed over Lucas, making him drinks and not letting him off the settee. At first, he insisted he was fine, but it didn't take long for him to give in and enjoy being pampered for a change. Her bandaged arm still hurt, a lot, but she tried not to show it.

'I bet you wish you hadn't taken on this job,' Stephanie said looking at his weary face as she handed him a drink of water.

Lucas looked sternly at her.

'First of all, Stephanie Rhodes, the only thing I regret is letting myself off guard. If I hadn't had been enjoying myself so much, I would have seen him coming. I can't believe I didn't spot him following us. The second thing is… I'm not being paid, Kate told me your story and I wanted to help. I did it as a favour to her and I wasn't doing anything much, so she organised it. I want you to know that I have been protecting you because I wanted to.'

'You're telling me that you agreed to come out here, to babysit a woman you've never met, and not get paid?'

Lucas chuckled. 'I know it sounds crazy. At first, I did it as a favour to Kate and I wasn't doing anything much, so she organised it. I have been protecting you because I wanted to. I heard some of your story and it intrigued me, and then I met you and your crazy friends, and you intrigued me. I must admit that I didn't think I'd be staying this long, but…I've been enjoying your company.' Lucas sat up straighter. 'Oh hell, that sounds like I only stayed to get to know you better. What I mean is, I did believe you were in danger, but I also enjoyed getting to know you better,' he gabbled looking more uncomfortable.

Stephanie started to pace up and down the carpet in front of him.

'You're not being paid?' she eventually said smiling.

She admitted to herself that she was happy to hear this as it meant he was there because he wanted to, not for money or to fulfil an obligation. The thought made her feel like she had a swirl of butterflies dancing in her stomach.

'I don't need the money,' Lucas said plainly.

He looked at her and Stephanie could see that he was searching for the right words. 'Do you know anything about my family?'

'Not really, I know that your dad and Kate have a lot of money, Mark told me that you are a bodyguard.'

Lucas chuckled, 'My dad used to work for MI5, and I am ex- Special Forces. I sometimes train agents and I work with them from time to time.'

'So, you are a spy?' Stephanie's eyes went wide.

Lucas laughed, 'Not exactly. A friend of mine has contacted Detective Jackson to tell him who I am.'

'Why does he need to know who you are?'

'Because I want to help, that's why I'm here.'

Stephanie turned at the sound of a car outside. A black Landrover pulled up and Detective Jackson got out, Stephanie walked to the door to let him in. She was beginning to feel like she had stepped into a spy film.

The three of them sat at the kitchen table and soon it was covered with postcards and photos of Sergei and people connected with him including Alex.

Two more people from the Skydive guest group were recognised, and it made Stephanie shiver to think that she nearly agreed to do the jump. Which one of them would she have been attached to when they threw themselves out of the aeroplane? Would they have unbuckled her in mid-air? She had a horrifying vision of her hurtling to the ground whilst watching the men laughing at her as they got smaller and smaller in the sky.

Detective Jackson noticed how pale Stephanie had got.

'The skydiving club were horrified to find out about these people, and they have been very cooperative. They wanted you to know, Stephanie, that they always insist on government photo ID before anyone joins their club, however their documents must have been fake. They will be long gone now I'm afraid. MI6 are using facial recognition and talking to the skydiving community, I feel confident that we'll find anyone who was connected to Alex,' Jackson added.

Stephanie remembered her friend Tracy had hung out with some of the skydivers and wondered if she had heard anything.

'My friend knows a skydiver named Craig. He probably talked to these people, maybe they said something that would be useful.'

'I remember Tracy,' Lucas said getting out his pen. 'Have you got her number?'

Stephanie gave him Tracy's details and realised that they were going to have to tell her about everything. Soon the whole village would be gossiping about Russian gangs, and they would be eyeing every stranger with suspicion.

It was scary but also fascinating listening to Lucas and Jackson discussing the sightings of Sergei and his gang members. Stephanie began to find out more about him. Sergei was a member of a Russian crime organisation that was smuggling drugs via the North Sea. The head of the syndicate was unknown at this time but there were two men who MI6 suspected. Stephanie realised that her small, sleepy village, a place that had always been a blanket of security, was now the setting of a serious crime drama, it seemed so surreal. She wondered what else might be still going on that they didn't know about.

'What about the burglaries in the village?' asked Stephanie

'The police searched their house and found a hidden area in the dressing room. It contained the missing jewellery as well as some other items we are trying to trace. Neither of them is saying anything. What we do know is that Sylvia and Gavin Smith are not their real names. They are experienced thieves and con artists minoring in extortion and violence. We believe that they were in the process of winding down before retirement and took a nice easy job for a while to build up the coffers in their retirement fund.'

'I don't understand how a few minor burglaries helps their retirement fund. They must already be loaded to build that house,' commented Stephanie.

'I believe they were recruited some time ago to keep an eye on things, local management if you like, I bet the house was a signing bonus.'

'Recruited by Sergei' Stephanie nodded. 'I've just remembered, tell your men to look inside the photo frame next to their bed. I accidently knocked it over when I was there, and there's a photo of them sitting on a very big yacht. The name was Viktor, which sounds Russian doesn't it?'

'I'll tell someone to check on that. Sergei is a big 'fish' in an international criminal organisation. They have hands in all kinds of operations all over the world. The operation in Hibaldton was just a small part of the network,' Jackson explained.

'We believe Sergei is a fixer and a builder, he sets these operations up using a combination of local and imported 'skills',' Lucas added.

'The smiths.' Stephanie sighed. 'But Hibaldton is such a small place.'

'As you know they wanted to bring in drugs via the North Sea and up the river, but we also think they wanted to use the airfield.'

'Wow, so the burglaries and the guest skydivers were connected with Sergei. Do you suspect anyone else?' Stephanie asked.

Jackson replied, 'We doubt Sergei is the main person in charge, but we've yet to find out who. Do you suspect anyone else Stephanie?'

Stephanie shook her head. 'I honestly don't know what to think. Alex said to me that he had orders from a new boss to kill me -- and that I knew him... or her.'

Lucas sat up straight at that comment.

'You didn't tell me that!'

'Didn't I? There was so much going on. But the more I think about it, and I have not stopped thinking about it, I don't believe him.'

Jackson asked, 'What makes you so sure?'

'He seemed really annoyed with me, and I don't even know what I have done to him. I think he was fed up with following me around and decided he wanted to get rid of me instead.'

Lucas pointed to a picture of Sergei looking mean, standing next to a jeep with a rifle.

'Sergei would want his revenge. Would he risk going against his orders?'

On cue, Jackson's phone rang, he looked very serious while he listened to the person on the other end, then hardly acknowledging the message he hung up.

Sitting back, he stretched and clasped his hands behind his head.

'Speak of the devil, I don't think we're going to get much info from Alex -- he was found dead in his cell just now.'

'Damn!' Lucas slammed the table and stood up which made Stephanie jump.

'How did it happen? Did someone get to him, or did he do it himself?'

'They're looking into it, it looks like poison. Stephanie, I think it would be best if you went away somewhere. Is there a place you can go for a few weeks?'

Stephanie thought of Mark in London, Lucas turned to look at her and was obviously thinking the same.

'You need to go Steph, it will be safer in London, they won't know where to find you.'

Jackson stood up. 'That's settled then, keep in touch, Lucas.'

He shook hands with them both and took his leave.

When the detective had gone, Stephanie watched Lucas pile all the documents and photos back into the file.

'How come he's let you keep all those?' she asked feeling worried.

Lucas dropped the file on the table and led Stephanie into the front room.

He explained, 'While I was in hospital, I had a long time to think. I can't let you keep living like this, looking over your shoulder, wondering when one of Sergei's people will strike next. He's got it in for you, and when a man like that bears a grudge, he's never going to stop -- unless someone stops him.'

'What are you trying to say?'

'I'm saying that I'm that person who's going to find him and stop him.' He placed his hand on her shoulder but she shrugged him off.

'Lucas, no,' she gasped.

'Please, listen, I know what I'm doing, I'm trained for this.'

They stood in the centre of the room facing each other.

'I want to do this Stephanie. I care a lot about you, and I can't stand to see this creep getting away with it.'

Stephanie felt her eyes filling up. 'I care about you too and if anything happened to you...'

'It won't, I'll be careful, I promise. I want you to go to stay with Mark in London, it's what you planned anyway.'

At the mention of Mark, Stephanie went quiet and bit her lip. Would he still want her to go stay with him? Were they even going out together anymore?

'Are you in love with him?'

Stephanie looked up at Lucas, 'I don't know… yes, but it's complicated.'

Lucas put his hands in his pockets and stepped back.

'Look, I know you have a history together and things haven't been going well but you need to go and find out how you two feel about each other.'

Stephanie felt confused, she had strong feelings for both men, and this had never happened to her before.

'I don't want to be the guy who got in between you and the love of your life.'

'That's the thing,' Stephanie blurted out, 'I'm not sure he is. We have something between us -- don't we?'

She had an urge to run up to him, to put her arms around his neck, to hold him close. Stephanie took a step closer to him and he put his hands out to hold hers.

'If you choose me, I want you to be certain. You might not want to be with someone who is in my line of work.'

Stephanie couldn't stop looking into his eyes, the thought that she might not see him again was too much to bear.

They stepped closer to each other, still holding hands but now their bodies were almost touching.

She whispered, 'What if -- I want to be with you?'

Lucas leant down, their mouths were so close that she could feel his breath tingling her lips.

'Let's take one thing at a time, shall we?'

Their lips touched and Stephanie allowed herself to relax into a slow and sensuous kiss.

When they parted, Stephanie laughed and wiped tears from her face.

'Why don't we just go somewhere else, where Sergei can't find us?'

'Because I know you love this place and we'll always be wondering about the two things that are standing in our way. That's why you need to go to London, and I need to find Sergei.'

43

RETURN TO LONDON

It was stifling hot in London, with higher temperatures than normal for mid-August. Lucas and Mark had helped Stephanie bring all her bags in and they stood at the entrance to Mark's flat to say goodbye to Lucas.

'Promise me you will be careful,' Stephanie said.

'I'm always careful,' Lucas replied.

Stephanie looked into his blue eyes and suddenly feared that she'd never see him again. Her eyes grew wide, and she hung on to his arm. 'I don't want you to go. What if something goes wrong? I might never see you again.'

Lucas soothed her with his warm hand on her face. She closed her eyes against it and a tear rolled down her cheek. Stephanie opened her eyes to see his face close to hers. He brushed his lips against her cheek and his breath felt hot on her neck.

'Don't worry.'

He stood up and waited until Stephanie had recovered. She smiled weakly and nodded.

'I know you'll take care of her,' Lucas said to Mark. 'I'll be in touch,' he called to Stephanie as he walked over to his car.

Bruce was panting out of the window of the Landrover, when he saw that she wasn't returning with Lucas, he whimpered and put his paw onto the edge of the door.

'Stay,' Lucas commanded gently.

Stephanie walked quickly up to Bruce and leaned in to hug the dog. He licked her face and then leaned his head against her shoulder, and she relaxed against the warmth of his soft neck.

'Be good and look after Lucas won't you boy?' she whispered into his ear and as she stood up to wave goodbye, he gave one bark as if to say, 'Will do.'

Mark was quiet as they went inside, and Stephanie sat down in the front room. She felt so tired, her arm hurt, and her head felt like cotton wool.

Mark sat next to her and said quietly, 'Are you all right? You look so… I… I'm sorry I wasn't there for you. God, I've been frantic these past few days.'

Stephanie took a deep breath and fresh tears pooled in her eyes.

'No, you weren't there.'

She searched his face and noticed that he looked exhausted, he was also trembling slightly. His voice, was hoarse when he finally whispered, 'I see you and Lucas have got close.'

'Yes, we have I suppose. I can't believe he's going away to find Sergei.'

'If anyone can find that man, it's him.'

Mark stood up, took a deep breath, then continued, 'You know he's Kate's brother, don't you? I wouldn't have agreed to it if I didn't know him.'

Stephanie was too tired to go all over this again.

'Look, Mark, I have forgiven you and Kate. I can see why you didn't tell me, but you need to stop keeping things from me. After I found out, Lucas has been working with me, not treating me like… like a fragile China doll.'

'Yeah, I can see that.'

Mark's voice took on a sarcastic tone as he looked down at Stephanie.

'What do you mean by that?' Stephanie asked, standing to face him.

'Have you slept together?'

'You sound like you've already made your mind up about that."

'That's not an answer.'

Tears fell down Stephanie's cheeks, she was exhausted and angry and felt guilty, but she had nothing to hide. Before she could answer, Mark pulled her into a hug.

'I don't care what your answer is Steph, you're alive and that's all I care about right now.'

They both held each other with Mark stroking her back soothingly. Eventually, they pulled apart and Stephanie gently wiped tears from under Mark's eyes. Mark smiled and looked around for her bags.

'Let's get you moved in, and I'll run you a hot bath, you look like you could use it.'

On shaky legs, Stephanie followed Mark out of the room into the bedroom where he put down the bags and then proceeded to turn the taps on in the bathroom. Stephanie stood at the end of the bed and looked around. It was a pleasant room with cream walls and a white fitted wardrobe. She noticed a different bedspread from the grey one from before, this one was a dark blue with daisies, a feminine touch she thought. As she looked at the bed, a thought struck her – did she want to share a bed with Mark right now?

Mark returned and gently took her arm.

'Can I see your arm? Oh sorry, does it hurt?' Mark let go as Stephanie flinched.

'Yes, it does a bit, I'm still on painkillers.'

'After you've settled in, you'll have to fill me in on everything I've missed.'

'There's a great deal to tell you.'

Mark nodded and walked towards the door, 'I'll leave you to it, make yourself at home.'

'Mark.'

'Yes?' He paused, hand on the doorknob.

'I… I'm really tired. I need a good night's sleep tonight.'

Mark looked over at the bed and then his expression showed that he understood.

'Oh, of course. I'll grab some stuff and sleep on the couch, it's not a problem.'

'Thanks, Mark.'

Stephanie watched the door close and felt relieved to be on her own for a while. She looked down at her hand and realised it was shaking. She touched the bandage on her arm.

'I was shot, with a gun -- a real gun!' she said out loud to herself as if it were finally sinking in.

In the bedroom mirror, her ghostly reflection stared back at her with wide eyes.

'Everything's going to be all right, Lucas is going to be all right,' Stephanie continued to tell herself as she walked into the steam-filled bathroom and shut the door.

❧❀❧

Wearing a fresh T-shirt and shorts, Stephanie padded in bare feet towards the front room of Mark's flat. She paused as she heard two voices and then realised one of them was Kate. She thought about turning around then decided to get it over with.

'Stephanie! Oh my gosh, you look awful my darling.'

Kate didn't beat about the bush. She took Stephanie by the hands and led her to the settee and sat next to her. Mark was sitting in a chair.

'I am so sorry Steph that you had to go through all of this. Lucas will find this thug, and everything will be all right, you'll see.'

Kate squeezed her hands and stared with concern.

'Mark darling, you must go out and get some food. Have you eaten Steph? No, of course, you haven't.'

She turned to look at Mark again.

'Go get something from that take way on the corner.'

When Mark started to say he could ring up, Kate ushered him out of the room and soon Stephanie heard the slam of the front door.

Kate returned to sit back next to her, and taking her hands once more she said, 'Steph, Lucas told me how he likes you… a great deal.'

Stephanie looked surprised and when she started to say that nothing had happened, Kate interrupted.

'I know darling, I know, but from your reaction, I can see that you like him too.'

Tears filled Stephanie's eyes again, she swiped at them in annoyance, it was all she seemed to be doing lately.

'What shall I do Kate?'

'Come and stay with me,' Kate quickly said.

Stephanie looked at her, then shook her head.

'I can't, what if it puts you in danger?'

'Darling, my apartment has guards at the desk and cameras everywhere. It's much more secure than Mark's flat. What do you say?'

Kate was getting excited about the plan. She continued, in a hushed tone, 'It will also give you time away from Mark, to decide what you want. You can spend time together, obviously, but you will be able to have time to yourself too.'

'I..I'll think about it. I'll talk to Mark tomorrow.'

'You know Mark, he'll change your mind like he always does dear. We need to go now before he gets back.'

Kate stood up and Stephanie dragged herself up feeling rather dazed.

'Is your suitcase on the bed? Come on, it will be fun living together. You need to have time away from both men and then you'll find out who you miss the most.'

'What about Mark?'

'Don't worry, I'll explain everything to him when we get to my place.'

KATE LED STEPHANIE up to her penthouse apartment. Stephanie was too tired to be excited about her posh surroundings or to notice the porters bustling around them with her bags.

Stephanie climbed into the luxurious bed and sighed as her head sunk into the soft, cool pillow. As she closed her swollen, weary eyes, she wondered what life was going to throw at her next. Should she stay with Kate all holiday, or go back to Mark's flat? Would it be exciting to live in London with Mark?

What about Lucas? Did they have a future together, and if so, where would that be? Stephanie quickly drifted off to a restless sleep. Her dreams were full of recent nightmares and endless possibilities ahead.

ACKNOWLEDGEMENTS

Thank you to my husband, Alan, if it weren't for him there would be no book. I love you.

Thank you to Janice, for help with proofreading the story once again.

Thank you to my dear friends Susie, Dave and Ruth, whose enthusiasm has kept me going and helped me to believe in myself.

Thank you to everyone who bought the first book and gave me such amazing feedback.

Finally, a special thank you to everyone at The Rabbit Hole bookshop in Brigg, including local authors and Wayne Oram.

Printed in Great Britain
by Amazon